Crank

Cover Design:
Kari March Designs

Photograph:
Adobe Stock

Editing:
Adept Edits

Interior Design & Formatting:
Christine Borgford, Type A Formatting

Books by
ADRIANA LOCKE

The Exception Series
The Exception
The Connection, a novella
The Perception
The Exception Series Box Set

The Landry Family Series
Sway
Swing
Switch
Swear
Swink

The Gibson Boys Series
Crank
Cross—coming December 2017
Craft—coming January 2018

Standalone Novels
Sacrifice
Wherever It Leads
Written in the Scars
Battle of the Sexes
Lucky Number Eleven
Twelve Days Until Sunday—fall 2018

USA *Today* Bestselling Author
ADRIANA LOCKE

chapter
One

Walker

"I'M NOT TAKING YOU TO the hospital."

Peck teeters on the edge of one of Crave's billiard tables. He sways back and forth, his sneakers squeaking against the cheap wood over the chatter of the patrons of the bar. "You don't think I can land a back flip off here?"

The truth is I'm pretty sure he could. My cousin has the reflexes of a cat. The problem is he also has nine lives, and I'm sure he's used up eight of them already.

"The question isn't if you can land it. It's how bloody the end result would be," I say, taking a sip of beer. "And I'm not trying to splint a head wound. Can you even do that?"

"*You* could. Look at my arm." He holds his left forearm in front of him, his watch catching the light from the new fixtures above. "This is some of your best work."

Memories of splinting Peck's arm with nothing but a belt, a bar towel, and a Playboy rush through my mind, as does loading him into the back of my truck for a quick trip to the emergency room.

"I really think I can do this," Peck insists, working his shoulders back and forth.

Downing another drink, hoping I'm good and hammered before Peck attempts this disaster, I look across the table. My older brother, Lance, is watching me as he brings an Old-Fashioned to his lips. We exchange a look, both of us waiting for Machlan to catch wind of Peck's antics and throw him out of Crave. Again.

"What's the worst that could happen?" Peck asks. "Another broken arm? I mean, I think I can get the rotation fast enough to not land on my head."

"I think it's your turn to take him to the hospital," I tell Lance.

He coughs, choking on his drink. "Yeah, I don't think so."

"Remember how hot that nurse was last time?" Peck asks, wiggling his brows. "Actually, that kind of makes me want to go for it now just in case she's on duty."

"She's not," Lance chimes in. "I think she was fired after the Hospital Administrator found her fuck-foundered in triage three the night of your broken arm."

"Peck! Get your fucking ass down." Machlan's voice rips through the bar, booming over the crowd.

Everyone quiets a few notches, not quite scared of my younger brother, but not willing to test his boundaries either. His reputation as a man you don't want to tangle with without a small army definitely helps his cause when it comes to managing his bar. Peck, on the other hand, just rolls his eyes.

"Just one jump, Mach! One. Uno. I got this." Peck gives Machlan his best shit-eating grin before looking at me and Lance. "If he throws me out, I'll be back in a couple days. Hell, he threw me out on Tuesday and I was back on Thursday for corn hole."

"I think that just means you're in here too much," Lance offers.

Peck starts to respond but his attention is redirected as Molly McCarter saunters by. The dim lighting does nothing to hide the exaggerated sway of her hips or the way she licks her lips as her sight sets on *me*.

Bracing for what may come out of her mouth, I fill mine with alcohol.

"Hey, Walker," she says, stopping at my chair. Her hands rest along the top rung, her fingertips sliding across the back of my neck. "Hey, Lance."

Lance tips his glass her way.

"I was thinking," she purrs, "my car is way overdue for an oil change. Maybe I could bring it to Crank sometime this week, Walker? Do you think you could *fit it in?*"

"I'm pretty full this week," I lie, ignoring her thinly veiled offer. "See what Peck has available."

A huff whispers through the air and she pivots on her heel. "Thanks anyway."

"I can get you in . . ." Peck's voice drowns into the Crave chaos as he follows her towards the bar.

He tails after her, all but drooling, as she slides onto a bar stool. Her gaze flicks to mine, her knees spread just a little farther apart than a lady ever should. Then again, no one has ever called Molly a lady.

"Ever fuck her?" Lance asks, downing the rest of his drink as he turns back to me. "I've been tempted to a couple of times and did get a decent blow job one Halloween when she was dressed up in this nurse outfit."

"What is it with you and nurses?"

"Think about it: they're smart, make good money, work a lot so you have free time, and they're used to getting dirty," he smirks. "It's like a straight shot to my dick."

"And they're good with needles, have access to medicines that can make you lose your mind, and I've never met one who didn't have a warped sense of humor," I counter. "They set off my crazy radar."

Lance laughs. "Did that radar just start working? Because I distinctly remember you getting balls deep with some psychologically-challenged women. One in particular."

"Are you feeling froggy tonight? Because if you keep that mouth runnin' like that, I'm about to knock those glasses off your face."

I'm kidding. More or less. The problem is Lance knows it.

"Oh, go to Hell," he laughs.

"Already there, brother. Already there."

He takes his glasses off his face and places them on the table. "I usually look at your life and think I'd hate to have it. But after the day I had today, I'd trade you places."

"What? Did the high school kids refuse to learn about the American

Revolution?" I laugh. "You have such a cush job."

"I'm a professional."

"A professional bullshitter, maybe."

He makes a comeback, but it's swallowed in the roar of the crowd as a popular song blares through the overhead speakers.

Crave, an old brick building along Beecher Street, is longer than it is wide, and pulses with the noise of the crowd and music. Alcohol ads, high school sports schedules, and a giant cork board adorn the walls. The latter is a good read and filled with letters and notes from one townsperson to the next. Affairs have been called out, coon dogs found, marriage proposals made, and entire conversations about who is working what shift at the factory have taken place on that thing. It's been a mainstay of the bar since our uncle founded it almost fifty years ago. When our younger brother, Machlan, took over Crave thanks to Uncle George's failing liver, he extended the wall of corkboards all the way to the door.

"That's new," Lance says, moving over one seat closer to me. Motioning to the phallic design made up of yellow rubber duck Christmas lights on the wall between the pool tables, he laughs. "Let me guess: that's Peck's handiwork."

"Naturally. Machlan wasn't thrilled, but Peck rallied the masses and they convinced him to keep it."

"It is nicely done," Lance says, chewing on the end of his glasses. "I can see the art in it."

"Fuck. I should've been an artist if that counts as art."

"Apparently things didn't go well with Molly," Lance says, twisting in his chair.

"She's never gonna give Peck a chance."

At the sound of his name, Peck walks through the front door. He stops just inside, the glow from the exit sign giving his mop of blond hair a pinkish hue.

Peck makes a beeline for our table, a look etched in the lines on his face that sends a ripple of concern up my spine. After growing up with him and then working with him for the last few years, I can read him like a book. Something is wrong.

"What's going on?" I ask, scrambling to my feet as he gets closer.

"Walker, man, you need to get outside," Peck says. "Someone just bashed the front of your truck."

"What?" I hiss, sure I misheard him. "Someone did fucking what?"

"Yeah, man. You need to get out there."

Blood ripping through my veins, I plow my way through the bar. Machlan lifts his chin, sensing something is off, but I shake my head as we pass. I know he loves a good fight, but this one is mine.

Lance is on my heels as we make our way through the crowd. "Who did you piss off now?"

"Someone who wants to die, apparently." My fingers flex against the wood of the door, the warm summer air slamming my face as I hit the sidewalk. "You sure you don't want to stay inside? I think getting into a street fight is against your teacher code of conduct."

"Fuck off," Lance chuckles. "I'll have Peck hold my glasses and I'm in."

"You, my brother, are an intelligent heathen."

"I'll take that as a compliment. I think."

The top of my black pickup truck comes into view, sitting beneath one of the few lamps lining Beecher Street. There are two people standing on the sidewalk next to my truck.

"Do we know them?" I ask Peck through gritted teeth.

"I promise you we've never seen them before."

"So it's not . . ." Lance doesn't finish his sentence. *"Holy shit."*

The two women turn to face us and I think all of our jaws drop. The first is tall with jet black hair and a strong, athletic build. It's the second one who has me struggling to remember why we're out here.

Long, blonde hair with faint streaks of purple and the brightest blue eyes I've ever seen, she assesses me in the hazy streetlight. She doesn't make a show of looking me over like most women do, batting their eyelashes like some damsel in distress. There's something different about her, a quiet confidence that makes her almost unapproachable.

Unapproachable, but still hot as fucking hell.

My gaze drifts down her ample chest, over the white lace fabric of the top that hugs the bends of her body. Cutoff denim jeans cap long, lean legs that only look longer next to the Louisville Slugger half-hidden behind her.

It takes a ton of effort, but my eyes finally tear from her body and to the body of my truck. Sure enough, there's a rip across the grill and a broken headlight that looks an awful lot like a slam from a baseball bat. It's nothing that can't be fixed in my shop, but that's not the point. The point is the disrespect.

"Either of you know what happened?" I ask, leaning against the hood. They remain silent. The only response is a dashed look between them.

Settling my scrutiny on each one individually, watching them squirm, I save the blonde for last.

"Did you see anything?" I ask, turning back to the tall one.

Her weight shifts from one foot to the other as she runs a hand through her shiny hair like we're talking about coffee or having a beer later. "Me? No. I didn't see a thing."

"Really? You were standing out here just now and you didn't see anything?"

"No," she smiles sweetly. "Nothing at all."

Peck steps between us and inspects the damage. When he turns around, he bites the inside of his cheek. "If I were a betting man, Walker, I'd say it looks like someone walloped Daisy with a baseball bat."

The blonde lifts a brow, something on the tip of her tongue that she holds back.

"You got something to say?" I prod.

"You named your truck 'Daisy'?"

Her eyes narrow, almost as if she's taunting me. That she has the guts to challenge me combined with those fucking blue eyes throws me off my game. "I did. Got a problem with that?"

"No. No problem," she says, twisting her lips into an incredibly sexy pout that I want to kiss off her goddamn face. "Just never met a man who named their truck after a flower."

"Me either. Now, before I go calling the Sheriff about this, I'm gonna give you two a moment to consider telling me what happened. And," I say, cutting off the blonde, "I'll give you a piece of information before you decide what to say. Doc Burns' office has cameras installed that will show everything. Just let that sink in a second."

Their eyes go wide as they instinctively move together into a protective huddle. The tall girl points to the blonde who responds with a frantic whisper. She's guilty as hell.

On one hand, I want to break her down and get inside her in ways she's never dreamed. On the other, I can hear my brain issuing an alert to back away slowly.

The longer they confer, the more time I have to watch. The blonde controls the conversation, the other deferring to her as they talk amongst themselves. It's hot as hell.

The light bounces off the wounded plastic of the headlight and draws my attention back to the fact that Daisy is damaged, and in all likelihood, one of these two did it.

"You really calling Kip?" Peck whispers. "He's not gonna do shit about this, you know."

"He might throw them in the back of his cop car and fuck their brains out. Especially the blonde," Lance whistles. "Can you imagine her in handcuffs? *Shit.*"

The thought shoots a flame through my veins that catches me off guard. The vision of her bound up with one of these assholes at the helm irks me. Bad. "You two stay out of this. Let me handle it."

The sound of metal pinging against the ground rings through the air. The girls jump, the blonde leaping away from the aluminum bat as it rolls across the sidewalk and lands in the gutter with a flourish. Her eyes snap to mine, guilt etched across her gorgeous face. "It was an accident."

"How, exactly, does a baseball bat accidentally strike the front of my truck?" I ask. "Did it just hop over there and smash itself into my headlight?"

"Well," she gulps. "I . . ."

"She was imitating her brother," the dark-headed one says. "So we stop using pronouns, I'm Delaney. This is Sienna."

"I'm Walker. That's Peck and Lance." I rest my attention on Sienna. She's leaned against the grey car, her arms crossed over her chest. "So?"

"I was swinging the bat," she says, "while Delaney puked over there and it slipped out of my hands."

"I think we're gonna have to see your swing," Peck chuckles.

Sienna rolls her eyes. "You do *not* need to see my swing."

Imagining her ass popped out, her body moving for our benefit, seems like a fair trade for the hassle of dealing with this tonight.

"How else do we know it was you? It could've been Delaney and you're just covering for her," I explain, loving the frustration on her beautiful face. "Gonna need to see the swing."

"No."

"Lance, call Sheriff Kooch."

"Wait," Sienna sighs. "It *was* an accident. I can cut you a check for the repairs but please don't call the police. I . . . I can't have a record. You don't understand."

Looking away, it takes everything I have not to laugh. The plea in her voice is so damn adorable it almost makes me give in. Yet, she hasn't shown any remorse, and that's something I can't get to sit right.

Swiping the bat out of the gutter, I extend it to her. The air between us heats, our fingers brushing in the exchange. The contact is enough to have her eyes flicking to mine. The light above may be dim, but it's bright enough to see the way her lids hood, her lips part just barely as she pulls her skin from mine.

A zip of energy tumbles through my veins and I remind myself I can't tug on the bat and pull her into me. There's no way I can cover her lips with my own, sliding my tongue across hers, making her attempt at resistance to this proposed swing futile.

Instead, I step back.

"Batter up." Peck motions for her to go. "Let's see it."

"Are you really going to make me do this?"

"Did you really just smash the front of my truck?" I ask. "The answer is the same to both questions, Slugger."

Her eyes narrow, but there's a fire in them that turns me the hell on. She steps away from her friend, zapping all the power I held just a few seconds ago with the flick of her tongue. It darts out, rolling across her bottom lip as the bat comes over her head. Sticking her ass out, bending her knees, her eyes still locked on mine, she slices the bat through the air . . . and stops it at the last possible second before impact.

It's everything I thought it would be.

"Any questions, fellas?" she asks, propping it up on one shoulder.

"I have one," I say, forcing a swallow, trying to redirect my thoughts. "If you could stop it that fast, then why the fuck didn't you do that the first time?"

"Very funny." She tosses the bat into the back seat of the car and crosses her arms in front of her again.

"Can I ask why you have a baseball bat to begin with?" Lance asks. "Do you belong to some softball league or something? If so, I just took a huge interest in women's softball."

Sienna laughs as Delaney's face turns red. "Delaney's car is like a scavenger hunt. You can find anything in there. So while she got sick, I just rummaged around in the trunk, found the bat, and fooled around." She looks at me, her eyes softening. "Are you going to be here for a while? I'll go home and get the money. I didn't bring my debit card with me tonight."

It'll cost fifty bucks to fix the damage and about an hour's time. Definitely not worth her going out of her way tonight. But it *is* worth making her come around again and say she's sorry. It might do her some good.

Might not hurt me either.

She clicks her tongue against the roof of her mouth, the motion driving me crazy.

"Come see me Monday morning at Crank. It's two streets over," I say, gesturing to the north, before I can talk sense in to myself.

"Smart," Peck whispers behind me, getting an elbow to the side from Lance.

Her jaw sets, a glimmer of resistance clouding her baby blue eyes. "I have plans Monday. I can try on Tuesday."

The nonchalant attitude cuts through me, like her fuckup is no big deal. I wasn't set on Monday morning, but I am now. "Monday or I call the Sheriff. Your decision, but make it quick. I got shit to do."

"Fine," she huffs. "Monday."

"Fine," I mock. "See you Monday morning."

We start back down the sidewalk, her gaze heavy on my back. I pause at the bumper of their car. "Peck got your license plate number, so don't think about not showing."

"I did not," Peck hisses, catching another elbow from Lance as their car doors open and slam shut.

"What the hell are you going to do with that?" Lance asks once we're out of earshot. "Because I have a list of suggestions if you need them."

As we get farther away, the air clearing of Sienna's perfume, I realize it's not suggestions I need. It's a heavy dose of self-control.

chapter
Two

Sienna

I DIDN'T EVEN SAY I'M *sorry*.

Groaning, I roll over and toss the magazine I was trying to distract myself with onto the coffee table. Out of all the things that could've kept me up last night, it was my conscience.

Tossing and turning all night, my brain feels like it's been through the wringer and my body through a fight.

Shutting my eyes, I see Walker's face just like I have every thirty seconds since I saw him. His thick, shiny black hair and bottomless brown eyes stare back at me. The controlled demeanor and intensity that swirled off him like a tremor foreshadowing an earthquake make me unsteady.

Putting him in a box seems impossible. He relaxes me with a smile and then puts my defenses up with an asshole remark. He's playful when asking me to swing the bat, yet demanding with his "Be there Monday morning or Sheriff." It's dizzying.

"Hey." Delaney's voice jostles me from my daydream. "How long have you been up?"

"A while. The neighbor decided to mow his lawn at the crack of dawn," I say, omitting the whole Walker thing for now.

She yawns, stretching her arms high above her head. "I just started a pot of coffee. Had any yet?"

"Nope. I'm too tired for even basic tasks this morning."

"Do you have a busy day planned or can you just chill out?"

"Well, since we wrapped up the project that would never end and decided to take a couple weeks off before jumping back in, I'm chilling out."

She curls up on the chair across from me. "We needed this break. *I* needed this break."

"Me too," I admit. "My brain needs to reset. We've done great this first year, but there are so many ways we could go starting this fall. I read some articles I want to show you."

Delaney nods, gazing into the distance.

The summer sun streams through the windows, a threat of rain rolling in from the west. Before we know it, it'll be fall, then winter, and another year will have passed.

Thinking of it like that causes a swell of anxiety to bubble in my belly, a reminder that another year will have gone by and I still feel like I have nothing figured out about my life.

I'm only in Illinois because of Delaney. When she came up with the idea for Boutique Designs, I was all in and didn't even mind moving up here despite my hatred of all things winter so she could stay near her family. But now our lease is almost up on the house we've been renting, and when I try to push forward on expanding our brand and getting a long-term plan in place, she drags her feet. I'm in this static state, unable to move.

"About all that . . ." Delaney says.

Sitting up, groaning as my back screams in distress, I push it aside and focus on my friend. "What's up?"

"Um, well . . ." She takes down her ponytail and puts it back up. "I want to thank you for being such a good friend."

"Okay . . ."

She takes a slow, deep breath. "Remember when I had dinner with my mom a few weeks ago and came home crying?"

"Yeah," I say, utterly confused as to where this is going.

"Dad got a new contract at the farm."

"That's great," I say, knowing her family had been struggling. "He must be thrilled."

"He is. Mom too. It's for production of organic dairy, which is all the rage, but there's all this red tape involved . . ." She looks at the floor, avoiding my gaze.

Shifting in my seat, I try to figure out what she's saying so she doesn't have to come out and say it. I got nothing. "What does this mean for you?"

"They need my help. Full time." She looks up at me, her eyes wide. "I couldn't design with you and work for them. It would be too much to do both things."

"Is that what you want?" I ask, my mind reeling. This would answer so many questions, explain her lack of motivation over the last few weeks.

"I don't know," she groans, getting to her feet. She walks a circle around the living room, kicking a gum wrapper as she goes. "I need to help my parents. I'm not sure they'll make it if I don't." Her voice breaks, and when she looks at me, her eyes are watery.

"I get it." Standing, I make my way to her and pull her into a hug. "Family always comes first, Delaney. I respect that."

She pulls back, wiping her face with the back of her hand. "You are the best person I know."

"Oh, I am not," I laugh.

"Yes, you are. You're so kind. You want to fix everything and you'd give anyone the shirt off your back. You're gorgeous and talented and—"

"Stop. You're making me feel weird."

She laughs too before taking her seat again. "I'll have to move back to my parents' property. Is that okay? I mean, I know you can afford the rent, but I feel like I'm abandoning you."

"It's fine. You do what you have to do." Even as the words come out of my mouth, I can't help but wonder what I will do. Where does this leave me?

"I didn't even want to bring this up until we finished the Paxton Project and were on vacation. I've been a wreck."

"Don't be nervous about talking to me. Ever," I tell her. "You'll just be a half hour away. I'll be fine here until I figure out how to navigate this little curveball."

She sniffles before getting back up, her nerves getting the best of her. "Enough touchy-feely. I'm going to get coffee."

"You do that," I laugh, listening to her grumble about not being a baby as she walks out of the room.

Falling back onto the couch again, I rub my temples. As if I didn't have enough stress with the truck issue, now I have this.

Looking around the place we've lived in for a year now, it suddenly feels less like home than it did ten minutes ago, and it didn't feel particularly home-like then. With Delaney gone, it'll be even worse.

A bout of loneliness creeps in to my stomach as I try to figure out what I'm going to do. Stay here? A place I know really no one but Delaney and a couple of her friends and a couple of guys I've seen here and there? Or go back to Savannah and feel like a failure for landing back there again?

What do I do with Boutique Designs? Can I run it on my own? Can I do the things I want to do as a one-woman show?

I bury my head in my hands.

"You're okay with this?" Delaney asks, coming in and handing me a mug of coffee.

"I understand you wanting to help your family. Of course," I tell her. "I hope someday you figure out how to follow your dreams in the process, but I get it. Truly."

"Will you stay here or go back to Georgia?"

"I don't know," I say, sipping the brew. "That's the beauty of our company, I guess. I can do it from anywhere."

"I'd go back. There are all those sexy-as-hell brothers of yours."

"Brothers, Delaney. They're my brothers. They're gross."

I attempt a snarl, but it doesn't come out that way. As gross as they are, I love them so much. Despite their overbearing and ridiculous antics, they are the best brothers in the world and have taught me so much.

Delaney smiles over the brim of her mug. "So stay here."

"Probably not," I laugh. "I'm definitely going somewhere warmer. Somewhere . . . inspiring."

"You know what I find inspiring?" she asks, wiggling her eyebrows. "We should go to the bakery over in Linton and get a donut and see if we can bump into anyone."

The tension in my shoulders evaporates as the notes of her giggle work through the room and I see right through her plan. "Yeah, I'm sure the guys from the bar are having a croissant there this morning, Delaney," I say, rolling my eyes. "Highly unlikely."

"Probably not. But we might run into them at the gas station. Or . . ."

"We are not stalking random guys on a Sunday morning," I laugh. "Even if they were totally cute."

"Cute? They aren't puppies, Sienna. They were *stallions*."

"You've officially lost it."

She grins, plopping down her coffee mug and tucking her legs up under her. The lightheartedness slips from her face as she clears her throat. "What are you going to do about the truck?"

The flip of my stomach at his smirk turns into a crazy knotted mess at the memory of last night.

Everything about last night was an epic fail.

"I don't know what I'm going to do about it," I sigh. "I've been thinking about it all morning. I don't even think I said I'm sorry."

"In your defense, none of us were prepared to be accosted by three men that good-looking at midnight in Linton of all places."

"What do they put in the water over there?"

"Sex appeal. Straight into the pipeline," she says, pumping a fist in celebration of our luck.

The lust dampens as my conscience takes over and guilt swamps me. "Now that I've had a second to clear my mind, I'm kind of embarrassed, Delaney."

"It was an accident."

"I know. But I messed up his truck," I wince. "And I probably came across as an unapologetic brat."

"No one uses the word 'brat' unless they're eighty," she teases. "And you are the least bratty person I've ever met."

"That doesn't mean he knows that."

She considers this. "Okay. I see your point and I have a suggestion."

Groaning, I set my mug on the coffee table. "I'm not sure I even want to hear this."

"Sure you do!" she says, her eyes dancing. "Go over there on Monday and offer up a night with you in exchange for the damage."

"I will do no such thing," I say, shaking my head. But two nights . . .

"But you want to. I know you do."

"That doesn't matter," I laugh. "I'm going over there on Monday to apologize and offer again to pay for the damage—with money. It's the least I can do. And hopefully he won't file a police report."

"He's not going to do that," she tsks.

"We don't know anything about them other than they're cute. They could be total assholes, Delaney. I can't risk it. Can you imagine Graham's reaction? Or my father's?" My eyes squeeze shut so hard my temple pulses. "I can hear them now. It would be a nightmare."

"Fine. You're right. Go see him Monday and say you're sorry. But if he offers any other exchanges, follow through and give me details."

My cheeks heat as I consider being in Walker's orbit again. All night, I kept telling myself I imagined the weight of his gaze and the crackle of energy that passed between us as he handed me the bat. It will do me no good to create some infatuation with the sexy stranger. When I see him again, especially being a desecrator of his property, I need to have my wits about me in case I need to think straight. That means not fantasizing about him. Again. Too much.

Delaney hops off the barstool and rinses out her coffee cup. "If you won't go to Linton, I'm getting a shower. Let's do something this after-noon. We could get manicures."

"Let's do that."

She flips me a thumbs-up and pads down the hallway towards the bathroom.

Gazing out the window, my heartbeat picks up at the thought of seeing Walker tomorrow. He was playful with his teasing, but there was a glimmer of seriousness buried in those deliciously dark eyes. Just pre-tending to feel them watching me has a rash of goose bumps flittering across my skin.

It may not be a bad way to spend a few nights while I'm still in town. Then again, something tells me spending even one night with Walker might be the worst thing to ever happen to me.

chapter
Three

Walker

"IT WAS THE ALTERNATOR AFTER all," Peck sighs, wiping his greasy hands off on a blue towel.

"I'll get a new one ordered. What about the tire for the Ranger? Did you get it on? David should be in this afternoon to pick it up."

"Done, boss."

Rolling my eyes, I push open the door to the office of Crank, holding it open for my one employee. "Why don't you go ahead and get lunch?"

"Okay." Peck tosses the dirty rag towards the hamper along the back wall. It hits the rounded top of the pile and spills onto the floor with an assortment of others. "That's getting a little out of control, yeah?"

"Yeah," I sigh. "Maybe I'll take them to the laundromat tonight."

Glancing around the shop, I take in everything that needs to be done. Shit I don't have time for. Shit I never thought about needing to do when I took this place over after my parents passed away a few years ago. I just saw the business that I'd wanted to have as my own since I was twelve and decided that being a bull rider might not be for me. Despite helping out here since I could walk, I never realized all of the little things that had to be done. I hate them.

Besides the shop rags, there's a coffee pot that hasn't been washed maybe ever. A bathroom with more discarded toilet paper tubes than actual toilet paper. Mud that was tracked in last week in the rain still dots the floor, and piles upon piles of receipts, work notes, orders, and shipping logs are scattered across the desk. And I have no time or energy to sort any of it.

"I'm going to head home and grab a bite to eat," Peck says. "Nana made fried chicken yesterday and sent leftovers home with me."

"The one Sunday dinner I miss and she makes fried chicken. Are you kidding me?"

"I think she was going to make meatloaf and then you skipped church. This was your punishment" he cackles. "Miss next week, will ya? Maybe we'll get dumplings."

"Get out of here while you still have a job. And bring me back some."

"That's the thing," he says, calling out over his shoulder. "She only sent enough for me. Seems like she knew you'd ask that."

His laughter trails through the room as the door snaps shut behind him.

Taking a quick look at everything I need to do, I do what I did all weekend and don't do any of it. I can't think of the last time I let things go like this. Normally when I'm stressed, I throw myself into my work and forget the world. Not this time.

A fog presses against my shoulders that hit me after the whole incident with my truck. It wasn't the truck that bothered me so much. It was *her*.

Something about Sienna flipped me sideways and I haven't been able to get upright. It, meaning *she*, has not been far from my mind since they pulled away from Crave. I can't shake it, can't escape this ripple in my stomach that keeps pulling me back to the memory of her.

Regardless, it's made me sleep-deprived, blue-balled, and as confused as I am after a fifth of Hennessy. I have no time or business dealing with this. I just need to shake it and move on.

Glancing at the clock, it's clear she's not coming by. As much as I hate admitting it, I was hoping she'd actually show. Best case scenario would include her saying or doing something completely horrible that would put an end to the fascination that had me up so late Saturday night

I missed church *and* Nana's dinner. Something has to give because I can't hack many more nights like that. Or mornings in the shower, squeezing one off in my hand while I imagine what the curve of her hip feels like beneath me.

Sorting through invoices, I force myself to be somewhat productive until the door chimes ring. Expecting to see Peck, I look up with a line on my tongue. Instead, invoices spill from my hands, scattering in a mess on the desk in front of me as I take her in.

A bright pink tank top showcases Sienna's perfectly round breasts, drooping not quite low enough for her cleavage to be visible. Long gold earrings hang from her ears and her hair is a wild mess, held back only by a pair of oversized sunglasses. On her legs is another pair of cutoff jeans. Thankful I'm sitting so my cock won't be visible, I try to keep my face passive. Hot or not, this *is* the girl who banged up my truck and ruined my weekend. "You're late."

She assesses me for a half a second. "That depends on who you ask."

"I said this morning. It's noon."

"And I said I'd be here today. It's still today."

She saunters towards the desk with the confidence of a woman that usually gets what she wants. With every step she takes, I can almost taste the sweetness of her perfume, feel the silkiness of her hair wrapped around my fist.

Still, she knows she's messing with me, and while it's a turn-on to watch her almost stalk her way across the lobby, it's also proving she thinks she can just flirt her way around this, the one thing I hoped she wouldn't do. Maybe I hoped she'd be different and take this seriously.

"Why did you even bother to come by?" I ask, my tone even harsher than I intended.

"I came to tell you I'm sorry."

The pen in my hand stops scrawling across the notepad in front of me, but I don't look up.

"I mean it," she adds. "I've thought about this all weekend, and I don't think I even apologized to you."

She waits for me to utter an acceptance of her apology, one I don't quite believe because believing gets you disappointed. But when I lift my gaze, the complete somberness in her features has me giving her the benefit of the doubt.

Sitting back in my chair, I press my lips together. "You're right. You didn't apologize."

"I'm embarrassed. I don't know what happened to me . . ." Her eyes drop to the floor, a tiny smile gracing her shiny lips. "Please accept my apology." She waits for my response, one I don't give her. Finally, after what feels like an eternity, she looks up at me. "So . . . you're still really pissed?"

"You took a bat to my truck, Slugger."

"Stop calling me 'Slugger.'"

I can't help but return her lopsided grin, despite my best efforts. I hate the way my anger is dissipating, the way my shoulders feel lighter than they have since Saturday night.

"You have one hell of a swing," I note, remembering more about what her body looked like moving the bat through the air than the actual mechanics of the swing. "I bet your daddy is proud. Were you a college softball standout or something?"

"No. Just a good learner."

I try not to frown. "Ex-boyfriend play?"

"Nah, just my brother," she says with a shrug. "I spent half my life at a baseball stadium or practice field watching him do his thing."

"Was he any good?"

"Decent," she says. "I take credit for any success he ever had. I threw him so many pop flies growing up he owes me."

"I'm sure he owes it all to you," I chuckle.

She grins, the damn thing lighting up the room. Leaning against the desk, she bites her bottom lip. "So, about Daisy . . ."

Before I can respond, the chimes ring behind her. We jump like we've been caught doing something we weren't supposed to be.

"Peck was right," Kip says, taking off his brown Sheriff's hat and purposefully *not* looking at Sienna. "And that's all I'm going to say about that."

"You called the Sheriff?" Sienna whips around, her eyes wide. "Damn it, Walker. I said I'll pay for it. Don't you believe me?"

"Sienna—"

"Let me introduce myself," Kip says, extending a hand. "I'm Sheriff

Kooch, the man in charge of this county. And who might you be?"

"Sienna." She squares her shoulders and bats her eyes once for good measure. "I told him I'd pay for the damage. There's really no reason for you to be involved. Don't you have a lot of other things to take care of today? Things that matter?"

Kip doesn't say anything, just turns to me with a slightly raised brow. He's putty in her hands. If I don't watch it, he'll be writing *me* the ticket.

"Daisy matters," I say, ignoring the rest for now.

"My legal footprint matters," she shoots back.

"Yeah, Walker," Kip adds in. "Peck told me what happened. Pretty silly to get the law involved in an accident."

"No, the fact that a grown man named his truck after a flower is silly." Sienna has a hand on her narrow hip and waits for my response.

"It's not named after a flower, smartass. Ever heard of 'The Dukes of Hazzard'?"

"I'm from Savannah. Of course I have. I didn't know Yankees were allowed to watch it."

Our gazes tangle together, heating the longer they hold. Her chest rises and falls, her bottom lip dropping just enough that I can see it. Instead of hurdling this desk and pressing her back against the wall in front of Kip, God, and anyone else who happens to walk in with not so much as a fuck given, I choose to break the spell in a different way.

"What do you say, Sheriff?" I ask, forcing a hot swallow down my throat.

Kip looks at me, then Sienna, and back at me. A smile slides over his face. "I say I just came in to tell you Nana is on her way over and she's fit to be tied. Seems as if her favorite grandson didn't show up to church yesterday."

Sienna's jaw drops. "You didn't call him, did you?"

"If he would've called me and told me about *you*, I'd have been here a lot faster, sweetheart," Kip laughs. A burst of static sounds through the air and instructions are doled out from the operator on the other side of his walkie-talkie. "I gotta go. It was nice to meet you, Sienna."

He's gone as quickly as he came, the rip of gravel sounding as he takes off to play hero.

As the chimes settle, Sienna slowly turns to face me. "You. Are. A. Jerk."

"It's been said."

"Were you going to let me think you called the cops?" she snaps. "That's not nice, Walker."

"I never told you I was nice."

She considers this as she leans against the desk, looking around the shop. "This place is a mess, if you don't mind me saying."

"I do mind, actually," I grumble, picking the pen back up.

"Forget it," she says, digging in her purse and pulling out a wallet. A wad of cash comes from one of the compartments. "Let's get this figured out. How much do I owe you for the repairs?"

"First of all," I say, shaking my head, "you never show how much money you have. Haven't you ever listened to Kenny Rogers, country girl? You don't show your hand while you're still dealing. You wait. Otherwise, someone will take advantage of you."

Her tongue darts across her bottom lip, leaving a trail of wetness behind. The light catches it, my eyes glued to her mouth as she speaks. "Are you going to take advantage of me?"

Grimacing and cursing whoever is on the other end of the phone ringing in my pocket to the pits of hell, I retrieve it. My eyes not leaving hers, I answer it because if this isn't a bailout, I don't know what is. "Crank."

The person on the other end talks, but I have no idea what they say. I can, however, recount every move Sienna makes in front of me.

I get off the chair, motion for her to give me a minute, and head into the shop area so hopefully I can concentrate on something other than taking deep, repeated advantage of this infuriating woman.

chapter
Four

Sienna

AS SOON AS HE'S OUT of sight, my whole body feels the void of his energy. My knees wobble, my breath whispering across my lips with a shaky sound. All this as I attempt to pull precious air into my lungs while searching for the filter for my mouth.

Are you going to take advantage of me? Did I really just ask him that?

Fanning my face, I watch him through the window. Delaney is right. *Cute* doesn't cut it. He's so far beyond *cute* that I'm not sure there's been a word created to encompass it all. He's not good-looking like the guys I usually date. Those guys are clean-shaven, hair gelled, politically-correct boys I've met at a fashion event or political rally. Walker is . . . not. He's nothing of the sort.

His five o'clock stubble begs me to run my fingers down it, feeling the coarseness against my palm. His skin isn't moisturized or evenly tanned, but rather rough and with tan lines that I can see around his watch. The words out of his mouth haven't been chosen out of a list of words his private school teachers drilled into him. He doesn't know me or my family, and even if he did, I bet he wouldn't care.

There's something raw and real about Walker. It's the way he looks at me, the way I can't quite tell if he wants to grab me and kiss the hell out of me or throw me out of the room. Either way, it burns my libido like it's a forest hit with a hot match. My choice: kiss the hell out of me.

I could leave. I could leave a stack of cash on the desk that I took from the ATM this morning and skate, getting back to reality. Like I should. But that option, as logical as it is, seems so . . . plain. Boring. Predictable.

Is this what the start of an addiction feels like? A hankering for more, even when I know taking it in large doses might kill me? Being absolutely sure I shouldn't be partaking, but not able to talk myself out of it either?

This place, this man, is a breath of oily-scented, testosterone-fueled air. It's as foreign to me as outer space. It's another planet, and while I was never the little girl who wanted to go to outer space, I'll sign up for this ride just to see what it's like.

The chimes ring and I spring around. An old man with a plaid golfer's hat and worn blue jeans, a man I doubt has ever played golf a day in his life, stands in the doorway. "Seen Walker?" he asks, his voice gruff like there's a pack of cigarettes in one of his pockets.

"He's in the back," I volunteer.

"I hope he doesn't take long," he murmurs, wincing as a hand goes to the small of his back.

He looks at the floor, the lines in his face so deeply etched that I wonder if he was born with some of them. Regardless, my heart breaks when he posts a hand on the wall and leans against it with a cringe, the hole in the toe of his shoe dark and unraveling.

"Let's get you a chair," I say, looking around. There's none in the lobby, but I spy the one behind the counter. I bring it around and help him get settled.

He pats my hand. "You are a doll. Thank you."

"You're welcome."

He seems unsure with his repeated head-to-toe scans of me, like he's wondering if I'm an imposter taking over Crank without anyone's knowledge. He'd be right, but for whatever strange reason, I don't feel like I *don't* belong here. I just feel like I haven't figured it out yet.

"Is Peck around?" he asks.

"I've only seen Walker. Do you need something I can help with?"

"My truck. I need to meet my wife for breakfast. I should've been there an hour ago but my neighbor was late picking me up and all that jazz."

"Where is your wife?" I ask.

"The nursing home." He forces a swallow. "She's been there two years now. I go by every morning for breakfast and I'm never late. She hates being late. That's all I heard for the fifty-five years we've been married—if you aren't early, you're late."

"Maybe she'll cut you some slack," I offer. "Especially if this is your first offense."

His eyes drift from the window to me, a sadness written so heavy in his features that I feel it in my soul. "She won't care. She doesn't even know I'm there. Alzheimer's is a son of a bitch."

Nodding is all I can do because if I say a word, he'll hear the lump in my throat.

"I walked into her daddy's lumber yard when I was fifteen and she was up to her knees in mud. She was the most beautiful thing I'd ever seen." He dabs at his eyes with a blue bandana, the tip of his nose turning red. "Fifty-five years is a long time to sleep next to someone and then they don't remember who you are."

"I'm so sorry," I say, my own eyes watering. Placing my hand on his over his knee, I squat in front of him. "That has to be very hard."

"It's the hardest thing I've ever done. Harder than going to war, harder than losing our baby at three months old. It's like having my heart cut out of my chest."

His other hand, wrinkly and cool, settles on top of mine. They shake, his knee vibrating with his valiant attempt at restraining his emotions.

"She loves you," I tell him, my eyes burning. "Remember that as you go to see her and think she doesn't remember you. She does. She just can't tell you."

His tears flow freely, dripping down his hollowed cheeks like a floodgate has been broken. "Thank you, hon. I needed to hear that today." As his face falls, his eyes sliding closed to the exhaustion riddling his old body, I turn away.

Heading to the desk, sensing his need to change the subject, I clear my throat. Discreetly wiping my face with the tail end of my shirt, I take a deep breath. "What kind of car did you have?"

"Black Ranger. I had a tire bust on me yesterday and Walker had a used one out back."

The desk is covered in receipts and notes, candy wrappers and invoices. There's no way anyone knows what's actually here. The further I try to dig, the deeper the mess becomes.

I look up when the chimes ring again. A tall, dark-haired woman with a baby wrapped to her chest and another child holding her hand steps inside. She greets the old man and then looks skeptically at me. "Walker around?"

"He's on a call," I say as the baby starts to scream.

"Shhh," she whispers, bouncing herself up and down. "Shhh, Gabriel. It's okay."

"Mommy," the other one whines. "I'm tired."

"I know, baby," the lady tells him. "We'll have the van in a second."

"You walk down here, MaryAnn?" the old man asks her. "All the way from Washington Street?"

Over the wails of the baby and the whining of the child, she tries to stay calm. "I hit a deer in the van last week and Mike had to work today."

"I still can't believe you walked all that way," the old man says. "That's a couple miles."

"The baby has a doctor's appointment this morning. He's having an allergic reaction to something and we can't figure it out. It's costing a fortune with co-pays, which is why Mike is still at work. He's been working all the overtime they'll give him." She sags against the wall, patting the older boy's hair. "It could be worse, right?"

Out of the corner of my eye, I see the exchange between the old man and the woman. It's nothing more than a slight tip of their chin, but they understand each other on a level that I don't. I don't know what it's like to be them, and to even consider it strikes a fear in me that I can't shake.

I can't imagine my sister-in-law, Danielle, walking two miles with Ryan because she didn't have another choice. Especially in this heat with a sick baby.

"I'll try to find your invoice," I volunteer, feeling so frustratingly helpless. "What kind of car?"

"A maroon van. I have no idea what year it is," she says, still bobbing the baby up and down. "I barely know what I had for breakfast at this point."

Thrust into what my mom calls "do-er mode," I scramble for something to do to make her day easier.

"Do you have your keys?" I ask, holding up a couple of random papers. "I found your invoices."

"Walker always leaves them on the floor mat," the old man says. "What do I owe him?"

"Well," I say, forcing a swallow, hoping this doesn't bite me in the ass. "You, sir, have no charge because the tire they used was going to be thrown away anyway. Right?"

"That's what he said," the man agrees, but doesn't look convinced.

"And you, madam," I say, hurrying along, "there's something here about insurance and write-off's, but Walker's writing is crap and I can't figure it all out. It just says zero with a circle around it," I shrug.

"You're kidding me." A flitter of hope casting across her face. "I don't owe anything? Are you sure?"

"I'm sure. Says it right here."

Holding my breath, seeing if they believe me, I wait until they prepare to leave. The woman opens the door and grabs the little boy's hand. "Tell Walker thank you," she says. "I'll send Mike over this week to double check. I just . . . I appreciate it."

I round the corner and offer a hand to the old man. "Do you need help outside?"

Groaning as he gets to his feet, he takes both of my hands in his. "I'm going to be fine. Have a blessed day, sweetheart."

"You too. Enjoy your breakfast."

"It's the best part of my day."

I take a quick step and open the door for him. As he heads to his truck, I move to the window and watch him make his way off the stoop and through the gravel. Rummaging around the floorboard, he retrieves his keys. He hobbles into the front seat, adjusts his hat, and pulls out.

"Was someone here?" Walker asks from behind me. "I thought I heard the door a couple of times."

Giving myself a moment to adjust before turning around, I scramble for an angle to talk myself out of this jam. I'm sure he's not going to be thrilled with this bit of news, but I'm just as sure I didn't have a choice other than to help them both.

"I was going to ask you," I say, turning around. "How much would a used tire cost for my car?"

Furrowing his brow, he shrugs. "Depends on what size you have."

"Um . . . the size of a Ford Ranger, I think."

Walker crosses his arms in front of him, the muscles in his thick forearms flexing. "Funny. I didn't have you pegged as driving a Ranger."

"Funny. How do you know me well enough to know what I would drive?"

"I don't," he admits. "I'd say that a used tire would run you thirty-five bucks or so."

He moseys across the room and stands next to me, so close I can barely think. He's a step from my personal bubble, his cologne knowing no bounds and filling it with his heated, working man scent that has me shivering despite the heat.

"Looks like I need to call Kip," Walker notes.

"Why?"

"Someone stole Dave Cooper's truck. A Ranger," he adds, watching me carefully.

Gulping, I take a step away. "I have another question. What would it cost to repair a car that hit a deer?"

He's not amused. Storming across the room, he swings open the door. "Where is MaryAnn Maylor's van?"

"Well, she was here," I say, taking a couple of steps to the corner. "And so was Dave . . ."

His face doesn't flinch. He doesn't even make an attempt to speak, just stares at me in a mixture of disbelief and disdain.

"Can you add their bills onto my tab?" I cringe, waiting for his eruption.

"You let them take their cars without paying?" he booms.

"No, I didn't. I mean, I did," I correct. "But it's okay. I'll pay for them."

He walks in a circle, shaking his head. "Dave's tire is about thirty-five bucks. But MaryAnn's van was about fifteen hundred." He stops and looks at me. "You have that in your pocket?"

"No, but I'll get it."

He flashes me a glare before heading back to the desk. One look at it and he's back to me. "And I suppose you just messed this up too?"

"Oh, no. That was a mess before," I shoot back. "I looked for the invoices, trying to do you a favor—"

"I didn't ask you for a favor. I asked you to come by and apologize for fucking up my truck, not waltz in here like you own the damn place and cost me another two grand."

"Fifteen thirty-five," I correct, hoping for the best.

I think he's going to explode. He turns away, his back heaving as he fills his lungs with air. The sound of it whooshing out of his body gushes through the room.

"What was I supposed to do?" I ask when he turns to face me.

There's a weakness in his glare, one that tells me I can make him see the light. I see this in my brother Graham every so often when he's trying to nix some idea I have. It's an opening, a small window of opportunity to appeal to their humanity and get them to come around.

I stand in front of the desk, game face on. "I felt sorry for them. Dave needed to go have breakfast with his wife who has Alzheimer's. She doesn't even know he's there every day. How sad is that? And MaryAnn walked all the way over here and it was like two miles with two babies."

This seems to weaken his resolve.

"Why didn't she call? Peck would've gone and picked her up," he says, the irritation in his tone a little less prevalent.

"I don't know," I rush, trying not to lose momentum. "But she was stressed out, her husband's working doubles, and they have a sick baby. So sue me for having a heart if you're that much of a dick. But I'll pay for all of it."

He fiddles with the papers in front of him, the lines on his forehead melting away with each passing second. The room settles, the only sounds the beating of my heart and the papers he's pretending to deal with.

"Don't act like you know what any of that is," I kid.

"It might look like a mess, but I actually do know where everything is.

Most everything, anyway," he grumbles. Retrieving two pieces of paper, one missing the bottom corner, he holds them in the air. "These are the invoices you were looking for."

"I'll take care of them."

He sets them back down and leans on the desk. His brown eyes are filled with something I haven't seen before, something that makes me feel like everything over the past few days comes down to this moment, like if I fall, I may never recover. Only it's not a fall from a ledge or a fall from grace, it's a fall into those chocolatey eyes. It's a delicious and yet uncomfortable feeling and all I can do is shift my weight from one foot to the other and hold on tight.

"How am I supposed to take your money when you won't take anyone else's?" he asks.

"One is not dependent on the other."

He looks over my shoulder and laughs. "Brace yourself."

"Why?"

"My Nana is two seconds from walking through the door."

The chime hits on demand and the entire feel of the room shifts.

"Walker Elder Gibson, what do you think you're doing?" The door latches closed as she sees me. "Oh, I'm sorry, honey. Are you busy?"

"No, Nana," he says, his chin dipping with a shy smile. "I'm never busy. I just come here to hang out all day every day."

"Don't give me that . . ."

She's in her mid-sixties, if I were guessing, wearing a white dress with tiny blue flowers. Her hair is gunmetal silver and set in a way that makes me wonder if she still visits the beauty shop on Saturday morning like the little old ladies in Savannah do. Her belly is round and in her arms is a wooden picnic basket.

She pauses in the middle of the room, giving me a quick once-over with the finesse of a professional. "I didn't mean to walk in on the middle of anything," she alludes, smiling at me. "Should I come back another time?"

"Stop it," Walker hisses before I can respond. He crosses the room and plants a kiss on her cheek. "Did you bring me lunch? I heard you made fried chicken yesterday."

"And you would've known that yesterday had you had your fanny in a pew at Holy Hills like you should've," she sighs. "I wasn't going to bring you any, then I prayed about it and thought maybe you had a good excuse." She looks at me out of the corner of her eye, a grin tipping up the edge of her lips. "She's awfully pretty, Walker, but she's no excuse to miss out on Jesus."

"Nana!"

Before I know what's happening, my laughter fills the room. "You tell him, Mrs. Gibson," I say, then cover my mouth with one hand.

"First, call me Nana," she corrects. "Second, don't cover your mouth. Women around here have to speak up or we're never heard. Remember that."

"I will," I say, relieved.

"And you are?"

"I'm Sienna," I say, offering a hand her way. She gives it a firm, yet gentle shake. "It's nice to meet you. But, for the record, I'm not his excuse for missing church." Peering over my shoulder, I give Walker a little smile. "How could you disappoint this woman and miss church?"

Licking his lips, he'd say something altogether different if Nana weren't standing here. That I know for sure. But she is, so he cocks a brow. "You better stay out of this, *Slugger*."

"Now, I didn't mean anything by what I said," Nana says, either not paying attention or choosing to ignore the look her grandson and I are exchanging. "It's just that I don't ask nothing of this boy, or any of 'em, for that matter, except they get their behinds to church on Sunday and come over for dinner most of them. That's it. I'm not gonna be alive much longer and I—"

"Oh, you are too," Walker sighs, cutting her off. "And I'm sorry about yesterday. I wasn't feeling good."

"You seem to be feeling better now," she points out.

"Yeah, well . . ." He looks at me through the longest lashes I've ever seen on a man. "I'll be there this week. Promise."

"You better." She hands him the picnic basket. "If I'd known you had company, I would've brought you extra. Speaking of which, is this your girlfriend?"

"Nana . . ."

"Oh, no," I say hurriedly, not wanting her to get the wrong impression. "I'm just here to settle up some business."

"He'll be fair and he does good work," she says, smiling proudly at Walker. "He's a good, good boy."

Walker's cheeks turn a soft shade of pink as he switches the basket in his hands. "Let's get back to the chicken. There's more you didn't bring? What are you saving it for?"

"For my grandsons who show up to church," she winks, heading to the door. "Sienna, make sure he shares with you. I'm not known around these parts for my fried chicken for nothing."

"Will do. Nice to meet you, Nana."

"Same here, honey."

"See ya, Nana," Walker calls after her.

He sets the basket on the counter. There's a sudden awkwardness, a void that needs filled and I don't know with what or how. I can't decipher the look on his face or the way my stomach is all twisted in knots. Despite not really wanting to leave, it's the only choice. It's the responsible choice. It's the one I don't want to make but do anyway.

"Let me pay you what I have and I'll bring the rest by later," I say.

His brows shoot to the ceiling as he fiddles with the edge of the basket. "Don't worry about it."

"Of course I'm going to worry about it."

"The damage is done."

"And I want to fix it," I insist.

"Are you still arguing over Daisy?" Peck, the light-haired guy from the other night, comes from the garage bay, a huge grin on his face. "Just take her money and give it to me."

"Fuck off," Walker laughs.

"Ah, Nana brought you lunch after all," Peck notes, knocking on the top of the basket. "It's sickening how favored you are."

The two of them spar back and forth, neither of them serious but both of them trying to win the argument. Walker fills him in on the Dave and MaryAnn drama and Peck continues to just give him shit about it. It's hysterical and reminds me a lot of my brothers back home. I didn't realize how much I missed this feeling of camaraderie, this sensation of family.

"I have an idea," Peck says, bringing me back to the present. "We have a lot of shit that needs done around here. Since y'all can't agree on money, why don't you just stick around and help out some?"

"Because she's not a fucking maid and that's what we need," Walker barks immediately, scowling at his cousin.

"Wait," I say, looking between the two. Walker isn't going to let me pay him back and I know he can't afford to be out that much. I can't live with costing him that much either. "That's not a bad idea, really. I mean, I'm not your maid and I'm not cleaning that filthy bathroom."

"That bathroom hasn't been cleaned in years," Peck sighs.

"I can believe that," I say, scrunching my nose. "But I wouldn't be averse to sweeping some of this mud up and maybe organizing that desk, because it's driving me nuts."

"It's not necessary," Walker says.

"It's *totally* necessary," Peck counters. "We were just talking about it before you got here. Well, the cleaning part. Not the you part. Although . . ."

Walker looks at me, the pools of chocolate dragging me in just like they did the other night. I'm not quite sure if he likes me or loathes me, but either way, I can't look anywhere else.

"I'm technically on vacation for a couple of weeks and am probably going to leave town after that anyway. I'm going to have some time on my hands," I point out. "I really don't mind working off what I owe. Heck, it might even be good for me and I know it would be good for you."

"I want it to be good for me," Peck deadpans.

Walker rolls his eyes at Peck. "You sure?" he asks me.

"I mean, if you don't want me . . ."

"We want you," Peck jumps in, standing between me and Walker. "We. Want. You. I want you, anyway. If he doesn't, I do. Let's make that clear."

Walker shoves Peck's shoulder, making Peck laugh.

"If you want to, that's fine," Walker says, once Peck makes his way back into the shop bay. "But I'll pay you. You aren't helping out around here for free."

"You aren't paying me," I toss back. "This is to work off the damage and today's freebies. What time do we start?"

He twists his lips into a hesitant grin. "I have a feeling you're going to show up whenever you want, so we open at eight. The rest is up to you."

It would be so easy to stay, to linger beneath his lopsided smile. I could pull up a chair and fix us both plates of Nana's fried chicken and listen to this gravelly voice tease me, grumble, whatever he likes, all day. Sometimes, though, the right option isn't the easiest one. Sometimes, it's the hardest.

"See you then," I say.

Before he can get in the last word, I head to the door. Without looking back, I tug it open and make myself walk away from Walker Gibson.

chapter
Five

Walker

PAPERS FLUTTER AGAINST THE CORK board, held in place by various thumbtacks, nails, and an occasional toothpick with the foil at the end that Machlan uses in Crave's famous cheeseburgers. There's nothing particularly interesting tonight. A coon dog that went missing out by the lake and a carpenter from Merom looking for help. Otherwise, it's just a bunch of jokes, shift schedules for the factory, and some pictures from when a couple of the Illinois Legends football players were in a while back.

Mach works behind the bar, wiping down the bottles that line the counter below the oversized mirror. He's the youngest out of us all. He shares my dark hair and a little above average height, but he's more like our sister in that he can be a hard nut to crack. Things are right or wrong with Machlan, and he's not above doling out justice when it's deserved. A time or two this has put him into spots with Kip since he took the position of Sheriff.

As if on cue, Mach leans against the bar across from me. "Blaire called this morning."

"Why?"

"She wanted to make sure I got my bartender license renewed. Apparently it was on her calendar as a 'to-do' item," he grins. "How does our sister even know when it renews? I mean, I wouldn't have known if my accountant didn't remind me last week, but I pay her for that shit."

"You know Blaire," I say, peeling at the label of the beer bottle I just finished. "She just likes holding it over our heads that we need her. It's her way of feeling relevant."

"I think that fancy corner office in Chicago should make her feel relevant."

"But to us?" I ask. "If she wasn't our older sister, would we even give a fuck that she's a lawyer with some hotshot firm? What do we care about law degrees?"

"Lance cares. He'd love to find some chick who could moan eight-syllable words as she got off."

Laughing, I lean back in my chair while Machlan heads down the bar to refill a customer. He pauses long enough to have a quick conversation, making the guy I haven't seen before feel welcome, but doesn't hover.

No one sits at the far end of the bar to chitchat. They're not even really there for the beer. They're there to get away from something, maybe even everything. Then again, maybe the majority of people in a bar are there for that purpose.

I mean, I am.

Crave was my last-ditch effort to rid myself of a certain woman with the most aggravatingly irresistible vibe. A woman I'd love to fuck until she can't respond with her quick comebacks anymore. Until all she can say is my name.

My phone glows on the bar-top. Swiping it on, I lift it to my ear. "Were your ears burning?"

"Should they have been?" Blaire asks.

"Machlan was saying you called him today and now my phone rings. Are you missing us, big sister?" I tease.

"Hardly," she scoffs. Despite the gruff, I hear her smile. "Just thought I'd check in with you guys. I haven't seen you in forever."

"That's because you're too good for us these days."

"Damn right I am," she jokes. "I had a case end today that I thought was going to kill me. I might sleep for a week now."

"You will not."

"Yeah, you're right. I just took on another case this afternoon." She unloads a slew of put-downs in a very ladylike fashion, the words muffled as a car honks in the distance. "Sorry about that," she says, coming back to the line. "Some asshole didn't understand how crosswalks work. So what are you doing?"

"Drinking a beer."

"Do you ever do anything fun?"

"All the time," I deadpan.

"You're a liar."

"Don't start on me, Blaire," I warn, resting my elbows against the counter. "I don't want to hear your shit."

"You have to hear it from someone, and Lord knows neither of our brothers is going to give you sage advice."

"Who said I needed advice?"

"You did when you just told me you're drinking a beer on a Monday night," she sighs. "Look, Walker, you need prodded along. I know you're all 'I'm fine,'" she says, mocking me, "but you're not. You're bored as hell. You're grumpy. You're stuck in a cycle that—"

"Blaire."

"What?"

"Stop it."

"This has gone on long enough, Walker."

I know where this is going, and I'm not heading that direction. "I swear I'll hang up on you."

She groans in the line. "If Mom were here, she'd tell you the same thing." With the reference to our mother, the octave of her voice drops and you can almost hear the mortal side of her that we don't see often.

"But she's not," I almost whisper.

"I miss them, Walk."

Blaire's admission makes me gulp. Of course she misses our parents. We all do. None of us expected them to not come home that Fourth of July. We didn't know they'd be hit in their boat and capsize, losing their lives on Lake Michigan. I know she misses them. I do too. But to hear her, the stoic one, the real badass of the family despite Machlan's attempts to prove otherwise, say it out loud throws me for a loop.

"I thought of her yesterday," she says, a lump clearly in her throat. "There was a woman her age with the same long, black hair in the court-house. She laughed a high, almost singing sound, and my stomach hit the floor. I couldn't stop looking at her . . ."

"It's almost her birthday," I say softly. "Dad would start bugging her right about now, asking her what she wanted."

"And she'd say she already had it." Blaire sighs into the phone. "I gotta go. I'm meeting a client in twenty minutes and I haven't even found a cab yet."

"It's ten o'clock at night, Blaire."

"So it is," she sighs again. "Talk to you later."

"Be careful. Love ya, sis."

"Love you. Bye."

The phone slides across the counter, hitting the napkin dispenser before stopping. The stranger takes another long draw of his drink, his fourth since I got here. Maybe I'm just not going at it hard enough.

Picking at the label on the bottle in front of me again, I allow my mind to go to the place it wants to go every time I stop purposefully focusing on something else—to Sienna.

I can't make heads or tails of this woman. She's too easy. Too sweet. Too confident. I've never seen a woman with the guts she has to do things like she does. I just don't know what to do with her.

The money is one thing. There's no way I can afford to go in the red on that kind of cash on a regular basis, although I see why she did it and I kind of love her heart for it. I wouldn't have charged Dave anyway and MaryAnn's husband would've worked off whatever their insurance didn't pay. But I'm still on the hook and can't afford to be out this much again. My customers' money keeps the lights on.

All of that is fair enough, but not the reason I try to shove it out of my mind. I try not to think about it because as much as I tell myself to be angry with her, I can't. Every time I tell myself to find a way to get a hold of her and tell her not to come in tomorrow, I don't. Each attempt I make to convince myself she's a potential thorn in my life that I really don't need right now, I fail.

The proposition of her coming into Crank to help is idiotic and driving me mad. Will she come? Will she not? Will she be even more impossible to shake off or finally bare some flaw I can't overlook? All afternoon, it's been a series of questions, of "what-ifs," of the dumbest fucking scenarios that I have no business toying with.

"Fuck it," I mutter, tipping the rest of the beer back. It slides down my throat with ease, the cool liquid pooling in my gut and joining the churn.

"Fuck what? Actually, let me guess. Peck gave me a head start," Machlan snickers. "Seems as if you're gonna have a helper in the shop."

"Not my idea," I point out. "It was Peck's."

"He said you weren't exactly against it. And I can't see what there is to be against if he painted the picture accurately."

Ignoring his leading, I keep things factual. "She owes me a lot of money," I explain. "And it just seemed . . ."

" . . . like a good idea. You don't have to admit that out loud because I might tell somebody, I get it. Lips are sealed."

I motion for another beer and wait until he places it in front of me. "It's a terrible idea. There's nothing good that can come out of this," I say more to myself than to him.

"Well, based on Peck's description, I can think of lots of good things to come out of that," he grins.

"You know what I fucking mean." I stare at him, hoping he drops his angle.

Blowing out a breath, he nods. "I do. I get it. You get her in there helping out and then you like her and God forbid you like someone. That would totally ruin your reputation as the loner."

Glaring at him, I swipe my phone off the counter and jam it in the pocket of my jeans. "I'd hate for people to confuse the two of us."

"I was going to suggest letting Peck take a shot at that, but I can see that wouldn't go over well," he jokes. When I don't budge, his lips frown. "Fine. Moving on . . . Let me toss an idea by you."

"Shoot."

"The two lots behind the bar are for sale. I was thinking about trying to buy them."

"For what?" I ask, half in the conversation, half wondering what Sienna is doing.

"I have lots of ideas. We could build a room for meetings and wedding receptions and that shit. We could build a couple of apartments and rent them out."

Machlan's talking too fast, his eyes darting around too much to be telling the truth.

"Why don't you tell me what you're really thinking?" I ask.

"That is what I'm thinking."

"Sure." Standing up, I snag a twenty from my pocket and toss it on the bar. "Go get into wedding receptions. Seems right up your alley."

I wait for him to give in, but he doesn't. "Have it your way. See ya tomorrow," I call out.

Stepping out into the late summer heat, I stop and breathe in the warm, humid air. It reminds me of nights at the lake with a girl in my arms and barbecues and homemade ice cream. All things that annoy me to pieces.

chapter
Six

Sienna

FLIPPING DOWN THE VISOR, I silently curse the yellow light illuminating my face. Taking a calming breath, I remind myself I don't need to look my best. I'm just going in to work off a debt. That's it.

"Why did I agree to this?" I whine. "You know why you agreed to it. It's the right thing to do." Snorting as I run a hand over the top of my head to smooth out a bump in my ponytail, I laugh. "Yeah, it has nothing to do with how sexy he is. Don't lie to yourself."

Stomach sloshing as I pick apart my appearance, I set aside the excitement building in my gut and focus on the reflection in the poorly lit mirror. My skin is decent, except for the pimple that decided to spring up during the night. My makeup is light and casual to go with my strategically ripped jeans and short-sleeved red and black plaid shirt with a lacy white cami underneath that took way too long this morning to choose.

"Stop," I chastise myself, working a strand of hair from the center of one of my large hoop earrings. "You're here to do the right thing. Walker doesn't even like you anyway."

Gathering my phone and lip gloss from the passenger seat, I slip them into my purse and open the car door. If this happened in any normal situation, I would've already paid him back by now. But if I tossed him some cash, I think he might actually be offended. Still, knowing enough money is tucked in my wallet to pay for the damage if things go south is a little balm to my uneasiness.

Confidence is one of my best qualities. I can walk into a room of political powerhouses or professional athletes and hold my own. It's a regularity of my life in Savannah, how I was raised. So why am I walking into a mechanic's shop in the middle of Illinois and feeling like I'm naked in Times Square?

Ignoring the roiling in my stomach, I take the handle and yank the door open. The chimes I'm already starting to hate ring as I step inside. The air conditioning is a welcome reprieve from the heat. It's almost as nice as the view sitting at the desk.

A tight black t-shirt grips his muscled frame as Walker sits in the chair and clicks around on a computer. He knows I'm here; there's no way he doesn't. But he doesn't look at me.

I wait a few seconds before finally clearing my throat. "Hello?"

"Hi." His head doesn't turn, his eyes unmoving from the screen. He couldn't pretend to be more bored with my arrival if he tried.

I pick at the hem of my shirt, silently begging him to have mercy on me and just speak. But after almost a minute, it's obvious he's not going to.

"Good morning to you too," I say flatly.

Readjusting my purse on my shoulder, I wait for him to respond. He continues doing whatever it is that he's doing, and I'm two seconds from walking back out when he shoves away from the desk. The sudden burst of movement startles me. Large arms cross his chest, and his eyes are darker than I've ever seen them before as they settle on me.

"I didn't expect you to come today," he says simply.

"I'm a woman of my word."

A hint of a smile plays on his lips, but never quite breaks free. I want to ask him why he's so constrained, why that sentence amuses him, why he didn't expect me—but I don't. Instead, I just stare back at him, giving as good as I'm getting.

He gives nothing away with his steady gaze, two-day stubble, and wild hair like his hands have been in it all morning. My heart strums in my chest, each moment that passes without any sort of break in the standoff giving me way too much time to examine him for all the wrong reasons. To smell him. To almost taste the energy spiraling off him in waves.

If I stand here much longer, I might start to pant.

"What do you want me to do?" I ask.

One corner of his lips lifts, catching on to my unintended innuendo, before he rolls his mouth around like he's tasting a sip of wine.

Blushed, I clear my throat. "Where do you want me to start?"

"How do I know?" he asks, his voice low and grumbly. "This wasn't my idea, if you'll recall."

"If you'll recall," I start back, "it's your business and you agreed to this. I assume you want a say in how I work off my debt."

"I can make suggestions," Peck laughs, coming out of the bathroom. "Wanna hear them?"

"Get to work." Walker shakes his head as Peck walks by. "The fuel injector came in for the car in the back. Can you get that thing on so we can get it out of the way?"

"Yeah. Got it." Peck leans against the door to the garage bay. His boyish grin is adorable, a dimple set deeply into his right cheek. A mop of blond hair sticks out from under a navy blue cap. "Nice to see you, Slugger."

"Go on, Peck," Walker rumbles as I release a little giggle that only seems to annoy him more.

Peck's chuckle remains a few seconds after the door swings shut, leaving us alone. Walker scoots his chair back and stands, sending a whiff of a woodsy cologne through the room. "There'll be a delivery this morning from the auto parts store. Just sign for it if you happen to be out here, okay?"

"Yeah, sure. Easy enough."

Moving around the desk, he stops just a few inches from me. I tilt my head up to look him in the eye, breathing in the masculine scent that I've already committed to memory. He's close enough that I could touch him, could run my hands down the sides of his face or trace the lines of his shoulders pressing against the cotton of his shirt.

His eyes narrow, his lips part slightly, as he takes me in. There's no uptick in his breathing, no tell-tale sign that he's thinking anything re-motely like what I am. There's just a hint of intrigue buried deep in his eyes that only fuels my need to make him react.

"Anything I should or shouldn't do today?" I ask, a little kiss on the words to hopefully drag some sort of response out of him.

"Don't give anything else away."

My shoulders fall. "Really? That's your answer."

"Yup. That's my answer."

"Fine," I grumble, sidestepping him. I don't mean to brush against him as I turn the corner of the desk. I don't really even know how it hap-pens because I move far enough out of the way to not make any contact at all, yet it happens.

Ever-so-lightly, my arm slips across his as I move. Not-so-slightly, a shiver rips through my body as his sturdy body doesn't flinch. It doesn't give at all. It's as if it needs the contact as much as mine in its refusal to get out of the way or at least recoil as any normal person would when touched.

He's hard and steady and I imagine him enveloping me with both arms.

My eyes flip to his immediately and are rewarded with the faintest glimmer of desire. It's there, just masked with a look of annoyance that is more tolerable knowing the other emotion lies just below the surface.

His nostrils flare, almost a taunt for me to press the issue. Like he's asking me to verbalize whatever the hell that was that just sparked be-tween our bodies so he doesn't have to.

I almost do. I almost give him the opening I think he wants, but think better of it.

"Where can I put my purse?" I ask, gesturing towards the desk. Again, I wait for a response I don't get. "I'd be happy to figure it out if you'll get out of my way."

He cocks his head to the side, twisting his lips together. "Why is it that when you come in here, I feel like you forget who's in charge?"

"Because I think we both know who's the calm, level-headed one here." I toss my purse on the desk.

"You?" he bursts, the word floating on a laugh. "The one who bashed my truck with a baseball bat?"

"That's a poor example. I was thinking more like the way you stomp around and try to snarl all the time."

It's a gamble calling him out, and I hold my breath while I wait for his response. I'm shocked when he laughs, his shoulders relaxing for the first time all morning. "I don't stomp."

"But you do snarl," I wink. "So, purse?"

He hesitates, his features smoothing as he resolves himself to some decision I'm not apprised of. Closing the distance between us, he stops when he's beside me. Reaching across my body, his arm intentionally brushing my shoulder as it passes, he lifts my purse up with two fingers.

Boxed in between the wall and his forearm, roped with a mass of veins and muscles, I keep my vision pinned on the calendar taped to the desk. As he drags the purse towards him, his bicep swipes against me again, stealing my breath.

He leans close, his lips a hair's breadth away from the shell of my ear. "It wouldn't be wise," he says, his voice a few decibels above a whisper, "to leave your shit lying out and getting stolen."

When he pulls back, it's like oxygen is freed up in the room again.

"You think I'm an idiot, don't you?" I ask, my cheeks heating. "From the truck to the stuff yesterday to this—you think I'm just a stupid girl who doesn't know anything."

He doesn't answer, just holds my canary yellow purse in his hand.

"Well, I'm not. The truck thing was kind of stupid," I admit, "but I didn't mean to do that. I just . . ."

Scrambling for words, completely thrown off by the mixed signals from Walker, I snatch my purse from his hand. He watches me, a confused look etched on his face.

"Let me just pay you and get out of here," I say, searching for the bank envelope.

"I'm not taking your money."

"Why? I owe it to you."

"Because I'm not."

The finality in his voice startles me and I look up. He runs a hand through his hair, the spikes changing position but still sticking up. The irritation doesn't leave his face, but it changes—from what and to what, I'm not sure. All I know is that the hand holding my purse drops to my side as I wait for him to find the words he's so obviously searching for.

"I, um . . ." He forces a swallow. "Put your purse in the cabinet back there. No one can get into it but me and Peck, and while he might be a dumbass, he's not a thief."

"Okay," I say quietly. There's a shift in the air, one that swirls between us and leaves us both a little wobbly.

"Otherwise, just, um, do whatever you think needs done. There'll be a few customers coming in this morning. Just knock on the window and Peck or I will come in and take care of it."

"You trust Peck over me?"

"Damn right I do," he replies.

"So I should just assume I'm not to take any payments or deal with invoices?"

His attempt at biting back his chuckle fails. "No. I can't afford to get behind anymore."

If I couldn't tell he was playing, I would be pissed. But the way his lip curls on the side dissolves it before it gets started.

"My business skills are on fire," I tell him. "You're making a mistake, Walker."

"I'm confident in my decision-making abilities, Slugger."

"Your loss," I shrug, heading towards the back cabinet. I lay my purse on a box and close it. When I turn around, he's still there. "You gonna work today or watch me?"

Shaking his head, he heads towards the door to the garage. "Behave."

Walker

"ARE YA EVEN LISTENING TO me?" Peck bumps my shoulder as he walks by. "I get it. She's hot as hell. But we still have to get shit done."

"Shut it."

"Just speaking the truth," he cracks. "You've managed to make it two hours without going back in there. I'm impressed."

Tossing a wrench into the toolbox with more force than necessary, I glare at my cousin. "This was all your idea."

"And a damn good one at that."

I pluck a screwdriver out of the container and head back to the SUV we've been messing with all morning. My stomach growls as I remove the screws holding in the faulty part that's taken two hours to get to. It falls into my hand with a heavy thud.

"Finally," Peck says, taking it from me. "Now can I go to lunch?"

"Yeah, may as well. When you get back, maybe the new piece will be here."

"Hell, at this rate, I'm tempted to go to the parts store in Merom and just buy the fucker. We've waited all day."

"And we'll pay double."

He grabs his keys and phone from the rack by the door and makes his way out. I watch through the window. He stops and talks to Sienna, telling her something that makes her laugh. I move closer to the glass without thinking, wishing I could hear the sound.

It's taken everything I have all day not to go back in there. It's taken more than I knew I had not to look up every three seconds and look for her.

She moves with grace—her chin always lifted, her back always straight. It reminds me of the ballerinas who used to perform with Blaire when she was a little girl. Always poised, always performing. The only difference is, with Sienna, it doesn't feel like a performance.

That's the fucking problem right there. That's the reason I can't shake this girl from my system despite every attempt at doing just that.

There's a confidence exuding from her that's overwhelming. How can someone be that sure of themselves? How can she just blaze into my world, my business, and make decisions like she'll just fix it if it's wrong? Who does that?

I laid awake last night with her on my mind. I've worked all day today and had a stream of Sienna rolling in the back of my brain the whole morning as I tried to fix this fuel pump. She's intoxicating, a drug foreign to me that I've somehow ingested and can't purge from my body.

But I need to. Desperately.

"Hey." Her voice sweeps through the garage, capturing my attention.

"There's a pump of some sort here. Peck said to tell you if it came in."

"Thanks."

She waits as I head her direction, holding the door open for me. I want to tell her to stop it, to stop making it so hard to dislike her, but I don't. Instead, I listen to the door shut behind me and spy the box on the desk.

"What's this for?" she asks.

"A fuel pump we've needed since nine," I say, leaning against the wall. "We order everything from Standski's, but their delivery has been shit lately. I don't want to order from one of the online places, but they're gonna force me to."

"You should've told me. I could've called and spurred them on."

"You think it would've helped?" I scoff.

"I can be really persuasive."

That, I have little trouble believing. Instead of agreeing with her, I glance around the lobby. "Damn. You've done a lot today."

You can see the cars in the parking lot, the trees lining the other side of the road through the now-clear windows. The floors don't shine, but they definitely don't have heaps of dried up mud on them either. And the desk is semi-organized with a handful of stacks of papers in a neat line on top.

"You like it?" She shoots me the brightest smile, one that hits something inside me it shouldn't. "I didn't know where to start, so I just started at the messiest place and moved on. I thought I'd take those rags to the cleaners when I leave."

"To the cleaners?" I ask, lifting a brow.

"I'm not putting those greasy things in my washing machine," she gags. "They stink too."

"Um, fun fact, Slugger: you take those to a dry cleaners and they'll laugh your ass right out of there."

"Do you just throw them away then?"

"There's about fifty bucks' worth of towels. No, I don't throw them away," I say like she's crazy. "We take them over to Suds N Spins and wash them there."

"That's a . . . what do you call it?"

"A laundromat? Haven't you had to do laundry there before? When your washer broke or at college or something?"

"Um, nope. But I'll take these there. What do I need to know?"

"Wait," I say, holding up a hand. "You've never been to a laundromat?"

"No. So what?"

"So who even are you?"

Something crosses her features as a hand goes to her hip. "Do you want me to take them or not?"

There's a laugh ready to expel, a reaction to how adorably sexy she is when she's all riled up and challenging me back. Not because I've never been challenged, but because I don't think anyone has ever given a fuck to actually help me and not gotten frustrated when it's not easy.

I bite back the reaction and instead answer her question. "I'll get to it."

"Why are you so hard-headed?"

"Me?" I ask.

"Yes, you." She points a white-tipped fingernail my way. "I'm trying to help you out. The least you can be is nonjudgmental."

"I'm not being judgmental."

"Yeah, you are."

As I take a step forward, she takes one back. Then another. And another until her back is against the wall. Her chest rises and falls at a spectacular speed, her blue eyes sparkling in the sunshine streaming through the window. Just standing this close to her, feeling her body this close to mine, is enough to fray any sensibilities I've managed to hold on to.

With the most caution I've ever used, I drag the back of my hand down her cheek. Her skin is soft, the quiet intake of breath so perfect that I find myself forgetting where I am.

God, I want to give in. I want to dip my head down to hers and kiss the fight right out of her. She would be so perfect in my hands as I pin her to the wall, feel her body squirm against mine as our bodies press together and she moans in to my mouth.

"Damn it," I groan, my voice more haggard than I wanted it to be as I drop my hand away from her face. "Why are you so frustrating?"

"I don't mean to be."

It's not the words, but the way she whispers them that shoots through me.

"I'm sorry," I say, forcing my feet backwards.

She sags against the wall, her fingers flexing against her sides. She searches my eyes, almost desperately, and my stomach sinks right along with her shoulders.

"What are you sorry for?" she asks.

"Nothing." I twist around and snatch the box off the desk. "Peck headed to lunch. If you wanna go, Carlson's Bakery has pretty good sandwiches. Tell Veronica I sent you over."

I don't wait for a response. I just hit the door to the bay and escape while I still can.

chapter
Seven

Sienna

THE TOWEL RUBS ALONG THE steamed up glass, squeaking as it wipes away the moisture. After a few swipes, I can make out my foggy reflection.

Hair up turban-style, my body wrapped in a soft pink robe, the streaks of dirt and dust from Crank are only a distant reminder. My cheeks are still rosy, though, and I wonder if it's from the heat of the shower or the fantasy of being pinned against the wall by Walker I just indulged while rinsing off the grime from the day.

My grin stretches from ear to ear, and with just me in the room to witness, I don't try to hide it. There's no point in pretending I'm not utterly perplexed by Walker Gibson.

Closing my eyes, the heat of the bathroom makes me remember the fervor zipping between us when he walked me back to the wall. There was an intensity etched on his face, lines dipping deep into his skin as he wrestled with whatever was causing the browns of his eyes to spiral like a storm. Each step towards me both a warning and a promise, a message that I couldn't quite grasp.

I wanted him to touch me, kiss me, break this barrier he's so obviously constructed between us. Most guys have no problem trying to see what they can get away with. Walker? I'm not sure I could beg him to.

As I take in my reflection again, the apples of my cheeks are even redder. The fabric tucked around my chest is unforgiving and I have to loosen it to breathe.

"Sienna?" Delaney's voice sounds from the other side of the door. "I'm going to grab some takeout. You want anything?"

"No," I say, blowing out a breath. "I'm good. Thanks, though."

"When I get back, you're gonna tell me all about your day. Right?"

"I've already told you everything," I lie.

"Sure you have. Be back soon and then you can for real."

Her steps soften as she heads to the doorway and end when the front door snaps shut.

Sagging against the counter, I really just want to go to bed. My body aches from all the mopping and wiping and sweeping. I did more cleaning today than I've ever done, despite the distraction Walker and Peck delivered through the window.

Peck, on his own, would be hard to not watch. He has this boy-next-door sweetheart thing going on and a personality like a magnet. But next to Walker, he doesn't exist.

I open the door, letting the warm, wet air trickle into the rest of the house. Everything is quiet as I make my way to the living room and plop down on the chair. The blue and red plaid material is rough against my legs. I've hated this chair since Delaney had me help her carry it in from a swap meet when I first moved here.

A few boxes sit half-packed against the wall and reality bowls me over. In a few days, Delaney will be gone. I'll be here. Alone.

Tears well up in my eyes as I take out my phone and pull up social media. My friends from back home smile from Tybee Island. My girlfriends are posting loop videos of themselves at dinner at one of our favorite restaurants there. Right before I click off, I see a picture my sister posted of her holding my father's hand. It's innocent with a text saying, "I love my daddy," but there's nothing in the picture that I recognize besides the scar running from his index finger down the top that happened one Christmas morning a long time ago. But there is the edge of what I suspect is a hospital bracelet and a blue and white checked fabric faded into the background that looks eerily like a hospital gown.

The longer I look at the picture, the more I can't shake the fact that something isn't right: Camilla posting something so intimate on social media. The odd location, the way the photo blurs and shows really nothing to the naked eye.

A chill tearing through me, I call Camilla. It rings twice, my heartbeat soaring with each tone, before she answers.

"What's going on?" I ask immediately.

"Did Graham call you?"

"No. Why would G call me?" I spring to my feet, my heart in my throat. "What's happening, Cam?"

"Calm down. It's nothing or I would've called you already. You know that."

"It's something or we wouldn't be having this conversation at all."

My tone almost reaches the level of panic, a ball of tension taking root at the back of my neck. Every possible situation that could be wrong screeches through my mind.

"Dad didn't feel well today," Cam says gently. "Mom took him to the emergency room to be safe. That's all."

"*That's all?*" I ask, aghast that she would downplay something as serious as a trip to the ER. The fact that he allowed Mom to take him has vomit threatening to spew from my mouth. "What did they say? Is he okay?"

"They said it was angina and he should make some dietary and exercise changes. He has to see a cardiologist sometime soon."

Red-hot tears dot the corners of my eyes, a ball lodged in my throat making it impossible to talk.

"He's going to be okay, Sienna."

"Do I need to come home?" I say, my voice sounding all gulpy.

"No. We'd love to see you, but don't race home because of this. He's irritated tonight. Graham showed up and tried to tell Dad what he was going to do, so that went over well."

"I bet," I chuckle. "Who won?"

"Mom," she laughs. "She told them both to settle down in that voice she keeps for the two times a year she actually gets mad."

Imagining my sweet mother's face angry, I'm able to catch my breath. When she goes into that mode, she gets shit done. She fixes the problem. It's where my siblings and I get our need to step in and take care of things.

"So Dad's okay?" I ask, taking a long, calming breath.

"He's fine right now. If anything comes of it, you know you'll be my first call."

Slumping back down in the scratchy chair, the adrenaline from thinking there was a crisis starts to wane. "You had me scared with your vaguebook."

"I didn't vaguebook. Dominic took the picture and I thought it was nice so I posted it. I didn't expect anyone to read that much into it," she laughs. "I should've known you would."

"Of course I would. So Dom was there?"

She chatters on about her new-to-the-family boyfriend, one who I knew about for almost a year before she told everyone. He's a good guy— he treats Cam like gold and he and I get along great. I know I should be thrilled that he was there for her, for my mother, tonight, but I can't help but acknowledge the jealousy that stems from him getting to be there and me not.

"He fits so well into the family," she continues to gush. "I don't know why I was so afraid of bringing him around. Ford loves having him work at Landry Security. Lincoln loves kicking his ass on the golf course," she giggles.

"Sounds great."

Stop. Biting my cheek, I have to remind myself that I'm not there because I chose not to be. I'm the one who opts out of living there. I'm the one who doesn't want to end up in pearls and heels alongside my mother and sister. I don't want to be a pawn in a world with reporters and security guards and paid drivers. I don't want to be a piece of something. I want something I'm *a part of*. Something that I need as much as it needs me.

"It's been great," she admits. "But what about you? What's happening up there? Tell me your good stuff."

I consider telling her about Walker's truck. I think for a brief moment about replaying my day in the auto shop, about Walker and Peck and

Nana and all the things I've done over the past few days, but decide not to. She'd understand, probably even love it. But the follow-up questions would be too much, and besides, what's the point? I'm leaving here soon anyway. There's no sense in making this anything more than a distraction. Instead, I focus on facts.

"Delaney is going to work for her family," I tell her.

"What does that mean for you?"

"Just that the business will be mine. I'm going to call Graham tomorrow and have him get the papers together for me," I say, wondering how our brother will take that bit of news.

There is a part of me that hoped I could impress my brother by striking out on my own. I understand design and I understand the business behind it and somehow, by Delaney leaving, it feels like I didn't keep it together.

"How do you feel about that?" Cam asks.

"She has to do what she has to do. It's her family, you know? I'd do the same for you guys."

"I was hoping you had happier news."

"Well," I start, an eruption of warmth swelling from deep within me. I can't stop it. "I met a hot-as-hell car guy."

"Oooh, car guys," she squeals. "Tell me about him."

"It's not like that," I warn.

"It is. I hear it in your voice."

"It really isn't," I say, the seriousness in my tone not matching the grin on my cheeks.

"Then tell me about him that's not like that," she laughs.

My mouth opens, but nothing comes out. The words get jumbled on my tongue, the descriptions, the place to start gets fuzzy as I mentally jump from one thing to another. I don't know where to begin.

Pacing the room, one foot in front of the other, I search desperately for words that I can't come up with.

"Got it," Cam says after a long pause.

"I didn't say anything."

"That's how I got it."

"Oh, shut up," I say, rearranging magazines on the coffee table for a distraction. "There's really nothing to tell. I just hit his truck with a bat and then—"

"Wait. You did what?"

"It was an accident."

"I . . . I don't know where to start with that."

"Don't, because that's not where we're going," I tell her. "So he owns a car repair shop and somehow I've managed to spend a little time down there to pay off my debt."

"Does he not take cash?"

"He does, but it's a long and convoluted story, Cam."

"So, let me get this straight," she says, clearing her throat to hide the amusement laced in her tone. "You damaged his truck and are now working it off. Like, manual labor? You. My twin sister, Sienna Jane Landry, working in a car repair shop?"

Laughing, because it sounds even crazier hearing it out loud from someone else, I throw up my one free hand. "Basically. That's it."

"Who are you and what have you done with my sister?"

"It's crazy, right?" I say, Walker's face now firmly affixed in my mind. "Thank God it's only for a couple of weeks. Or, maybe it was just for today. I'm not sure, actually . . ."

The words no more than enter the world and I wish I could take them back. Even I can hear the way my voice dropped off at the end.

"Tell me about him," she says easily, prying me for information in the most unobtrusive way. "What's he like?"

Heading into the kitchen, I try, once again, to figure out where to start. As I try to come up with a good description, I grab a bottle of water out of the refrigerator and take a good, long drink.

Finally, after I've put the cap back on and wiped my mouth with the back of my hand, and stalled for as long as I can, I suck in a deep breath. "His name is Walker. He's infuriatingly difficult. A total grump. Broody."

"And . . ."

"He wears a plain black t-shirt almost every day. His eyelashes are the longest I've ever seen on a man. When he's amused but doesn't want me to know it, the left corner of his lip turns up." The words come out in a rush and I know I've said too much but can't stop myself from saying more. "Walker tries really, really hard to be an ass," I say, rolling my eyes, "but I think he's probably really kind. His grandma, Nana, makes dinner every Sunday like our mom does and expects him to show up, and when he doesn't, she comes in and gives him hell."

My laugh is free and easy, my downtrodden spirits now lifted. "He has a cousin named Peck. I have no idea why they call him that or if it's his real name. The two of them remind me of Lincoln and Ford," I say, thinking of my two brothers that can be oil and water. "They're always nitpicking each other, but you can tell if someone messes with either, it's game on for both."

Cam gives me a second to catch my breath. "Sounds like you like them."

"They're . . . interesting."

"Maybe they're more than interesting."

If Delaney had said that, I'd fire back with some reply as to how I'm not interested in Walker Gibson. But it's not Delaney, it's Camilla, the one person in the world I can't lie to.

"They remind me of being in Savannah," I admit, looking at the gold ring on my right pointer finger. It's a thin band with a rustic teepee design. My brothers got Cam and I both one for Christmas. They blamed the whole thing on Ford who deflected any responsibility in getting his two baby sisters something so sweet for the holiday. In truth, I'd bet it was Barrett found the jeweler, Graham funded it, although I'd bet Ford probably did come up with the idea, and Lincoln probably picked it out. But we'll never know. "They remind me of our brothers in a weird way, but without the expectations. They don't care if I say the wrong thing, and if I came in with a new tattoo, they'd probably like it or at least find it interesting," I say, finding a warmth spreading inside me. "They don't know our last name, but if they did, I don't think they'd care."

"That's hard to find," she notes.

"Almost impossible, but I think I might've," I say, feeling a swell in my chest. "They're just easy, even though they're difficult. It's hard to explain."

"Do you think you'll stay there then?" she asks softly.

"No," I scoff, running a hand through the air. "No way. I don't know what I'm going to do, but I'm not staying here. Have you ever seen an Illinois winter?"

"No. Can't say I want to."

"Exactly."

"Maybe you'll come home then?"

My mind settles back on my father and the image Camilla posted. "Maybe this time I won't go as far away. Maybe I'll look into Atlanta or Florida or something."

"Can I ask you something, sis?"

"Sure."

"Would it be that bad to come back? To settle down here. Meet me for lunch and go shopping and take yoga at Mallory's . . ."

I imagine my sister's face, all twisted in hope like she does when she's afraid someone is going to tell her no. I sit at the table and feel my spirits drop with my body. "It wouldn't be *bad*, Cam. It's just not for me."

"What's not for you?"

"I just . . . Mom gave up everything when she married Dad."

"She did not," Cam says, defending her. "She had a role in Dad's campaigns, in Grandpa's campaigns. She's spent her life changing other people's through her charities and raised six kids."

"I know that. But Mom could've rocked her own political career. Probably better than Dad. Think about what she could've done had she not stepped back and fallen into this other role. She could've ruled the damn world."

"I think she does," Cam says sweetly. "Her world is Dad and us."

What Cam is saying is true. I know that. But it doesn't negate what I'm saying. "Isn't that kind of sad? That her world shrank to the size of the Landry Estate just so she could fill some stupid role?"

Cam sighs. "I get what you mean."

"No, you don't," I scoff. "You've wanted to be our mother since we were little girls."

"That's true. I've always thought our mother was the most amazing woman I've ever met."

"So do I," I insist.

"But here's where we differ," Cam says gently. "I don't think she gave anything up. I think she chose a role that could give her heart more than she ever could've gotten out of politics or business or whatever else. Look at what Dad accomplished. Look at Landry Holdings. But he never got to do the fun stuff with us, Sienna. He gave up a lot of things to create his legacy for them, for *us,* while Mom got to do other things. Important things, just in a different way."

"Maybe . . ."

I see her point, but I still don't agree. I watched her for years sit back with the answers to my father's quandaries and only offer them up in the solitude of their bedroom after we'd all gone to sleep. I watched her friends jet off to Europe on vacations and go to see Broadway shows and she stayed behind, raising us. I don't want that life.

I want ripped jeans, nights with whiskey slurring, and laughing with no regard to who is taking a picture. I want to experience Yosemite on a whim. To live my life without the constraints of someone else's.

"I need to go, Cam," I say, taking the towel off my head. My hair falls to the small of my back as I run my free hand through it. "Keep me posted on Dad, okay?"

"Okay. And, hey—don't call out there tonight. He's pissy that anyone knows at all. Lincoln showed up when I was leaving and I think the only reason Dad tolerated that was because he brought the baby. Mom has her hands full, you know?"

"Okay. I won't call tonight."

"Thanks. Talk to you soon."

"Goodnight."

chapter

Eight

Sienna

"I CAN'T BELIEVE I LET you talk me into this," I hiss as Delaney leads me down the sidewalk towards Crave.

"You put up little to no fight, my friend. Stop acting like you're shocked you're here."

"You said you wanted to go out. That it would be one of the last times we got to hang out for a while."

"And, here we are. Mission Hang Out is commencing." She tugs open the door before I can say no. "After you."

Sounds of the bar spill onto the sidewalk, as does the multi-colored glow of beer advertisements and signage. The air smells of salt and I'm turning on my heel when I hear a familiar voice inside calling my name.

"It's the blond," she whispers. "What's his name?"

"Sienna! Get in here," Peck lures me in from somewhere in the depths of the building.

With a deep breath and an eye roll, my nerves on high alert knowing that if Peck is here, there's a decent chance Walker is too, I step inside.

It's brighter than I imagine and not as busy as I would've thought. Delaney stands beside me as we get acclimated to the venue.

"Hey," a bartender says. He has short, dark hair and wide, broad shoulders. A goatee dusts his chin, and with the five o'clock stubble spattering his face, he's right up Delaney's alley. "I'm Machlan. You must be Sienna."

"This really is a small town," I sigh.

"It is, but that one," he says, nodding towards Peck, "is my cousin. Being that you are working with my brother, you can bet I've heard about you a time or two . . . dozen." His lips part into a smile as his gaze settles on Delaney. "I haven't heard about you yet, love. Wanna fill me in?"

"I'd love to." She bats her lashes, taking a seat at the end of the bar. I nudge her in the back, in shock she's leaving me alone, when she waves me off. "Go on. Go have fun."

"I hate you," I whisper. She fails to respond, too enchanted with Machlan's smirk.

Peck, a beer in one hand, sidles up to me. "What brings you by tonight?"

"Her." I nudge Delaney again. "I didn't imagine I'd see you here."

"No, right? So totally crazy and random. Why would we be here, the place we met you?"

I force a swallow past the lump in my throat. "You say 'we' . . ."

"Walker's sitting back there by the pool table. Wanna come say hi?"

"No."

Laughing, he motions for me to follow with his head. "Let's go."

"But Peck," I whine.

"What else you gonna do, Slugger? And let's be honest, you came here to see him." He stops. "Unless you came to see me?"

"Peck . . ."

"That's what I thought," he sighs. "It's never for me. Come on."

Against my better judgement, but totally in line with my libido, I follow Peck through the small groupings of people. As we near the end of the bar and the billiards area comes into view, I see Walker. And he sees me.

There's no indication of whether this makes him happy or pissy and all I can do is try not to let the spiraling anxiety swirling in my belly take over.

"Look what I found," Peck tells him. "Just standing up there by the bar, waiting on Tommy to find her."

"Who's Tommy?" I ask as a flash of something fierce flickers through Walker's features.

"You just get here?" Walker asks, ignoring my question.

"Yeah. Peck thought I should say hi, and in case you saw me, I didn't want to be rude."

He roughs a hand down his face. When he puts it back on his lap, rocking his chair on the back two legs, he averts his gaze to his cousin. "Get her a drink, will ya?"

"It's fine," I say. "I'll go up there and get one in a minute."

"What'll it be, lady?" Peck grins.

"Um, an amaretto sour?"

"Typical chick drink. Be right back."

Peck dashes away. A couple plays pool on one side and another half-dances, half-copulates on the other beneath the dick-shaped duck lights, but we're alone otherwise. Tucking a strand of hair out of my face, I wait until I can't take the awkwardness anymore.

"I'll go get the drink. It was nice to see you," I say.

"Wanna sit?" he gruffs out.

"What? No, I'm fine."

"Sit down," he sighs, sitting on all four legs again. "I won't bite."

"I'm not totally convinced of that," I mutter.

He leans forward, gripping a bottle in front of him with both hands. "If I did," he whispers, "you'd like it."

His tone dances across my skin, the words pooling in between my thighs. It takes every bit of self-control I can muster to remain unaffected—at least on the surface.

Walker's attention rests with me, every blink, twitch, and gasp duly noted. The power, although never completely mine, is slipping away quickly and I have to get some of it back.

Sitting across from him, I let him wonder what my response will be before I finally give it to him. "If I didn't," I say, "that would be embarrassing for you, wouldn't it?"

A slow smile plays on his lips before he lifts the bottle and drains whatever is left in it. It sets with a thud. "What brought you to Linton, anyway?"

"Tonight or in general?"

He shrugs.

"My friend wanted to come in tonight, so that's why we're here. She's also why I'm in Linton at all, really. What about you?"

"Born and raised here."

"I was born and raised in Georgia," I tell him. "Went to school in Los Angeles. Ended up here for the time being."

"How the hell did you go from LA to Linton?" He leans forward, his brows pulled together.

"Delaney had a business idea and I thought, 'Why not?'" I say, lifting my shoulders and dropping them back down.

"What is it you do?"

"Design things. Clothes, merchandise, marketing material—whatever someone needs, really."

He looks beyond me with a slight shake of his head. "Can you design Peck a brain?"

"Why?"

I turn around in just enough time to witness Peck bent on one knee in front of a brunette, a beer extended in the same way a person would a ring. "Who's that he's . . . proposing to?" I giggle.

"A girl who doesn't deserve him."

Lifting a brow, I can't help but smile. He flinches.

"I didn't mean it like that," he insists. "Peck is just way too good for Molly and he doesn't even realize it."

"I take it we aren't big Molly fans?"

"She'd fuck a dog with two dicks, if you catch my drift."

Not sure whether to laugh or vomit at that imagery, I just squeeze my eyes shut. "That is so disgusting."

"Then you catch my drift."

The rhythm between us slides into motion, calming my nerves and settling me down. His body relaxes too as we watch each other across the empty field of bottles on the table.

"Did you drink all of these?" I ask, motioning towards the maybe ten bottles lined up.

"Nope. I think I've had two."

"I can't drink beer. I don't drink a lot at all, actually."

A touch of surprise floats across his features as that sinks in. "Not even wine? Don't all women drink wine?"

"Not me. I don't care for the taste of it, to be honest. And I really hate the feeling of not being clear-headed. If I drink, I'm home with my friends or sister or something." Biting my lip, considering how that makes me sound, I make a face. "Guess I'm not much fun, huh?"

He leans forward again, his cologne drifting my way. A shiver trickles down my spine as I sit under his heavy, wonderful gaze. "I think fun can be described a lot of ways. Alcohol usually takes a lot of that out of the equation."

"What about you?" I ask, needing the focus off me for a moment.

"What about me?"

"Are you fun?"

He does this half-snort, half-chuckle thing that only increases my curiosity.

"What's that about?" I poke, picking up one of the bottles and sloshing the mouthful or two left around.

"Why are you so full of questions?"

Placing the bottle in the middle of the table, I contemplate my choices. Sit here and let him navigate the conversation or walk away for a bit and let him come to me.

Decision made, I stand. "No more questions. See ya later."

I flash a smile at his slightly puzzled reaction and walk away before I change my mind.

There are a few more people now than before, and by the time I reach the bar, I can't spot either Delaney or Peck. Machlan is still behind the bar, wiping up a spilled drink.

"Hey," I say, taking a seat on an empty stool. "Did Peck order me a drink?"

"Nope. What do you want?"

"Something colorful, light on alcohol, but fun?"

"Fun is my specialty," he winks, heading off towards the blender.

His back flexes and pulls as he works the bar, grabbing bottles and scooping ice. He reminds me of Walker in a lot of ways, but lacks that mystery that drives me insane.

"Why do you do this to yourself?" I mutter, turning in my seat only to bump into someone beside me.

Blond hair, emerald eyes, and teeth so perfectly straight they have to have been designed by a dentist smile back at me. "Well, hello," he drawls. "Haven't seen you before."

"Not from here," I confirm, swinging back around in my seat.

This man is off-the-presses hot, and if I were a gambling girl, I'd say he's modeled before. The way he moves his long, lean body is something that's taught, not something you're born with.

"Can I buy you a drink?" he asks.

"She ordered one." Machlan sets a glass in front of me with more force than necessary. "What can I get you, Tommy?"

The man I now know as Tommy looks at me as he answers Machlan. "I think I'm good right now."

"Make sure you're still good the next time I check on ya," Machlan says, a warning written in every syllable. "Feel me?"

I slide away from the two of them, some unspoken pissing match firing between them. Machlan's hand hits the bar, making Tommy flinch.

"I, um, I think I need to find my friend," I say, climbing off the stool.

"What's she look like?"

"It's fine," I say, unable to shake the feeling from moments ago. "I'll find her."

"I just walked through. Maybe I know."

His hand touches the small of my back as he follows me towards the area I last saw Peck. It's too heavy for someone who just met me, too intimate for anyone who wasn't invited.

"Really. I'm okay. I'll find her," I reiterate, increasing my speed in hopes he'll drop his hand.

As I feel the coolness return to my back, my sight is drawn to the billiards area. Walker is standing, his arms over his chest, a look of death aimed at Tommy.

"Where are you, Delaney?" I mumble, sorting through the crowd. With each step I take, I feel Tommy take the same one, his voice behind me, but I can't hear what he's saying over the music.

I don't find Delaney, but do spy the red sign for the restroom. Tommy's hand again on my back, I spin around. "Gotta use the little girls' room. Thanks for your help."

Before he can say anything, I'm off through the doorway.

Walker

"WHY DO YOU LOOK LIKE you're two seconds from committing murder?" Peck's question rings out from beside me.

"I'd say two seconds is a stretch. Probably more like six."

My sight pinned on Tommy Jones, I follow that asshole through the crowd. He stops at various women, kissing their cheeks, grabbing a handful of ass, depending on what he can get away with.

"Where's Sienna?" Peck asks.

"Bathroom."

"She hasn't met Tommy, has she?"

"Yup."

"Oh, shit."

I wonder, vaguely, how long you can have your blood pressure as high as mine without your heart exploding. From the moment he touched her—no, from the moment he sat down beside her—my veins have pulsed with a tempo that can't be healthy.

I hate that motherfucker more than anyone on Earth. He's a worthless, pussified cocksucker who tried once, only once, to pull his shit on my sister. He got some free dental work out of that encounter.

Sienna comes out of the restroom, her eyes darting around Crave. She's tucking her hands into her pockets, not harboring that swagger of confidence that usually rolls off her. That alone pisses me off because I know it's Tommy who took it. But when I see him head her way, my body vibrates in anticipation.

"Patience," Peck warns. "You can't just go over there balls to the wall."

"I know." And I fucking hate it.

Someone like her shouldn't be in the same room with the rest of us. She's a good chameleon, blending in with whatever environment she's in, but I can tell she's just that—a faker. She doesn't hang out in shithole towns with shitty bars. You can see the little nuances if you watch for them, like the way she looks at what everyone's drinking before she orders or how she'd have no idea what a place like this would even serve. It's adorable, really, highly entertaining. And it leaves her vulnerable.

"I don't think she likes him," Peck notes as Tommy tries to step in front of her.

"Me either."

She moves backwards, laughing, but the way her hands clench at her sides isn't how she usually looks when she's giggling. She's not lifting her chin or cocking her head a touch to the left.

Tommy reaches for her arm, grabbing her just behind her elbow.

It's one motion, one jerk of her arm away. It's one moment of lip reading as she forms the word "Ouch," that has me storming towards them.

I can barely see straight and it has nothing to do with the two beers I drank. My body shakes so fucking bad, ready to break this asshole's face for a second time. By the time I get to them, they see me coming.

Sienna sags against the wall, Tommy taking a giant step away from her.

"You okay?" I ask her before I even get there.

"Yes," she sighs, looking at me with wide eyes.

"You," I say, turning towards Tommy, "are not okay."

"I had no idea she was with you—"

My fist slams into his mouth before he can even get his excuse out of his trap. The explosion is a perfect cross, shoving all the way through until my arm is extended with his face at the end.

Sienna gasps, her hand flying to her mouth, but wisely stays to the side next to Peck.

Tommy is crouched on the floor, one hand tapping at his mouth. He swipes a trail of blood down the side as Machlan shoves through the crowd and takes in the scene.

My muscles flex, ready to lunge forward and hit him again. Machlan positions himself so I'd have to go through him to do it.

"What the hell did you do now?" Machlan looks down at Tommy with no pity.

"Your brother fucking hit me! Did someone call the police?"

No one says a word, the song on the radio overhead wrapping up the only sound. Tommy looks around, getting to his feet. As he realizes everyone is watching, you can see the anger and humiliation building.

"You're going down for this one," Tommy snarls. "I'm calling the police."

"You do that." Sienna steps to my side, her head held high. "Call them. I'd love to talk to the Sheriff about how you grabbed my arm."

"You little bitch—"

He doesn't get that one out either before I rock him back with a left hook. His body weight twisting him around with the force of the punch, he lands again on his feet like a fucking cat.

"Tommy," Machlan booms, "I'm going to suggest you get the hell out of here while you can walk. Because if you open your mouth again, it'll be the last time for a while."

"Fuck you and this hillbilly town." Tommy spits a mouthful of blood on the floor. "Fuck all of you."

The crowd parts as he storms through it, the front door smashing so hard it sounds like the glass breaks. It's the trigger that gets everyone talking again. Before I know it, it's just me, Sienna, and Machlan.

As the adrenaline settles, the blood shining in the light, I realize what I've done.

"Fuck," I growl, so many things floating through my head that I can't make sense of any of them. The only thing that clears them for a brief moment is Sienna touching my hand.

"This is swollen," she says softly, holding my hand in both of hers. "Can we get him some ice, Machlan?"

"I'm fine," I grumble.

"You aren't fine." She lifts my hand to inspect it, her eyes full of concern. Watching her trying to get a plan together to fix me makes me forget about all the pain.

"I gotta get this mess cleaned up," Machlan breathes. "You okay, Sienna?"

"Yeah. He just grabbed me. I think he pinched a pressure point or something."

"Let me know if you need anything," Machlan says before disappearing to the store room.

She's right in front of me, her soft skin against mine. Kindness and worry about me, even though she was the one hurt, is all I see on her face.

Taking my hand away, even though my head screams inside not to, I lift her arm carefully. Her skin is smooth, a creamy white, and I'm relieved there are no bruises.

"I'm fine, Walker. Really."

"It doesn't hurt anywhere? You sure?" I run a hand down her arm, feeling for any lumps, watching for her to cringe. She doesn't.

"I'm sure."

Nodding, not trusting what will come out of my mouth, I place her arm back to her side.

"Thank you for doing that," she gulps. "I don't really know what to say. Just . . . thank you."

"Yeah. No problem," I say, exhaling roughly as the pain throbs up my wrist.

"I'm worried about you," Sienna says, reaching for my hand again.

Letting myself give in for a split second, I touch the side of her face. She leans into it, her eyes filled with something I can't put my finger on. Before I can do anything else, I flip her a nod and a tight smile and leave out the back door.

chapter
Nine

Walker

"THAT OUGHTA DO IT." MACHLAN takes a step back and examines our handiwork. "Looks good to me."

"I think it's sturdy," I note, gripping the edge of the gutter and giving it a shake with my good hand. The other is still swollen from Tommy's face. "Yeah. That's solid as shit."

We walk back to my truck and lay our tools on the bed. My brother fishes around in the cooler until he retrieves a bottle of water. Popping it open, he takes a long, leisurely swig before wiping his mouth with his shirt.

"You just left a smear of black shit across your face," I say, nodding towards the line going from one cheek to the other ear.

"Yeah, well, I gotta get a shower anyway."

The sun barely streams over the tops of the trees lining the back of Nana's property. Deep purples and pumpkin oranges streak the sky as a flock of birds fly into the evergreens. I'm not sure what's written on my face, but when I turn to look at Machlan, he's smiling.

"What?" I ask, unlatching the toolbox bolted into the top of the bed of my truck.

"What's on your mind tonight, Walker?"

"Nothin'."

"I'm gonna have to call you out on that bullshit."

Resting my forearms on the bed, I look at him like he's a dumbass. Of course there's a lot of shit on my mind. Even if I could stop thinking about Sienna, my throbbing hand would remind me every time I go to move it. But I don't want to talk to him about that. "Now how in the world do you know what's on my mind?"

"Because I'm your brother. I know you almost as well as I know myself."

"You don't know shit," I tell him, picking up the hammer and screwdrivers and tossing them into the toolbox. They clamor as they land on top of a variety of other tools.

"So I can assume everything Peck said is false?" he asks.

"Don't we always assume everything he says is false?"

"Not everything," he insists. "Sometimes he's right."

"Like when?" I snort.

"Like when he said I should dump Janette because she was a whore."

"I fucking told you that too. Peck doesn't get credit for that when the whole damn town knew it."

"Easy there, tiger," Machlan says, wagging a finger my way. "Let's not start talking about our history of whores. I believe you have—"

"Enough." Flashing him a warning glance, I slam the toolbox closed. In typical brotherly fashion, he laughs again. Louder this time. More *pointed* this time. "Machlan, I think it's time to call it a night."

"I think we're just getting started."

"See," I say, swinging the truck door open as my jaw sets in place, "this is where you're wrong. You never know when to shut the fuck up."

"No, I think I always know when you want to avoid shit and I force you to think about it."

"You don't force me to do anything besides want to punch your face in."

"Well, by the look of Tommy's face the other night, your skills seem to be pretty sharp. You might even be able to hang with me for a second or two." He opens the passenger side door and looks at me through the cab. "You really like her, don't you?"

"Who?" I deadpan.

"Come on, Walk."

"You want to say goodbye to Nana or just get out of here?" I ask, deflecting his stupid fucking question.

Climbing into the cab, I ignore my brother as he takes his seat and buckles his seatbelt. I usually give him a hard time about strapping in like a good little citizen, but I let it slide this time. I simply don't have the energy to rile him up. I expended every ounce of energy I could muster today trying to seem like I wasn't paying attention to Sienna.

If it wasn't her ass in those shorts as she stood on a chair and washed the windows, it was the way she chewed on her bottom lip as she sorted invoices. If I got really lucky, her laugh would float into the garage bay and I'd fight a hard-on while changing someone's oil.

Sienna is organized. My customers love her. She got Standski to get parts to us within an hour all week. I can't find a reason to dislike her no matter how hard I try.

The logical, maybe even compassionate, side of me wants to tell her to call it even. That's what I should do. That's the smart option for both of us.

The stronger side of me, the one that's laced with testosterone, wants me to give Peck the day off, lock the doors to Crank, and just strip her down on the office desk. I'd start at her sweet lips, kissing my way down to her—

"You still here?" Machlan asks, nudging me in the side. "I mean, I'm happy to sit here all night, but let me know so I can get comfortable."

Rolling my eyes, I start up the truck and pull down Nana's lane.

"Guess that settles that," he mumbles as we pass her house. "So, Peck says Sienna is super hot, which I already knew, but he also said she—"

"Peck needs to stop talking about her." I say it too fast, with too much force. Keeping my gaze on the road, I don't look at my brother because I don't want to see the victory in his eyes that I know is there. "You, too, for that matter."

"That's hard, in more ways than one, if you catch my drift."

He's saying it to piss me off. It works. My knuckles turn white as they wrap around the steering wheel, imagining it's Machlan's neck.

"You can keep your thoughts about Sienna to yourself," I say through clenched teeth. Just thinking about him thinking about jacking off to her makes me want to come undone. I hate this feeling of not being able to control my reaction to Sienna and having to listen to these assholes poke me about it.

"Well, if it's nothing to you, I don't see why it can't be something to someone else. If she finds her way into Crave this weekend, you know what'll happen. Every cocksucker in there will have his number in her hands."

I don't have to look at my brother out of the corner of my eye to know he's pulling my chain, but I do anyway. When I take in his cheesy smile and arched brow, I cut the steering wheel hard to bounce him around in his seat.

Laughing, Machlan adjusts his shoulder strap. "I haven't seen you like this in a long time, brother."

"Let's not go there."

"I'm not going there," he promises. "I'm just saying, it's fun to see you like this."

"Like what?"

"She's gotten under your skin."

It's a simple phrase, one I've heard used to describe people in songs and even, sometimes, in real life. But never have I truly understood what it meant until this very moment.

He's right. She's burrowed her way into my mind, maybe without even trying. Something about her just sparks a match deep inside me, one I can't put out no matter how hard I try. In a perfect world, I'd ask her to dinner. I'd ask her about the little drawl to her voice and what the ring on her finger means. I'd ask her why she chose purple to streak her hair and why she always hums the same catchy ditty to herself.

But I don't. Because that would be stupid. Because scratching this particular itch would only spread it. This isn't a bug bite. This is poison ivy.

I take the final turn to Machlan's house and pull up in front of the two-story brick home that was our parents'. The house where we all grew up.

Flicking the transmission into park, I look at him. "Thanks for helping me tonight."

"Yeah. No problem. I'm gonna grab a shower and then head into Crave. Our orders for the week go in tomorrow and I don't know what we have and what we don't." He grabs the handle, but stops. "Walker, look, I know I was giving you hell, but really . . . I think it's good you're finally starting to come around. You've done everything right, brother. But fuck it. You deserve a life too."

"It's not like that."

"Let it—"

"Mach," I warn, cutting him off. "Don't. All right? Just don't."

Fists clenched at my sides, I look at the house and not at him.

"How long you gonna do this?" he asks. "Up until now, I get it. There hasn't been anyone who's worth a damn. But Sienna is different, Walk."

"You getting out or what?" I ask.

Heaving a breath, he climbs out of my truck. "See ya on Sunday."

"Later."

As soon as the door closes, I peel out of the driveway. I should turn left to go home, but that would only make things worse. Instead, I take a right and drive aimlessly into the darkening night.

chapter
Ten

Walker

A ROCK SONG BLARES ON the overhead speakers as I fish under a table for a dropped bolt. The tune is one of my favorites, one that I play when I need to zone out and focus on a job. After getting here two hours early and getting nothing accomplished, I tried my luck with music. Turns out, my luck is out.

My hand rolls along the cool concrete floor, grasping wildly for the errant piece. My mind is just as desperate for a resolution of its own.

The lyrics, lines I've heard dozens of times over my life, sound brand new this morning. I've never picked up on the innuendo or the suggestive undertones before. As the words thump through the room, my mind is drawn further and further away from the broken axel on the pickup in front of me and closer to the blonde who should be walking in the door at any minute.

The truck has been a headache, but Sienna is a fucking migraine. At least with the truck, there are procedures and handbooks and common knowledge that can be applied to solve the riddle. With her? It's madness. There's not a handbook besides the back of a whiskey label to fix this.

"Hey," Peck says, breaking me from my spell. His head is stuck around the door, having just arrived. "Donaldson is in. Where's his invoice?"

"Fuck if I know," I grumble. "Sienna filed all that shit."

"Where?"

"All I know is the folders were all sparkly. There's still glitter on the floor back there. I'd just follow the glitter trail, Peck."

"I'd like to follow that glitter trail," he smirks.

Flashing him a look, my lips pressing together so hard they hurt, I watch as he laughs.

"I heard the guys at Crave talking about her last night. You have three calls on the answering machine right now with men wanting to bring their trucks in for basic shit they usually do themselves. You get what I'm saying?" he asks.

"Charge Donaldson fifty bucks. Get what I'm saying?" I ask, lifting a brow.

Peck laughs again, the sound cut off by the door closing. I go back to the truck and try to ignore the pain across the back of my shoulders. The lug nut is almost tightened when my hand falls from the tool. It dings off the concrete, making a racket, but I stay squatted down and wait. Within a few seconds, her laugh spills from the lobby and floods my ears.

The grin that settles over my lips every morning when I feel her presence does its thing, but because no one is here to see it, I let it go. I let my stupid body react while my brain screams at it to stop. It's like I'm trapped in a madman's world where the two parts of me are in a constant battle. My brain is right. My body is wrong. We all know it. It's common with men. But the override button I can usually press on my physical reactions is broken and that's why I'm fucked.

Angling my ear so I can hear her better, the faint pitches and dips of her voice as she teases Peck melt away a bit of my stress.

She showed up. Again.

Rocking back on my heels, I let out a breath before standing. As I turn around, the door is opening behind me and Peck's dumb ass is whistling as he comes in.

"Good Lord almighty," he cackles. "You need to go see that."

"See what?"

"See what," he scoffs. "I don't know. That ass. Those fucking legs.

Hell, even her purple hair is hot. But the best part is, she brought in blueberry muffins." A hand clamps on my shoulder. "She cooks, Walk. She fucking cooks."

"So what?" I say, rolling my eyes for his benefit. "I cook. Nana cooks. Veronica at Carlson's cooks. It's not a thing."

"And as much as I love Nana, she doesn't look like that."

Heading towards the sink in the back, I use every bit of self-control I have not to look at the lobby window. "Don't you feel guilty for mentally cheating on Molly McCarter?"

"Ah, don't bring her up," he sighs. "I saw her this morning at Goodman's gas station. She waved at me."

"Don't you think it's a little pathetic you have that look on your face because she waved at you?"

"Don't you think it's a little pathetic you have that look on your face because Sienna is standing out there and you're too chicken shit to go out there and talk to her?"

"What the hell are you talking about?" Flipping on the tap with more force than necessary, I rub my hands together beneath the freezing cold water with gusto.

Peck follows me and leans against the wall. "No one is going to think badly of you if you—"

"Is that what you think this is?" The faucet squeals as the water shuts off. "You think I'm worried what any of you will think?"

"Yeah. I do. I think you think we're gonna judge you."

A low rumble escapes my throat, the mountain of morning irritability now focused solely on him. "When have I ever given a fuck what anyone thinks of me, Peck? When I walked away from the football scholarship at EIU so I could help Dad out around here? Did I care then? Or when I beat the shit out of Tommy Jones for laying a hand on Blaire? Did I care that some people around here thought I was some kind of barbarian fucking up the golden boy of Linton? Because I don't remember that."

"I think this is a little different."

"You would."

Stomping across the garage, I glance quickly at the window but don't see Sienna. A bit of relief runs through me that she can't see my face. I have no idea how pissed off I look, but it can't be any match for how pissed off I feel.

Fuck Peck for pushing in places he shouldn't. To hell with him for insinuating this is anything but me trying not to twist up a girl who clearly doesn't need wrapped up in my bullshit. As irritating as she is, Sienna doesn't deserve this. And even if my life wasn't such a fuck-up, there's no way that girl, one I can't figure out for the life of me, would be able to handle all the baggage I come with.

Glaring Peck's way, I throw it all to the wind and fling open the door to the lobby. I try to ignore the legs and hair and scent of her pineappley perfume that's as unavoidable as a category five hurricane. Marching around the desk, I fiddle with the mouse and wait for the computer to wake up.

"Good morning," she chirps. Her voice is sunshine, a bright reprieve to my otherwise bland day. "Sorry I'm a little late."

"You mean you actually have a starting time?"

She giggles, stepping off the stool she's perched on, wiping at the window blinds. "I've tried to be here when you open every day. Haven't you noticed?"

I've noticed a fuck lot more than that. "Yeah, now that you mention it . . ."

"Aren't you going to give me a cookie or something?" she sighs. "I hate getting up this early."

"We open at eight. That's early?"

"No, but seven is." She tosses a rag into the bin. "I don't work on other people's schedules often. You should be honored."

"I'll remember that."

She hops up on the desk, her ass planting on a calendar I need to see. The way her back arches, her hair spiraling down almost to her waist, has me gulping. Her legs swinging back and forth, she watches me. "So, what's happening today?"

"Work."

The door chimes and two boys walk in wearing navy blue t-shirts with white writing on the front. "Hey, Mr. Gibson," the one on the right says. "We're here seeing if you'd like to help our science club."

"What are you raising money for?" I ask.

"We want to go to camp in Houston this winter," the one on the left says. "It's an astronaut camp. It's going to be really cool, but really expensive. That's why we're selling these." He holds out a box of chocolate bars wrapped in gold foil. "They're really good and they have a coupon on the inside for pizza. You really can't lose."

Grabbing at my wallet in my back pocket, I narrow my eyes. "So you want to be astronauts?"

"I do," the right one says. "But he wants to be an engineer."

"But camp would help me learn so much to do that," the left one says earnestly.

"How old are you?" I ask.

"Eleven," they say in unison.

Sienna watches from the side. She's itching to interject, opening her mouth a few times, but closing it before she does.

"How many do you have to sell?" I ask, doing a quick perusal of the contents of the box.

"As many as we can," the left one groans. "We have until Monday to finish selling this box but people don't want to buy them. It's chocolate! What's wrong with chocolate?"

Chuckling, I open my wallet. "How much are they?"

"They're a dollar a piece."

"How many do you have?"

"Total?" the right one asks. He does a quick count. "There are twenty-two in here."

"All I have is two twenties," I say, fishing out the bills. "I'll trade you."

"We don't have change." The right one closes the box. "I could ask my mom to bring it by to you tonight."

"Just use it for astronaut school," I say, taking the chocolates. "And when you get to the moon someday, do a shout out to Crank for me, okay?"

"Yes, sir," the right one says, his smile stretching from ear to ear. "Thank you, sir."

"No problem."

They skip out the door, high-fiving each other when they hit the parking lot. My eyes drag to Sienna. "What?"

"Nothing. That was just super sweet of you. I didn't know you had it in ya."

I shove my wallet back into my pants. "There's a lot you don't know about me."

"Want to tell me?"

"Nope."

"Can I ask you something? About cars," she adds.

Scooting the mouse away from the keyboard, I turn towards her. "Sure. What's up?"

"There's a light on in my car." She sets off describing it in the most girlish terms I can imagine. She's animated today, rambling on and on about calling the shop but wanting to know what it means so she can go in there armed to the teeth and not get taken advantage of. "Do you know what that is?"

"It's your oil light. When's the last time your oil was changed?"

She shrugs. "When I was in Georgia."

"How long ago was that?"

"Last summer."

My head falling back, I sigh. "You're way overdue. You can't let your car go that long."

"Well, my light should've come on before now," she insists. "I have an appointment after I leave here at the dealership. I just don't want them lying to me. I usually have one of my brothers take it in and handle it. Or Troy."

"Who's Troy?" I ask, not sure I want to know.

"My brother Barrett's guy."

"Is he gay?"

She bursts out laughing, leaping off the desk. "That would be a no."

She prances around the room, making a pot of coffee and wiping off the table where sugar appears to have been spilled. This is why I can't start looking at her—I can't stop. As she buzzes around the room, fiddling with everything she can, I don't even get annoyed. It doesn't even bother me. I'm too absorbed with a plethora of questions to pay attention to all the things she's moving around.

Before I know what's happening, she stops. "Something wrong?"

Looking at the floor, I shove around the desk and head for the garage. "Nope. Have a good day, Sienna."

"You too . . ."

———

WIPING MY HANDS ON A towel, I push the door to the lobby open with my shoulder. My brain is calculating the quantity of line I need to order when I stop in my tracks. Sienna is standing beside Nana who has a half-eaten muffin in her hand.

"Oh, there you are, Walker," Nana says, popping the rest of the muffin into her mouth. "I came in here looking for you and found this sweet girl instead."

I look at Sienna out of the corner of my eye. Smug doesn't even begin to describe the look on her beautiful face, like she won over Nana. Like that means something.

"I just got out to the garage yesterday and had a look at the work you and Machlan did for me. Such good boys, the both of you," she says, patting the side of my cheek. "What would I do without my sweet grandsons?"

"It wasn't a big deal," I say, feeling a little smug myself.

"If you come to dinner on Sunday, I'll make a pecan pie."

"Are you bribing me with pie?"

"Would you rather have cake?" Her hand drops from my face with a sigh. "I need your behind in a pew on Sunday, Walker. You can go out on Saturday and be friends with Jack and Jim, but I need you friendly with Jesus the next morning."

Sienna bursts out laughing, the melody like a song.

"What's so funny?" I ask.

"That Jack and Jim line. My mama would love it, Nana."

Nana's attention switches from pie to Sienna. "Does your mama expect you to attend services on Sunday?"

"Well . . ." Sienna blushes. "We go on Easter, Christmas Eve, Grandma's birthday when she was alive. But not every Sunday, no."

Sienna doesn't know the pass she just gave me. As Nana heads her way, the pie all but forgotten, Sienna looks at me. I wink, watching her cheeks turn an adorable shade of pink.

"Well, dear, I expect your behind at Holy Hills church on Sunday. Services start at nine and run just under an hour. Surely, you can find it in your heart to give an hour to God."

"I . . . um . . ." Sienna looks at me for help. "I'll try."

Shaking my head, I cross my arms across my chest and watch her struggle against my grandmother. It's a battle of strong-willed ladies, and I'm not sure who will win.

"It's next to the library. Big ol' cross in the front. You can't miss it," Nana says. "I'll see you there. Both of you."

"I'll be there," I tell her, watching her beam. "You know how much I love pecan pie."

"Don't come for the pie, Walker. Come for the lesson. Then the pie." She turns towards the door, calling over her shoulder, "Your muffins were delicious, Sienna. I'd love the recipe."

"I'll bring it on Sunday?"

It's more of a question than a statement, but it lights Nana's face up all the same.

"You do that. Have a good day, both of you." She sends me a knowing grin before fluttering out the door.

The chimes settle and the room draws smaller. Shoving my hands into my pockets, I look at the girl next to me.

Her legs are capped with a pair of navy shorts and a brown tank hugs her curves, dipping low enough to showcase the tops of her breasts. As if the roundness weren't enough of a draw, she's added a long, gold necklace with a heart at the end that snuggles just above her cleavage. It's like a warning sign and an invitation all at once.

"You two seemed comfortable," I note, trying to start us out on neutral ground.

"Who?"

"You and Nana."

"Your Nana is a pistol," she says, circling around the desk. She lifts a tray into the air. "Want a muffin?"

A muffin is the last thing I want right now. I know not to do it and the entire time my eyes draw up her arm, over her chest, and up to her gorgeous face, I tell myself to stop. Pleading with my brain to take over and force the rest of me to get in line, I continue to roam over her, committing each little curve and dip to memory.

I'm an asshole for doing this. I'm a complete dick for letting myself pretend anything with this girl is possible. Yet, when I settle on her bright blue eyes, they twinkle happily, which only makes me feel worse.

"Is that a no?" she asks. Setting the tray down, she watches me with a confidence that I want to fuck right out of her. Ignoring me as I start to speak, she snaps up the landline. "Crank," she singsongs into the line.

Adjusting myself while she takes notes on a scrap of paper, I grasp for some equilibrium. I think I have it until she looks at me again, sending me off-kilter.

"This is Rusty Carmine. He said they have a welding issue at their warehouse. He said you usually send Peck out to fix it and that it's urgent."

"Yeah. Tell him he'll be there," I say, signaling for Peck. Before she gets off the phone, Peck is on his way to his truck.

Pouring a cup of coffee after finding the coffee pot that has been moved, I wait for her to finish the call. Once I hear the "goodbye," I turn to face her.

"I've been keeping track of your hours," I tell her.

"Good for you." She ignores where I'm going and changes subjects instead. "What do you think of the place? Looks nice, huh?"

The floors aren't quite as dirty as before. The place has a floral smell to it and there aren't any towels spilling over the bin in the back. It looks nice.

"It's okay," I say, taking a sip.

"Okay?" she barks. "It's more than okay! It's a one-eighty from where it was."

"I can't find anything."

"Because you don't know how to look. Typical man," she mumbles. "I clearly marked all the folders in here. You can find everything super easily." She looks up at me. "I never thought I had it in me to like paperwork. Must've been buried deep in my genes."

"I'd love to be buried in your jeans," I say before I can think twice. Hoping she didn't hear me, my gaze snaps to hers, but it's obvious: she heard. Not only did she hear, she's not going to let it go.

My blood hotter than the coffee in my hand, I pivot on my heel towards the garage.

"You would, would you?" she teases, her voice dangling in the air.

All I can think about is what she'd look like sprawled in my bed, her body pressed against mine, her breath hot against my flesh. Shaking my head, ridding myself of the delicious vision, I say, "I shouldn't have said that out loud."

"So you've been thinking it?"

"Come on, Sienna," I sigh.

She leans against the desk, her bottom lip protruding. "Why are you so grumpy?"

"Grumpy?" I laugh, grateful for the change in direction. "What are we? In kindergarten?"

"No. But it's the best word to describe you. Grumpy. You're grumpy."

"I am not."

"See? And argumentative. It's a wonder I even show up here."

It's my turn to lean against the desk. There's an honesty in the way she speaks, and an edge of class or sophistication, that, at the end of the day, is both the worst thing and best thing about her. It's what people respond to—Nana, Peck . . . me. It's what she responds to in me that I don't understand. I surely don't give her much to go on. Most women are out the door by now.

"Why *do* you show up here?" I ask.

The levity from her features melts away and a somberness takes its place. "Because I owe you."

"Is that why?" I press, not able to fight the hope swelling inside me that it's not. "What's your story, Sienna?"

Her story isn't one I need to know, and if she responds, it'll just fuck me further. I need distance from this chick, not her family history.

This is the problem I knew from the beginning: dipping even a toe into this pool will drown us both.

"There you are." The door swings open without warning, causing Sienna and I both to exhale sharply. "I have a giant problem, Walker, and I need your help."

"What's up, Stuart?" I ask, clearing my throat.

"The tractor went down on me this morning. I hauled her up here, hoping you can take a look at it. I know it's a huge job and you have other stuff happening, but I'll pay you double. You're the best and I need this fixed by tomorrow morning. Is there any chance you can swing it?"

The garage bay is fairly empty, just the truck and a van in so far today.

"How many appointments are there today, Sienna?" I ask. "Do you know?"

She looks at a calendar and lifts her eyes. "You have two. A van and a car this afternoon, although a bunch of people said they're walking in."

"Yeah," I say to Stuart, leading him outside. "Let's get it in the shop and I'll start on it in a bit. What's it doing?"

As he goes ahead of me, rambling about the problems I should be paying attention to, instead, I focus on what's becoming the biggest problem in my life.

Sienna

I TURN THE KEY AND my car's engine roars to life outside of Goodman's gas station. Getting situated in the driver's seat, I buckle my seatbelt and get the radio set to a station playing upbeat and happy music.

Today was a good day.

Every time I think of Walker, I remember his little slip about my jeans. Giggling, I reach for the gear shift to put my car in reverse and stop.

The oil light isn't lit.

It doesn't come on when I put it in reverse either.

Peck comes out from inside the gas station where he was just buying a drink and sees me sitting in the parking lot. He heads my way.

I roll down the windows, the warm breeze making me even happier. "Hey," I say to him as he gets near. "Did you change my oil today?"

"Nope."

My back falls against the seat as I try not to act as giddy as I feel.

He leans against the door and takes me in. "What are ya thinking?"

"I mentioned it to Walker earlier and now the light is off. Does that mean he changed it?"

"Someone did," Peck grins, "and it wasn't me. Walker is a good guy. And I'm fairly certain he thinks a lot of you."

"You think?" I ask, my hopes whizzing upwards.

"I do." He taps the hood as he stands up again. "I got to get back to the job. Just came by for a drink. Be careful going wherever you're going."

"Will do. Thanks, Peck."

"Later."

I don't pull out quite yet. Instead, I sit there with a huge smile on my face.

As much of a jerk as he can be, he can also make me feel like this. Between protecting me with Tommy to changing my oil, it feels really, really good.

chapter
Eleven

Walker

"AH, FUCK." THE TOOL SLIPS out of my hand and clamors onto the floor two inches from my head. I'd jump—that's my immediate reaction—but the steel hanging right above me as I lie beneath the tractor keeps me from it.

Blowing out a hiss, my eyes fall closed as the aches in my back from lying in this position for the last few hours start to compound. My shoulders throb from holding objects over my head, my eyes burn from the oil and gas fumes. It's been a hell of a day.

Twisting just enough to get a glimpse of the clock on the far wall, I realize Peck isn't coming back. The welding job took all day, and by now, he's with the community center people helping the summer sports program. Annoyance that I'm still here, alone, now doing a job that would be so much faster with two people, would come easy except I know how much it means to Peck to give back to the program he credits for saving his life.

The massive piece of equipment straddling me is going to take all night, but I expected as much. Farm equipment is never a quick fix. But for all the headaches it gives, it also provides two things: a lot of money and an inability to think about anything else. Stuart coming in this morning with this giant pain in the ass was a godsend.

Cringing, my hand falls to my stomach as its rumbling sounds over the garage. Sienna left a couple of muffins on the desk when she left a few hours ago and I devoured them. That's all I've eaten today, another by-product of this project.

Lifting the tool I dropped, I start to attack the problem again when I hear a sound across the room. A set of tanned legs stop just in front of the tractor.

The tool drops slowly to my chest. There's no reason for her to be here now, just as the sun is starting to set. As my heart races so quickly I feel it pulse in my throat, I wait for her to speak. To explain. To leave again so I can breathe.

"Walker?"

"Yeah?" I croak, watching one of her legs bend at the knee. The light reflects off her skin, drawing me in like a fucking Siren.

"Why are you still here?"

"Working. Why are you here?"

She shifts her weight, a hand going to her hip. I wonder if she's rolling her eyes and shaking her head like she usually does when I don't just answer her questions, and if she is, I hate that I'm missing it.

"I drove by a few minutes ago and saw your truck and the lights on. I figured . . . I don't know," she says, clearing her throat. "Maybe you need some help?"

Chuckling, I slide myself out from under the tractor. Lying on the creeper, the heels of my work boots pressed into the concrete to stop me from sliding, I look up. She's looking down with a soft, inquisitive stare that makes me feel more vulnerable than I care to admit.

Resting my hands on my stomach, I force everything out of my mind except the fact that she shouldn't be here.

"Did you bring someone with you?" I ask.

"For what?"

"To help."

The glare I fully expect doesn't take long to come my way. "No. I meant I was coming to help you."

She's changed clothes from earlier today. I would guess these to be the clothes she doesn't care if she messes up. A pair of black cutoff sweat pants that hit only a few inches down her thighs, a tight grey t-shirt with spatters of pink and white paint, and lime green flip-flops. I can imagine her stretched out on the couch reading a book or curled up in a chair watching a fire, two thoughts I have to force away.

"Slugger, you can't work in a garage in flip-flops."

"Why not?"

I lift a brow.

"Fine," she sighs, turning to the table by the door. Motioning towards a plastic bag, she tucks a strand of hair behind her ear. "I brought you something to eat. Maybe you aren't hungry, I don't know, but I know you didn't break for lunch and—"

"I am. Hungry, that is."

Her chest falls, her shoulders relaxing, a soft relief smoothing her forehead. "When I saw you still here, I figured as much. I ran by Crave and Machlan made you a sandwich. I didn't know what you'd like."

"You're on a first name basis with my brother?"

"He's so sweet," she coos. "And he adores you, Walker."

"About as much as he adores syphilis." I get just close enough to grab the bag. Peering inside, I count three burgers and fries. "Think I'm hungry or what?"

"One of those is mine. Machlan just put it all in the same bag."

"Oh."

She kicks at an invisible rock on the floor, the toe of her flip-flop squeaking against the concrete. "I wanted to tell you thank you for changing my oil today. And for the new wipers."

Having forgotten all about that, I feel a weird sensation in my chest. It's not guilt, but more like being caught. "It's no big deal."

"You didn't have to do that. I didn't mean for you to do it, if that's what you were thinking."

"No," I say in a rush, not wanting her to feel guilty for my deeds. "I figured I'd just check it really quick so you didn't break down, and the oil was filthy. Almost like syrup. So I just changed it. We have all the shit here to do it, no sense in you taking it somewhere else." She starts to speak, but I know what she's going to say, so I cut her off before she can. "And you aren't paying me back for it."

A shy smile covers her gorgeous lips as she looks at me, eyes shining. "And for the wipers. How did you even know they sucked?"

"It's what I look for. Again, no big deal."

"Well, thank you."

"You're welcome."

The bag ruffles in my hand, the sound the only thing breaking the awkward silence between us. I'm not sure what to do or say. What I want and what I should do are at such opposite ends of the spectrum that I can't see through the fuzz to think clearly. Then I make the mistake of looking up.

Her hair is pulled on top of her head, the earrings and bracelets she usually wears are gone. If she's wearing any makeup at all, I'd be surprised.

As she looks at me with wide eyes and a hesitation I can't deny, I fight a smile at the realization: she *was* coming to help me.

The idea of this girl getting greasy and handling tools heavier than she is, is laughable. And the sexiest fucking thing I can think of.

Letting the testosterone swooping through my veins call the shots, I'm talking before my brain can tell my mouth to shut up.

"Want to eat with me?" I ask.

"Sure."

Her smile has me forgetting all about how empty my stomach was a few minutes ago. She holds up a finger, asking me to wait a minute, and then disappears into the lobby. Every second she's gone is a second longer for me to remember exactly why this is a bad idea. Busying myself with the task of washing my hands, I half wonder if she'll come back and half hope she doesn't. When she comes back with two large drinks, that all goes to the wayside.

"I brought the drinks," she says shyly. "I couldn't carry them in, so I left them in my car."

"You thought of everything," I say, unwrapping a sandwich.

"Not really. I was just going to drop yours by and take mine home."

"Why were you over here, anyway?"

"Um," she gulps, picking up a fry. "Well, to be honest . . ."

"Yeah?"

"I was worried about you." She looks at the ground, popping the fry in her mouth. "I'm sure you've done this a million times, but you were in here all day. I hardly saw you at all. And I knew Peck didn't come back . . ."

Resting my sandwich on the foil wrapper so it doesn't fall from my hand, the corner of my lips lift to the ceiling as I try to wrap my head around the fact that she cares. Maybe not about me, per se, but about what I'm doing. I don't really know how to process that.

"Really?" I ask.

"Of course," she says. "Why is that so hard to believe?"

"I don't know. I guess I'm used to doing a lot of this on my own. It's weird having someone looking over my shoulder."

"Oh, I don't want you to feel like that," she pushes. "It's not what I mean."

"I didn't mean it like that. I'm, um, I'm not used to having someone pay attention." I hold her gaze, my stomach twisting into a bigger mess than the tractor.

"Yeah, well, it's what I do," she says, dismissively. "I get it from my mother. My siblings are all like that. We try to fix everything. And I mean everything."

"Like the Ranger?"

"Like the Ranger," she agrees shyly.

Lifting the sandwich, I take a bite of Crave's famous barbecue bacon cheeseburger and think about what she said. "What's your family like?"

"They're great. Nosy, all of them, and pains in the ass. But I don't know what I would do without them."

"You seem like you miss them."

She considers this, leaning her head to the side as she focuses on a spot on the wall behind me. "I do. I miss them like crazy. It seems like the older I get, the more I miss them."

"Are they like you?"

"What do you mean, 'are they like me'?" she presses.

"Exactly what it sounds like."

"How would you describe me?"

Beautiful. Sexy. Intriguing.

"Capable," I suggest.

"Oh, gee. Thanks."

"What?" I laugh before taking a sip of my soda. "Capable is a good word."

"If you're talking about a soldier!"

"Fine. You're determined."

"I think I'm taking my burger to go," she laughs, tossing her half-eaten fry at me. It misses, hitting my cup and falling to the floor.

Setting my burger down, I focus my attention solely on her. "What about interesting?" I offer, more quietly this time. "Or classy? Or good-hearted?"

"You think I'm interesting?"

Her eyelashes bat together, the apples of her cheeks glowing. I want to show her just how *interesting* I find her to be, how her classy mouth sounds when it's crying my name in the dirtiest way.

"A little bit," I grumble instead, bundling what's left of my burger up in the wrapper. Her gaze sits squarely on my shoulders and I know if I look up at her, she'll be expecting an explanation. So I don't look up. "I have to get back to the tractor. Thank you for dinner, Sienna."

"Any time," she whispers.

Turning to toss my stuff in the trash, we nearly collide. The scent of pineapples rushes across me, mixing with the heat of her body. It's a connection I can't break, the way my body wants to crash against hers. The way I don't have to look in the morning to know she's here because I can sense her walking into a room. There's a definite link somehow from something in me to something in her, and even though I fight with everything I have to break it, I can't.

"Do you need help?" she asks. There's a twinge of hope in her tone that I can't let go.

"What do you know about tools?"

"I know you think I'm a silly girl who's never touched a hammer before, but that's both sexist and not true." Hand on her hip again, she throws her shoulders back. "If you don't want my help, that's fine. I'll go."

"So you know the difference between a socket and a screwdriver?" My question is quick, the desperation that she says yes thick—maybe too thick. I think she starts to read into it, but like me, tempers her hopes.

"Of course," she huffs.

"Fine," I say, turning away so she doesn't see my smile. "Let's get dinner cleaned up and get to it."

chapter
Twelve

Sienna

"CAN YOU GRAB ME A wrench? Inch and a half."

"Sure." Nearly skipping to the back wall that's lined in front by giant toolboxes, I'm relieved I actually know what a wrench is. The last two things he's asked me for have sounded like he made them up. My quick online searches have provided me with proof they were real, as well as an image to reference as I scan the thousands of implements in Crank and retrieve the one he's looking for.

Grabbing the wrench, confirming the dimension printed into the steel, I hand it under the tractor. His fingers rub against mine as he takes it, sending a pulse zipping through my veins.

"Thanks," he says. Just like the last two times, I can hear he's impressed that I got it. Just like the last two times, I feel my grin grow wider. "How do you know about tools, anyway?"

"Oh," I say, darting around for some answer that's not Google. "We have a farm. I mean, not lots of tools or farm animals anymore," *or ever,* "but I have lots of brothers," *who know nothing about cars.*

I try to imagine one of my brothers in their polo shirts working on a car in front of what we affectionately call the Farm. It's nothing more than an old farmhouse that's been in our family for ages and is the far-thest thing from a place to do farm activities. It's been the headquarters for my family's political activities, held family Christmases, and was even photographed for a piece about Southern homes in a fancy magazine last year. But actual real-life farming? Nope.

"How many brothers do you have?" he asks.

"Four. They're all older than me and my twin sister."

"You have a twin?"

"Yeah. And, no, I can't read her mind or feel it when she stubs her toe."

His chuckle floats from under the tractor and wraps itself around me, making me light-headed. "Weird answer."

"Everyone thinks that," I say, taking the last sip of my drink. "Maybe some twins have telepathic abilities, I don't know. But we don't."

"Hey, can you hand me a tractor pin?"

"Sure."

Whipping my phone out as I head back to the toolboxes, I punch in *tractor pin*. An image pops up of a small stick with a key looking thing attached to it. Going from one box to the next, I look for anything similar.

My blood pressure shoots up as I near the final one. There's nothing that looks remotely like what popped up online. I could tell him I can't find it, but I'm three-for-three. Maybe I want to impress him in his realm.

"Find it?" he calls out. "I think Peck stuck them up against the side of the box on the right. Top drawer. Probably hard to see."

Sighing in relief, I jump to the right box and retrieve the pin. "Got it. This is the last one, just so you know."

"Yeah, we don't use those much." His hand is sticking out from under the equipment awaiting the pin. I place it gently in his palm, letting my fingertips touch him as I let it go. He snaps his hand closed, catching my fingers for a brief, sudden hold.

Neither of us pulls away for a long second, the feel of his touch, however small, is like the spark of a match on a dark night. It's warm and bright and with it comes a flash of hope that may or may not pan out.

As I draw my hand back, white noise roaring past my ears, I fall back into my chair.

Fiddling with a straw, I watch him scramble around under the tractor.

Before long, he's adjusted his position and I can't see him anymore. A part of me wants to walk around the equipment so I can get a glimpse of him again without him knowing, but I stay put just in case he's paying attention. I don't want to look thirsty.

"I heard a lot about you in Crave tonight," I tell him. "There are some interesting stories floating around about you."

"Is that so?"

"Yup. You were a football star."

"Hardly," he snorts.

"That's what they say," I sing-song. "You also had lots of girlfriends."

A tool hits the concrete. "That's not true."

"Oh, come on," I laugh. "That's the one I believe. How would you not have a ton of girlfriends?"

"Who was telling you all this shit?" he asks, clearly annoyed.

"Machlan. Peck. A guy named Cross at the bar. They also said you once burned something in Merom's football field before the big homecoming game."

"That wasn't me," he laughs. "That was Machlan and Cross's dumb asses."

"Who is Cross?"

"Machlan's friend. They've raised absolute hell together since they were kids. Cross owns the gym on the other side of town."

The sound of his laugh, something I don't get to hear often enough, makes me smile.

"Do you have any questions for me?" I ask.

"I have no interest in hearing about your dating life."

"Good because I don't have one," I grumble. "My brothers made it terribly hard growing up. Dating is something that never came easy to me."

"How would it not?" he scoffs. "Look at you. You could get any man you wanted."

I don't say anything, point out that the man I want is under a tractor and refusing to take the bait.

The sounds get louder from him banging on the tractor, so I sit in the chair and let my mind wander. I wish I could ask him all the questions I have, get to know him better, but he's so locked up and I don't know why. Even more, I don't know why I'm so awkward with him. So unsure. So . . . not me.

"You still here?" he calls out.

"Yup."

"Can you grab me the hayfork?"

"Sure."

Hopping to my feet, I put the word in the search bar of my phone. A list of sites about real estate pop up. *Shit!* I add the word *tool* after it and stop in my tracks. The image it loads is of a shovel with prongs looking thing, something I can't imagine him using under there.

"Find it?" he asks.

"I'm looking!"

"What the fuck?" I mutter, looking at the wall, scanning helplessly. The hayfork looks more like a gardening looking thing, not something for a tractor. Why would he even have one?

"Can't find it?"

I jump, Walker's voice just inches behind me. His hair is a disaster, flecks of dirt all over his face. He's filthy, smells of sweat and oil, and is the sexiest thing I've ever laid eyes on.

My mouth waters as I try to look away, my face certainly flushing from the knowledge of how wet my panties are right now.

"What are you doing?" I exclaim. "How did you get behind me so fast?"

"Find the hayfork?" His lips twist, clearly entertained, as he crosses his arms in front of him.

"Um, no. Not yet."

He looks at me, then my phone, and back to me again. "Let me see your phone."

"No."

"Come on," he says, holding out his hand. His palm is streaked with grease, beet red in some spots from grinding against the machine. "Let me see it."

"Why?" I ask, my breathing getting shallow.

"You were looking up those tools, weren't you?"

"What? I . . . Why would you think that?"

"You were, weren't you?"

His tone is teasing, but there's something else in his eye that tells me it's more than a joke to him. It's almost as if he's angry or bothered. Either way, it makes me self-conscious.

While I'm trying to figure him out, in one abrupt move, he snatches my cell out of my hand.

"Hey!" I say, leaping for it but missing. "Give me that back!"

"Were you or were you not looking up those tools?"

His eyes narrow and I narrow mine right back. If he thinks he's about to make me feel bad for trying to help him, he has another think coming.

"What's it to you?" I ask, mimicking his stance. "Why do you care how I found them?"

"Just admit it."

"Fine," I all but growl. "I didn't know what a pin was or lubricating oil or a socket. But I figured it out to help you, you asshole."

He flinches, not expecting my tirade. Glancing at my phone, he quickly offers it back. I snatch it out of his palm without touching him.

"I don't understand you," I tell him, turning away. "You're an impossibly frustrating man."

Heading across the garage to where I set my things, I gather the garbage from dinner and toss it in the trash can. I feel his gaze on my back, the crackle of the energy between us as confused as I am, but refuse to turn around.

Instead, my phone goes into my purse, along with the paper and pen I was doodling on earlier. When I do finally turn around, I'm surprised to see him smiling. My head spins, one way with irritation, another with lust, another with confusion as to what he's even smiling about.

"Thank you for helping out tonight," he says. His eyes swirl with a softness to them that pulls at my heartstrings.

"Why do you do that?" I ask.

"Do what?"

"Act like you're so hard, like nothing bothers you. So black and white. And then I see in your eyes that you might not be that way at all."

"You don't know what you're talking about," he dismisses me. Even as he says this, I know even more assuredly I'm right and that just eggs me on.

"Oh, I think I do."

His jaw sets. "You think you have everything figured out, don't you?"

"No, quite the opposite. I don't think I have the first thing figured out about you."

The silence is heavy, like a wet blanket, almost strangling us with its weight. We have a standoff, the wits of two hard-headed people going to battle and neither wanting to give in.

Grumbling under his breath, he stands straight. I'm not sure if he's going to walk out the door or climb back under the tractor, but he surprises me. He walks towards me.

My breath catches in my throat, the bite of the metal table behind me scratching into my back as I lean away, needing distance between myself and this man stalking my way.

With each drop of his boots, I struggle harder to seem unfazed by his posture. Hooded eyes. Squared, flexed body. With each second he gets closer, I breathe faster. Gulp quicker. Feel the spot between my legs get wetter.

"Why do you keep coming around?" he asks when he's standing right in front of me. The top of my head is just beneath his chin, his chest at eye-level. It's rising and falling as quickly as mine as he takes over every inch of my personal space. With every inflation, a whiff of his cologne shuffles to my nose and my senses continue to be obliterated, completely consumed in every way by him.

"I don't know," I say. "It surely isn't because of your award-winning personality."

I think he's going to laugh, but he doesn't. Just like every time I think he's going to resemble a normal person, he stops himself. "Then why?"

"You want me to stop? Is that what this is about? Because I was just trying to help you tonight, Walker."

When he doesn't answer, doesn't flinch, I throw out an exasperated sigh.

"You win. Whatever game you're playing with me, you win. I quit," I say, reaching for my purse. "Figure out what I still owe you and send me a text. I'll get you the difference on Monday."

Just before I swipe up my things, his hand lays on my arm. I just stare at it wrapped around my forearm, his hand almost twice the size of one of mine. It's cut and bruised and in desperate need of a little tender loving care, but I ignore all that and pull my eyes to his.

Big. Mistake.

I can almost see the guard being pulled down, the shield he erects being cranked back. All the confusing emotions that are usually present are still there, only en masse.

I can't think. Can't respond. Just remind myself not to reach out and pull him into me and give him the hug I think he needs, maybe even wants on some level.

"You think I'm fucking with you?" he whispers.

"Aren't you?"

"Not a chance, Slugger. As a matter of fact, I'm trying my damnedest to not fuck with you at all."

"Noted," I say, a little snottier than I intend.

Sucking up my pride, I try to shake him off. He just squeezes my forearm firmly until its clear I'm not going to move. Then he eases up.

"I don't mean it like that." He moves himself so we're face-to-face.

"I think you do. I'm beginning to think a whole lot of what I see sometimes is more hope than reality."

"What do you think you see?" he asks, taking another step so I'm almost standing between his legs.

"Stop this," I whisper, my voice as shaky as I feel.

"Why?"

"It's confusing. I can't read you."

He catches my chin with his hand, lifting it so I'm looking at him. His Adam's apple bobs as he forces a swallow, his delicious lips parting with a small sigh. "Can you read this?"

"Wha—"

His lips capture the rest of the words from mine as his mouth covers my own.

chapter
Thirteen

Sienna

THE KISS ISN'T KIND. IT isn't sweet. There's no consideration given to anything besides the fervor between us.

He moves forward until my back is pressed against the edge of the table, my face cupped firmly in his hands. His lips part mine, urging them open, until I give in.

My head is spinning, my personal space completely obliterated by Walker Gibson. His solid body is against mine, his scent flooding my airways, the taste of his mouth rocking through my veins and wanting, needing, craving more.

He wastes no time, dipping his tongue past my lips with such a strong, purposeful motion it verges on ownership. I taste his desire, feel the heat radiating off his body, experience the raw, unhinged lust he's explaining without ever saying a word.

Moaning softly, my hands working their way into his thick strands, he holds me in place with the pads of his thumbs resting on my cheekbones. Each lick, each delve into my mouth, becomes more frantic. More heated. More on the cusp of spiraling out of control.

Moving so he's straddling me, one foot on the outside of each of mine, I can feel his cock rest against my belly. The length presses against me like a steel rod ready to burst the denim covering it.

Releasing the tufts of hair laced through my fingers, I wrap a hand around the back of his neck. My palm lying against his uncovered skin, feeling the sweat beaded there, sends a full-body shiver racing down my spine. Working my hands down his back, each movement causing the thick muscles to flex and bend under my touch, I make it to the hem of his shirt and then down the backside of his jeans until they're resting on his ass.

Taking my bottom lip in between his teeth, I moan into his mouth and jerk his body towards mine. My head is buzzing, my blood screaming, my pussy begging for relief.

Opening my eyes, I see his settled on me. He lets go of my lip and takes a step back, his breath as frenzied as mine.

His pupils dilated, his hair a wild, sexy mess, he sucks in a haggard scoop of air. "Does that feel like I'm just fucking with you?"

"You stopped, didn't you?"

He starts to smile but stops himself. "I stopped for your own good."

"I'll put it to you like this," I say, letting my libido do the talking. If he shuts me down, I'll leave and never look back. "I need fucked. I'll let you decide by whom."

That's all it takes. With a growl coming from deep within his throat, he stalks the short distance between us.

"I can always find someone else," I say, my voice betraying me. "If you don't wanna—"

"Stop talking."

My mouth clamps shut, like it's controlled by the man peering down at me. The heat of his focus warms my skin and my mouth opens again to drag a cool breath of air into my lungs. Only it's not cool. It's as heated as the stare firing down from Walker.

He grabs the edge of my shirt and yanks it over my head in one quick, unceremonious move. I have no idea what he does with it; I'm too busy watching him watch me.

My thighs clench together in a worthless attempt at quelling the incessant throb between my legs. I think he notices, the corner of his lip twitching in what I would guess is a halted smirk.

Biting down on his bottom lip, perhaps to avoid any further accidental giving-away of what he's thinking, he hooks a finger in the waistband of each side of my shorts. The roughness of his finger running down my skin as he drags them to the floor causes my back to arch, a soft sigh escaping my throat.

As the fabric falls south, he bends along with it, until his face is level with my pussy. My shorts pooled at my feet and wearing only a faint pink lace bra and panty set, I gulp when he doesn't immediately stand.

Crouched, he grips the table behind me with both hands, boxing me in. When he looks up, I almost melt. My knees threaten to give out as I take in the decadent smirk playing on his handsome face.

"The best part about this," he says, his voice low and gravelly, "is going to be hearing you speechless for once."

"I'm never speechless," I lie. "You're welcome to try though."

A chuckle rumbles from his chest, the sound whispering over my bared flesh. I don't even attempt to stop the quiver that comes as a result.

He places his hands on the globes of my ass, making me stutter a breath. His palms are splayed, his fingers covering my entire backside and kneading into my skin.

Before I've even processed this, before I can even wrap my brain around how we got here, his head falls forward.

"Ah," I moan as his face buries into the crook of my legs. His breath is hot against my skin, his tongue working its way around the lace of my thong. "Walker . . ."

Instinctively, I begin to pull back, but I'm yanked forward and harder into his face. Catching myself on his shoulders, partially bent over his crouched position, he hums against my pussy.

"Oh, God," I groan, threading my fingers into his hair as my eyes roll back in my head. As the warmth of his tongue slides down my slit and then back up again, I whimper.

"Words, Slugger," he chuckles.

"Ah . . ."

The flat part of his tongue rolls against my clit, the swollen bud pulsing against him. He works it around and around, working me into a frenzy. I press his face against me by the back of his head, moaning as he slides one finger into my opening.

Widening my stance, wanting to give him as much access as necessary, I almost come when he inserts another finger.

"Walker," I hiss, working my hips around. "Damn it. That feels *so* good."

As if that was some kind of challenge, he draws them both out and then slides them in again, repeating this movement as I bury my finger-nails into his shoulders. He tunes me like a car, making me hum like a well-oiled motor that revs only for him.

He sucks in my nub, caressing it with his warm, wet mouth until he feels my legs begin to shake. As my body nearly comes apart, my legs threatening to give away, he lifts me up and sits me hard onto the table. The tools sitting on the far end roll to the floor, clamoring about as they find the lowest point in the room to stop. All the while, Walker leans me back on the table, my legs dangling off the end as he fingers me relentlessly.

"My God . . ." I say, my voice bouncing with each thrust of his fin-gers. "Walker!" I shout as the sound of my wetness echoes off the walls of the shop.

"You're still talking," he laughs.

Despite the noise of the incessant strum of blood pouring by my ears, I hear the tear of lace as my panties break free from my body.

I don't even look down. I can't. All I can do is feel the heat of his mouth going in for the kill.

As soon as his lips hover over my clit, everything explodes. "Oh!" I moan, my knees pulling back as he laps up the juices that begin to coat my legs and the table beneath me.

His fingers work me every which way, a thumb hovering over the opening of my ass. I suck in a breath, only barely registering what he's doing, but the pressure just adds to the chaos wreaking havoc in my overstimulated body.

The orgasm is so hard it's almost painful, everything so sensitive it almost aches. As I land from the climax of my life, I open my eyes to see he's watching me.

"Feel good?" he asks, slowing his fingers between my legs.

I only nod, my throat dry, yet my need for this man unquenched.

He grins at my reaction, an easy, free kind of smile that I've only seen him use with other people. If my face wasn't already so red, I'd worry he would catch me blushing.

Narrowing his eyes as he undoes his belt, he licks his lips for my benefit. Not wanting to give up all the power over an orgasm, I pop up on my elbows.

"How do I taste?" I ask.

His hands falter for a moment before he nods his head. "Like a girl who hasn't been fucked enough."

"I'd say that's true."

The belt comes off with a snap. "It's your lucky day then, Slugger. I'm about to fuck you into tomorrow."

Walker

MY BOOTS, SOCKS, AND T-SHIRT lie scattered off to the side. Standing in front of Sienna in only a pair of dirty work jeans, the threads held together by the grease of the day, I watch her absorb the situation. Watch her absorb me.

I never know what to expect from this girl, the girl who I can't shake. The one I can't dislike even when I try, and damn it, how I try. I haven't scratched this itch for fear the irritation would spread far too deep, only to come to realize tonight, as she threatened to quit and never see me again, that I'm already fucked in all the ways that matter. Sinking into her sweet pussy at this point is a side note.

She stands next to the table in nothing but a light pink bra that does nothing but hold up her full, heavy tits. Her nipples are obvious through the lace, dark brown buds peaked and waiting for me. The sight of her alone has my cock throbbing so hard it's already ready to come.

"Come here," I say, unfastening the top button of my jeans.

She takes the few steps between us, her cheeks the color of her bra. Standing before me, her hair swept up in a messy up-do she must've created while I was stripping, she's never looked more beautiful.

Bowing my head, I press my lips to hers. One toned arm slips around my neck, tugging the kiss deeper. My hands grip her sides before grazing over her ribs and thumbing the tips of her breasts. She responds with a shudder and breaks the contact. It's just as well.

"Take off your bra," I instruct, taking a step back.

"Not before you lose the jeans, Gibson."

"Oh," I say, arching a brow. "You think you get to call the shots tonight?"

"I think you want my pussy as bad as I want your cock. That gives me a certain leverage, yes."

Shutting my mouth before I say something and piss her off, I look her dead in the eye as I unzip my jeans. She seems pleased as she reaches behind her back and fumbles with the catch to her bra. As my jeans drop to the floor, so does the lace. Both are tossed aside together.

As she eyes my cock and does the math, figuring how all of it is going to fit inside her tight body, I grab the length and give it a stroke for good measure. A bead of pre-cum pools on the head.

With the sway of a goddess, she moseys in front of me. Knocking my hand to the side and off the shaft, she wraps her smaller hand around the base of my cock.

"What are you doing?" I groan, her touch alone almost setting me off.

"Just seeing if you really want me," she teases. Before I can stop her, she's swirling her tongue along the head like it's a Popsicle.

"Sienna," I groan, flexing my hips forward. "Stop."

"Stop talking."

"Well played," I say, accepting my own words back at me as I fight the urge to fuck her mouth. She's every wet dream and grounded hope I've ever had, all wound up in this gorgeous body. It's almost too damn much to take.

Looking at me through her thick, black lashes, she licks up the length and then drops her mouth over my swollen head. As she starts to take me in again, I clasp my hands under her arms and tug her to her feet.

Walking away, feeling her silent objection behind me, I dig through a drawer in the back and retrieve a condom. Ripping the package open and rolling the rubber over myself, I'm ready to turn around when her hands wrap around me and lay on my stomach.

She strokes the lines in my abdomen, her touch soft against the harshness of her breath whispering against the middle of my back.

"I want you, Walker," she says, pressing a kiss between my shoulder blades.

Knowing myself too well and that I'll start tripping up if I allow those words to settle, I whirl around. "I know you want me. You just came all over my face."

The sting of her smack adds to the flame in my gut that's already burning entirely too hot.

"The nice thing would be for you to say you want me too," she says, forcing a swallow.

"Come on," I sigh, pointing at my dick. "Does this look like it wants you?"

"Of course it does. But do you?"

I can't answer that. Instead, I sweep her into the air, her legs locking around my waist. I'm surrounded by her sweet scent, the pulsing of her pussy riding up against my dick. She's wet, so damn wet, that she slides up and down my shaft with every movement.

Just this feels good, so fucking good, that for the first time in a long damn time I don't care about anything or anyone other than the two of us in this room right now.

"You're fucking gorgeous," I breathe, my teeth nipping at her ear. She squeals and tries to move away, only giving our bodies more friction to work with.

Her heels locked at my back, her nails digging into my skin, I crash my mouth onto hers. She meets it with matching eagerness. Need and lust make me dizzy, blocking out everything but what comes next.

Spinning us around, her foot catching a tray of bolts and screws and knocking it to the floor, I scramble to find somewhere to sit her. Pin her. Lay her out for the taking because if anything is true, it's that I'm gonna fucking take her.

Our breathing is ragged, her hands yanking on my hair to lift my chin for more access to my mouth. She kisses me like a starved woman and I'm the last oasis in the desert.

"Get. Inside. Me," she begs between breaks in the kisses.

"Stop being so bossy," I say, tugging at her bottom lip.

"You apparently need told since it's taking you so long."

Slamming her back against the wall, I pin her and dig between us, freeing my cock, and lining it up with her opening. It's my intention to take it easy, to go slow and enjoy it, but the frenzy of the moment puts all of that aside.

With a slight twist of her hips, she sinks down. Taking me in with a sharp gasp, her fingernails biting into my shoulder, she arches her back and takes in as much as she can get.

"Walker!" she yells, a stuttered breath punctuating the final syllable.

"Is that hard enough?"

"Ahhh . . ."

"Come on, Slugger," I tease. "Words or else I'll think you're speechless."

"Never," she manages to eke out as her eyes roll to the back of her head.

My hips flex, giving my cock to her with a brutal urgency. She groans, her eyes giving up and staying closed, as I press into her like I've wanted to since the first night I saw her.

She squeezes around me, the muscles of her pussy pulsing. Grasping under her ass, holding her up, she grips my shoulders and holds herself in place as I pound her into the wall.

"I'm not hearing anything," I say through gritted teeth. "Don't let me down now."

"Can. You. Go. Harder?" she asks, her tone coated with a plea for more.

"You sure?" I slam into her so hard I think I'm going to break her.

"Yes," she almost whines. "Like this."

The clock to the right of her head bangs against the drywall with the rhythm, the metal table beside us clamoring with each thrust. It's a dizzying staccato effect, an almost musical element to the situation. As she constricts harder, her moans getting louder and more urgent, I suck in a beaded nipple and feel her come apart on my cock.

Her body gushes over me, the force of the ejaculation almost shoving me out of her. I drive harder into her, nipping and kissing my way from her breast to her mouth, swallowing her pleasured moans.

As she goes limp, letting me hold almost all of her weight up on my hands, her head falls onto my shoulder. I have to move, change things up, before this is all I remember.

Gazing across the garage, I spot an old eighties Corvette Peck has been restoring for someone in town. The curves in the hood almost make a makeshift alley for a body. Walking over to the hood, my feet slapping against the cool concrete, I lay her down on the hood of the car.

Her eyes go wide as she squirms against the sleek carbon fiber material. "What are you doing?" she asks, cupping her breasts in her hands. They spill over her fingers, a decided difference from the flatness of her stomach. "Isn't this someone's car?"

"Yes, it's someone's car. And I'm going to lay you down on the hood and make you come all over it. Sound good?"

Her eyes roam my body, down my jaw, across my shoulders complete with the imprints of her fingernails, and down the lines of my abs. She flicks her gaze back to mine, her legs falling to the sides. "You going to start now or what?"

A victorious smile stretches across my face and it's reflected on hers. Bending over, I press a kiss against her lips as I find the opening of her pussy and work my cock back inside. It's tighter now than it was.

Grabbing her hips and pulling her down the hood, I position her calves on my shoulders. Her tits bounce as I drive into her. "You feel so good," I tell her, my brain getting fuzzy as I get lost in the rhythm.

My balls slap off her ass, her body squeaking against the car as I deliver us both higher and higher towards climax. Her blonde hair with faded purple streaks looks like a halo against the black paint of the 'Vette, her porcelain skin like an angel.

Digging my hands into the dips of her hips, I hold her in place as I drive into her pussy. Each thrust, each penetration into her delectable body, brings me closer to the edge.

"I . . ." she says, trying to warn me she's going to come. But I know. I can feel it. "Ah . . ." She moans, lifting her hips even higher.

Stroking as deep as I can get, hitting the back wall of her body, I feel the gush of her orgasm just as mine hits.

Her legs stiffen against my shoulders, her back arching off the car. She shouts my name, along with a stream of unmentionables, as I unload into the condom.

The orgasm feels like it's ripping me apart, decimating every cell in my body, yet the best part might be watching her fall to pieces. The way her full lips part, her cheeks flush, a gloss of sweat dots her forehead. Knowing the contented look on her face is because of me is, quite possibly, the best thing I've ever witnessed.

And then it's over.

My blood still roaring through my veins, unable to find its equilibrium, I pull out with a gentleness so as not to hurt her. Still, she gasps, sitting up and looking mildly embarrassed.

I want to tell her not to be, that she just gave me the best orgasm of my life. That I'll never look around this building and not think about the way she looked on the hood of this car. But I don't. Because I'm a dick. I have to be.

Guilt hitting me head-over-fist, I know what I have to do, even if I really don't want to do it.

"Need a hand?" I ask, offering her one.

She takes it and scoots off the car. Looking back at where she just lay, she bites her lip. "Can we, like, buff out where my body was?" she says, peering up at me.

"I'll do it later."

"I'd rather no one sees that, you know."

Instead of telling her there's no fucking way I'd let anyone see that, I shrug. "I'll get it tonight. No worries."

Sienna watches me for a long moment. "So, what now?"

"What do you mean, 'what now'?" I ask, even though I know exactly what she means. I also know what I need to do. I have to turn away from her to do it. "Now you leave."

I cringe as the words fall out of my mouth, hang my head as I say them. She doesn't say anything and I close my eyes and wait for it.

"Well, okay then. Now I leave."

"Sienna . . ." I swing around on my heel, my heart striking so hard I think she has to hear it. There's nothing I want more than to pull her against me, hold her, tell her how amazing she is. But what good would that do? None. "Um, thanks again for helping me tonight."

She smiles, but it's not the sweet grin I'm used to. It's cold. Angry. Embarrassed. "Sure. No problem."

She scoops up her clothes and disappears into the lobby. I see the light flip on in the bathroom as I get dressed. After a little bit, the door opens and the light goes off and I make out her shadow as she heads to the front door.

She pauses, maybe waiting on me to stop her. My hand reaches for the door, maybe to take her up on that. But for the first time in a while, my body and brain are on the same page and I do us both a favor and don't. I just watch her go to her car, making sure she makes it safely inside, and then pick up a hammer and chuck it against the wall.

chapter
Fourteen

Sienna

"I HATE THIS FOR YOU."

"Yeah, well, I don't love it for me either," I laugh, looking across the table at Delaney.

Shoving the food into my mouth, I settle back in the cozy chair of Peaches, a warm buzz settling over me from the glass of wine I've already consumed.

Peaches is a quaint, oddball place in Merom that serves a little of everything. Want pizza? They have it. Mexican? There are offerings. A sandwich? Some of the best I've ever had. It was the first place Delaney brought me when I got here last year and it's remained my favorite spot, especially on the weekends when I can people-watch.

Tonight, the tables are all but full with patrons ranging in every age group and demographic. Even the area reserved for large parties is bustling with a group of screaming kids with baseball hats. The chaos is just what I need to lift my mood and keep me from going home and overanalyzing this thing with Walker until I'm ready to cry like the girl I'm not. Like the girl I refuse to be.

"Do you want to talk about it?" she asks, running a finger around the rim of her glass.

"Not without more wine."

"I should've known something was wrong when you already had a glass sitting there when I walked in."

Motioning to Chester as he looks up from the table he's cleaning, I gesture for two more glasses of white wine and then turn my attention back to Delaney.

She wastes no time getting to the point. "How was it?"

"We really need to separate this into 'sex' and 'after sex,'" I say and then take another bite of my dinner.

"Let's start with sex."

"Unforgettable," I offer. "Amazing. I've never felt so . . . catered to. Does that make sense?"

"It makes me jealous."

I fall back in my seat. "You know how sex can be almost transactional? Like you're with a guy and it's hot and then it's over and there's really nothing there. You might sleep with him again, but it's an exchange of an orgasm."

"Yes. And for one, I appreciate those."

"I have nothing against them," I tell her. "But this . . . I don't know. It just felt like there was a connection. He kissed me, you know? A lot. Touched me. Caressed me, even. It wasn't just fireworks and explosions. There were moments that felt like . . . moments." I look at my wine glass and wish it were full already.

"I don't see the need for all the wine," she points out.

"Because we haven't gotten to 'after sex' yet." My fork hits my plate with a clatter. "You know what he said to me? He said, 'Now you leave.'"

The words sound as harsh coming from me as they did from him but hearing them the second time just makes me angrier.

"He did what?" she exclaims.

"You heard me right," I laugh. "He told me it was time for me to go. Fucking asshole."

"Who's an asshole?" Chester sets two glasses of wine on the table. With his white-blond hair, bright blue eyes, and thin frame, he's the polar opposite of Walker. Still, he's charismatic and handsome in a metrosexual kind of way and someone I've found minorly attractive. Until now. Now, nothing is even presentable if he's not wearing a black t-shirt and a scowl.

"So, asshole?" he repeats.

Delaney gives me a sideways glance. "Do you know Walker Gibson?"

"Lives over in Linton, right?" Chester asks. "Runs a car shop or something?"

"That's him," she confirms.

"I don't know Walker personally, but his brother, Machlan, the one who owns the bar over there—he and I were in school at the same time. He's mean as hell," he laughs. "A good guy, I think. I've never had an issue with him. But I've seen him in a few situations that I was really, really glad I wasn't on the other end of his fury, you know?"

"But what kind of guy is Walker?" Delaney presses. "Would you want your little sister dating him?"

"I don't know much about him like that," he says. "Why? Is he the asshole?"

"No," I say, injecting myself into the conversation. God knows what Delaney might say. "We just saw him the other night and were wondering about him. That's all."

"Well, I'm not an asshole. Just for the record," Chester winks.

As he scampers off, I look across the room. The kids are thinning out from the pizza party, just a few adults and colorful balloons left behind. I'm turning away when my eyes lock on Peck's. He's leaning over the bannister, a hat matching the kids' on his head, his hands locked in front of him. An inquisitive look is painted on his face before he turns his attention to a kid jumping up and down, tugging on his shirt.

My stomach drops, not wanting to deal with any more Gibson boys tonight.

Giving him a little wave, I face Delaney and down half of the fresh glass of wine.

"Whoa," she says, eyes wide. "What's that about?"

"Peck is over there," I mumble, hoping he's not still watching and can't read lips. "I can't deal with any more of them tonight."

"Heya, Slugger." Peck's at my side before I know what's happening, scooting himself into the booth beside me like we're old friends. "What's happening?"

"Make yourself at home, why don't you?"

He laughs in his easy way, running a hand through his floppy hair. "I didn't expect to see you here."

"Having dinner with Delaney," I say, nodding across the table. "Delaney, this is Peck. I know y'all met the other night, but, you know, we're all here, sober, so . . ."

"Nice to meet you again," Peck whistles.

"Likewise." Delaney tucks a strand of hair behind her ear. "Sienna has told me a lot about you."

"Have you?" he looks at me. "It better have been good."

"Of course it was good. What could I possibly say bad about you?"

"This is why I like you," he says, bumping my shoulder with his. "So, what's happening?"

"Not much. Why are you here?"

"End of the year baseball party. Fun times, y'all. Fun times." He cranks his neck, strumming his fingers on the back of the booth. "How'd work go today?"

He's clearly prodding for information, sensing something is off. Peck usually isn't serious, nor does he care about how work went today. Him asking this makes *me* curious.

"Got a tractor in," I say simply. "Walker spent the day on that."

"Ah, shit. Those are a bitch. I wish he would've called. I could've skipped out on the end-of-the-year party for the little league if he had."

Taking a deep breath, I lift my glass to my lips and try not to squeeze the glass until it snaps. "I went back tonight and helped him."

"You helped him? Work on the tractor?"

"I'm going to use the ladies' room," Delaney cuts in. "Be back in a minute."

I wait until she's gone before I continue, my stomach sloshing with wine and anxiety, the acid almost starting to burn. "He's a complete asshole, Peck."

Peck leans away as if he needs the room to comprehend this announcement. "Okay. What the hell happened?"

I sigh, taking the drink I've been holding. The liquid rolls down my throat with ease, the two glasses before this one making it an easy trek. My fingertips are warm; a slight numbness I've been chasing all evening washes over me.

"You okay?" he asks, a look of concern settling over his features. "How many glasses have you had?"

"Not enough."

"What the hell did he do?"

My laugh displays the fury I'm trying to keep in check, the load of embarrassment that's turned to so much anger I can barely hold it in. "I'm over it."

"Oh, fuck."

"Yup."

"Look, Sienna," Peck stumbles, getting comfortable in his seat. "I don't know exactly what just went down, but please stay cool."

"Stay cool?" I ask. "He just fucked me and then dismissed me, Peck. My ability to stay cool is broken."

"Stupid, stupid, stupid," he mutters, resting his forehead on the table.

"I'm mad, naturally, but I'm madder at myself," I say, still working it out in my head. "I let myself get in that position. I let my guard down. My fault."

Peck raises his head and looks at me. There's no judgment in his eyes, no callousness or amusement. Just a sincerity that makes me want to hug him.

"I can only imagine what happened and if it's as bad as I think it is, I'm not making excuses for him," Peck says quietly. "He's a grown man. But I will apologize on his behalf because you don't deserve to have any of his issues put on you."

"You're darn right I don't." I pick at a slice of lemon I removed earlier from my plate. "I obviously won't be back at Crank. I don't want to see him again."

"I can understand that."

Taking in his handsome features and the sweetness in his eyes, I give in. Wrapping my arms around his shoulders, I give him a quick, simple hug. "Thanks for being so nice to me."

"I'm really sorry about Walker," he says. "If you need anything, just call. Okay?"

"I'll be fine."

"Yeah, I know you will, you little badass," he laughs. "But I mean it. I can move furniture, pick up food, listen to you cry but that's not my favorite. Only call me for that as a last option."

"Okay," I laugh, watching Delaney come back across the room. "Thanks, Peck."

"For what?"

"For being my friend."

He slides out of the seat. "I got a few things to do. Again, you need anything, call me."

"Will do."

I watch him walk out of the restaurant, stopping to say hello to a few people on the way out, and wonder if I'll ever see him again.

chapter
Fifteen

Walker

THE MUSIC SWITCHES FROM A hip-hop beat to a country song. Patrons of Crave raise their glasses, inebriated cheers that only come at this point on a Friday night ringing out through the bar. I sit near the phallic ducks in the back and watch everyone celebrate the end of the workweek and what might be the end of my reason to get up in the morning.

Nora, Machlan's steady Friday night helper, catches my eye through the dim lights. Casting a glance over her shoulder, ensuring there's no one waiting for a drink, she sits backwards on the chair next to me.

"You look like hell," she says.

Her short blonde hair is all tousled, sweat lining her forehead from buzzing back and forth across this place a million times over the past few hours. Eye makeup smeared, giving her a rock star look, I could tell her she looks like hell too, but I'd be lying. I could also be wrong because everything is kind of blurred.

"What's it to you?" I ask instead, taking the last slug of whiskey from the glass in front of me. The burn of the liquor is gone, dulled by the whiskey before it. And the whiskey before that.

"It's not shit to me. I was just pointing it out."

"Well, thank ya for that."

She rolls her eyes, resting her arms over the back of the chair. "What's happening with you, anyway?"

"What does it look like is happening with you? I mean, me?"

Grimacing, I close one eye in an attempt to steady myself and also to see if it helps me see her clearly. It doesn't. My hand slaps against the table as I catch myself from falling onto the floor.

Nora laughs, her red lips spread wide at my state of undoing. "I've never seen you this toasted."

"Ah, I'm not toasted," I say, struggling to regain my composure. "I'm just enjoying the Friday night. Isn't this what people are supposed to do?"

"Sure." She watches me closely, narrowing her pretty green eyes. "Is she back—"

"Nope. I'm not that drunk, Nora."

Leaning back, she blows out a breath but is stopped when Lance shows up at her side. This causes her to sit upright and smooth out her shirt. "Hey, Lance. I didn't know you were coming in tonight."

"I thought it was odd you were wearing pants," he says, testing her reaction.

"Careful there, Nora," I say, wagging a finger in her direction. "It'll be you falling out of the chair now."

"Fuck you, Walker," she says, getting to her feet and storming off as I chuckle at my own joke.

Lance flips the chair Nora just vacated around. "You look like hell."

"Will you stop saying that?"

"I only said it once, but I take it someone said it before me." He works his head side-to-side. "What the fuck happened to you?"

"Who invited you here?"

He leans in, his eyes glimmering even under the dull light at my state of inebriation. "I'm actually here because I had to get out of town," he grins wickedly. "There's this girl—"

"This story is starting like all of your other ones."

"Which means I have the best stories, right?"

I don't want to hear his damn stories. I want to sit here and brood over my own mess, replay my own story, and pretend like I didn't just write "The End" on it with the tip of my cock.

"Want to hear it?" he asks.

"Let me guess—you fucked her."

"Senseless," he laughs. "I had her sprawled out on top of my desk, my tie shoved in her mouth, as I fucked the shit out of her."

He goes on about his fuckfest, but all I can think about are the hours before now. I've come to the conclusion there's not enough whiskey to block that out.

Her scent is still nestled in my pores, the taste of her pussy fresh in my mouth. Every now and then, my shirt catches on one of the indentions on my shoulder from her fingernails and I'm reminded, yet again, of Sienna.

My body, naturally, wants to have her again. I want to get off on seeing her respond to me, want me as badly as I want her—almost desperately. A craving to see her in my t-shirt, on my sheets, digs at me to the point I feel like screaming until I pass out. I almost don't care if it meant waking up to a reorganized kitchen and that's the scariest part of all. Is this what happens when you lose your mind?

If I lose it, I know the exact moment the fall began. It's not the look in her eye as she moaned my name or the pleasure glossed on her skin as she came. It's the way she watched me pretend like it was a transaction to me, another night with another woman. That is what's going to haunt my nightmares if I'm even able to sleep.

Of all the ways to stop her from feeling, I chose that. I did that. To someone who just might've given a fuck.

"You still here?" Lance asks, waving a hand in front of my face.

"Get that away from me before I break it."

"I'm going to guess that tonight I could actually take you," he laughs. "What the fuck happened? You don't drink like this."

"I'll tell ya what happened," Peck says out of nowhere.

"Peck—go home," I say, trying to focus on his face.

"Nah, Peck, sit. Stay, little cousin," Lance laughs, pulling a chair out across the table from me. "Tell me what my brother did."

"Well, I don't know for sure," he says, cringing as the song gets louder. "But I will say I just sat down with Sienna over at Peaches."

Both palms splay on the table, trying to root me in place. "You did what?"

"I don't know what he did," Lance says, pointing to Peck, "but you," he says, dragging his finger through the air until it's pointing at me, "fucked her, didn't you?"

Narrowing my eyes, I lean towards Lance. "Enough."

"Was she everything I dreamed she'd be?"

"Enough, Lance," I growl.

"I don't think he was everything she thought he'd be," Peck says, eyeing me cautiously, "considering she never wants to see you again."

Lance forgotten, my gaze switches to my cousin. His arms are crossed over his blue t-shirt, his hat twisted backwards on his head, as he gives me a look he's never given me before—like it's *him* calling *me* out on my shit.

Fuck that.

"She's not quitting," I say, although I'm not sure I believe me. "We talked about it."

"Before or after you shot your wad?"

"Damn it, Peck," I warn, my temples pulsing as I glare at him.

"This isn't about her quitting, moron," Peck fires back. "This is about you doing whatever you did and her never wanting to see you again."

Lance places a hand on my shoulder, gently guiding me back into my chair. I don't know who to be more pissed at—Peck, Lance, Sienna, or myself. All I know for sure is I'm ready to come out of my fucking skin, my blood boiling so hot I'm going to erupt.

Why am I surprised she's leaving? Wasn't it always in the cards? Didn't she even tell me that originally? Isn't this what women do?

"Don't 'damn it' me," Peck says. "You wanna be pissed at someone, be pissed at yourself. Or at the woman who caused all this."

"He's right," my brother says, motioning to Nora for a beer. "Any of this bullshit you're aiming at us, or Sienna, is misplaced."

"I know where to fucking place it," I seethe. "I don't need you two telling me what to do."

Peck stands, twisting his hat back around. "Then be my guest. Make a mess of everything and see who loses in the end because, I'll tell you what, it'll be you."

"I'd rather it be me than Sienna," I say, snatching the beer Nora brings for Lance. I down half of it before she gets it out of my hand.

"Machlan said no more for you," she says, wrestling the bottle away. Holding it up in the air, she smirks. "I love telling you no."

"You wouldn't tell me no if your life depended on it."

"Hey, Walker," she says, bending forward. Her cleavage is on full display, her lips painted and ready to wrap around a cock. None of it does anything for me. "No."

"Hey, Nora," I say, watching her eyes grow wide. "Good."

"I hate you tonight," she says, storming off.

"I'll add you to the list," I mutter, slumping back into my seat. Peck's gone when I look up. "Where'd he go?"

"Hell if I know," Lance sighs. "Spoke too soon."

As an eighties hit blares across the speakers, Peck jumps onto a table in the middle of the bar. Everyone cheers, bottles going up in the air, as he hooks his thumbs in the belt loops of his jeans and starts dancing. The song can barely be heard as the women catcall, the patrons urging him on as they do every time he pulls this non-Machlan-approved stunt. It's a sideshow act, one that drives my brother insane.

"Get off the fuckin' table," Machlan shouts, his voice swamped by the crowd.

Lance and I kick back and watch the circus, knowing just how it'll end.

Peck turns around, shakes his ass towards Machlan, and starts some pelvic thrust move that he's known for and perfected over the last few years.

We watch as Machlan sorts through the crowd and leaps onto the table. Peck abruptly hops off. The crowd boos while Lance and I laugh, Peck making his way to the front. He stops at the front door, bows to his adoring fans, and walks out the door like a soldier, complete with a one-fingered salute to Machlan.

A girl springs onto the table with Machlan, digging her hands onto the crotch of his pants. He winks, turning his head to the side and kisses the fuck out of her as she grinds into him from behind. The crowd goes insane, beer sloshing as the bottles are raised at the scene in the middle of the room.

Machlan breaks the kiss, smirks at the crowd, then hops down and heads back to the bar.

"Do you think Peck does that just to get kicked out?" Lance asks, taking a fresh bottle from Nora, who pointedly ignores me.

"Sometimes. It's his calling card or something," I say, ending the sentence with a yawn. "Like if he doesn't get kicked out of here at least once a month, people will forget about him."

"Is that what you're trying to do?"

"What?"

Lance takes a long drink before answering me. "Make sure Sienna doesn't forget about you. That's why you did whatever fucked up shit you did tonight. You figured she'd leave anyway."

The pit of my stomach quivers, the tell-tale sign I've drunk entirely too much. I focus on his face, his features swirling together in one colorful mess. It's the moment you wait for when you drink to forget—the moment when you feel all the problems finally give in to the alcohol.

"Fuck off," I tell him, struggling to get to my feet. "You can drive me home in Daisy."

"Oh, lucky me," he laughs.

"Damn right lucky you."

We slip through the throngs of people, Lance's arm around my waist, giving Machlan a wave as we pass. Lance is deep in conversation with me, meaning himself, as I tune out and enjoy the blur I've been searching for all night.

chapter
Sixteen

Sienna

WINDOWS DOWN, RADIO UP, WIND billowing through my hair, I zoom down the country road towards Merom. There's hardly any traffic as I make my way back to town after having dropped off a bunch of Delaney's things at her parents' house. Her mom and dad took us to lunch, her dad going on and on about the dairy industry and almost boring us to death. Still, being bored to death was a nice reprieve from everything else.

There's no one to blame this thing with Walker on but myself. I should've taken his hints and left well enough be. Maybe I pushed him. Maybe I overstepped my bounds coming in after hours, regardless of my intentions. I was a willing participant and he's entitled to his behavior afterwards. Just as I am mine.

"I don't get it," I mutter to myself, turning down the volume. The sappy song about true love and second chances is not doing me any favors.

I pilot the car around a big box lying in the middle of the road, wondering if it is some kind of analogy from the universe. Sometimes you have to go around stuff to keep going.

"I'll go around him all right."

Cornfields zip by as I step on the accelerator, my mind going just as fast around last night. The terseness of his tone. His initial refusal to look at me. The look in his eye when he did.

"Shit," I groan, hearing a loud pop. The car lurches to the side as a *thump-thump* smacks against the pavement. Slowing the car as quickly as I can, I bring it to the shoulder. It sinks to the right.

Resting my head against the steering wheel, I try not to cry. "Lord, please help me."

Turning off the engine, I get out into the warm afternoon sun. There's nothing around but tall stalks of corn and high, puffy clouds as far as the eye can see. It takes all of five seconds to confirm a flat tire and to spot the nail sticking out of the rubber. Air gushes around the gouge making it impossible to limp it to the nearest gas station which is, if I remember correctly, miles away.

Leaning against the trunk, I slip out my phone and call Delaney. It goes immediately to voicemail.

"This mailbox is full and not accepting messages. Please try again later. Goodbye."

"No," I groan, stomping my foot against the dirt. A rock rolls down the shallow embankment and into a ditch.

Pulling up the text app, I shoot a message her way and hold my breath. The "delivered" tag doesn't show and I wonder if she turned it off to take a nap to ward off the migraine she was getting like she said she was going to.

Another rock meets the toe of my shoe and joins the other at the bottom of the ditch. It's littered with trash and weeds and another bunch of rocks I kick in too.

"Damn it," I say to the corn. "Why can't I just go freaking home?"

Looking both ways down the road, there's no one in sight. I didn't even pass anyone when I was heading out here.

"I'm going to die a horror show death."

Tossing my phone from one hand to the other, I weigh my options. I can wait for someone to find me and hope they aren't a serial killer and come before nightfall. I could hold my breath that Delaney wakes up and checks her messages. Nine-one-one is an option, although this isn't an emergency and I would feel like a dick. Or I could call Walker.

"Ha," I sigh, thinking about calling him. "I'd rather feel like a dick."

Scrolling through my contacts, I see Peck's name. Swiping on, I make it to the R's before I go back. My finger hovers over his name. I gulp before I click on it. My breath holds while I wait for it to connect.

"Hey, Slugger," he says after the first ring.

"Hey, Peck. I, um . . ." Looking around at the corn, my spirits cave. "I need some help."

"Sure. What's up?"

"I'm stuck out here on Route 9 somewhere between Merom and Honnerton and just got a flat tire. I don't know who else to call," I sigh.

"Did you call Walker?"

"Nope. I'd rather walk home."

There's a small chuckle through the phone. "So I shouldn't tell him you have a flat tire and need me to come get you?"

"Absolutely not," I insist. "Look, you said to call you if I needed anything and I—"

"I'm already in my truck," he says, cutting me off. "I'll be there in a few. Just down Route 9?"

"Go to Merom and take it towards the bluff. I'm like sixty-eight million miles into the corn."

"Be there in a bit."

Tossing my phone into the car, I cross the ditch and sit on the other side. No cars pass as I sit there and lace little flowers together like we used to do at recess in elementary school. It's methodical and intricate and takes all my attention which is a godsend.

The first car I hear comes at me like a bat out of hell. Hopping to my feet, I see Peck's hand out the driver's window. Taking a step towards the ditch as he slides in facing me, I stop. His smile does nothing to smooth this over.

Walker climbs out of the truck. His expression is unreadable, even for him, and I grind my teeth together as I turn to Peck.

"Hey," Peck says, his tone way too cheery.

"What the hell are you doing?" I ask him, marching across the ditch next to the driver's side door as he gets out.

"Coming to fix your tire." He leans into the back of his truck and yanks out a toolbox. "Which one is it?"

"Did you not hear me when I said I don't want Walker here?" I hiss. "I'd rather have walked back, Peck. I meant that."

Popping one arm on the rail of the truck bed, he looks at me. "He was standing next to me. Did you think I was getting out of there without him when he found out it was you?"

"Yes, I did. Because you're a grown man who can tell him no."

"Sure," he laughs, carrying the toolbox towards my car. He passes Walker at the front of his truck, muttering something to him that I can't hear.

When I finally look that way, I ignore the wariness in his gaze and shoot him the dirtiest look I can manage. He starts to speak, but I turn away.

"Sienna . . ." he says, his voice fading.

Taking in the expanse of the cornfields, I calculate how long it would take me to just walk back to town. The rows are straight, which would kind of be like a path, and it would be relatively safe because no large animals could fit in there so I ultimately shouldn't die a gory death.

His hand rests on my shoulder. I pull away.

"Why didn't you call me?" he gruffs out, standing way too close for comfort.

"Really?" I ask, pivoting in a half-circle to face him. "Why in the world would I call you?"

His jaw clenches as he works it back and forth. "Oh, I don't know. Because that's the logical solution."

"Logic? You want to talk logic? This should be fun," I glare, crossing my arms over my chest. "Can you just go help Peck or something?"

"Peck doesn't need my help, Sienna."

"Then why the hell did you come?"

"You know why I fucking came," he says, his eyes darkening. "I came to talk to you."

"I don't have anything to say to you."

He takes a step towards me, his hand flexing in the air like he wants to reach for me but wisely refrains. "Maybe I have a lot to say to you."

"You know what? Maybe you've said enough."

We have a mini-standoff on the shoulder of the road, a flock of birds flying overhead. The music Peck is streaming into his earbuds a few feet away as he crouches at my tire floats through the air right alongside the irritation passing between his cousin and I.

"Damn it, Sienna."

"Don't use that tone with me," I bite, jabbing a finger in his direction.

"Will you just stop it for a second and let me talk?"

"No, I won't. You've said everything I need to hear already."

He growls, running a hand through his hair. "You are so damn hard-headed."

"Me?" I ask, dropping my hand. "I'm hardheaded? What the hell does that make you?"

"At least I'll listen to you."

"Well, listen to my steps walk away." I get a few steps towards Peck when Walker spins me in a circle. "Hey!"

"I just want to talk to you. Hear me out."

"Why? It doesn't matter what you say because whatever comes out of your mouth right now, you'll contradict later. Look at last night . . ."

I fight the tears hitting the corners of my eyes like a prize fighter, imploring them to reabsorb into my eyes. I'd rather do anything instead of letting him see me cry.

His gaze settles on the lone tear slipping down my cheek, sliding down my cheekbone, near the crease of my nose, and over my lips. He watches it fall all the way to my shirt.

"I'm crying because I'm pissed," I tell him, omitting the part about my feelings and how they hurt more at the hands of him than they ever have over a man.

"I hate seeing you cry."

His eyes rise to mine. My cheeks are hot, warmth exuding from them as I stand in front of him. Even now, I can see something in his eyes that pings at my heart and I have to force it away.

"I kept thinking I saw something in you that proved you weren't really an asshole. And, you know what," I say, biting back a sob, "that's what hurts."

He grimaces, walks in a circle, but refuses to dispute anything.

"I'll be honest," I say, my voice dropping a couple of notches, "I liked you. I enjoyed spending time with you. And I thought you did too. Maybe it's what I hoped would happen, maybe I wanted you to like me."

"You know I like you, Sienna," he says, standing still. "That's not the problem."

"So this is what you do to people you like?"

"No," he groans, looking at the sky.

"You do this on purpose. You're hot and cold intentionally, making me wonder where I stand and what you're thinking."

"You know what I'm thinking," he says, his body almost shaking. "You know how I feel."

"Do I? Because the last interaction we had made it perfectly clear how you feel, if that's the case."

My words stop him in his tracks. He takes a deep, measured breath as he sticks his hands into his pockets.

"Do you want me to hate you? Fine. Done. You win," I say, holding his gaze for half a second and then turning to Peck. "You done?"

"Let's go somewhere and talk," Walker says from behind me.

"Peck?" I say, ignoring Walker.

"Yeah, I'm done. You sliced it pretty good." Peck brushes off his hands, leaning the old tire next to his leg. "That one will get you around for a while, but you'll need a new one. It's the only one we had in the shop."

"I'll order a new one," Walker says.

I look at him over my shoulder. "I'll go to the dealership. Don't worry about it." Turning back to Peck, I hold up a finger. "Hold on a second." My hand shaking, I get into the car and sift through my wallet. Pulling out a fifty-dollar bill, I get back out and hand it to Peck. "Here. It's all the cash I have—"

"Stop," Walker cuts me off.

"Take it, Peck," I demand.

"I'm not taking your money," he laughs.

I shove the money in Peck's hand. "Then give it to him. But I won't owe either of you."

Peck studies me for a long second before nodding. "Fine. You still coming to church tomorrow?"

"Doubt it," I say, my heart softening as I think of Nana. "Tell Nana I'll mail her my blueberry muffin recipe."

"She'll be pissed," Peck grins. "You really want to risk that?"

"Thanks for coming." I send him a small smile before walking around the back of my car. "I appreciate it."

"Any time. I told you that."

With a final look Walker's way, I ignore the look in his eye that would typically make me stop and ask him what's wrong. Today I don't give a damn.

Jumping into the car, I flip on the ignition and take off down the road, leaving Walker behind.

chapter
Seventeen

Sienna

THE SUN IS BRIGHT, BIRDS chirping, grass still dewy as I make my way from the parking lot of Holy Hills Church to the front steps. Scanning the gatherings of people scattered in front of the brick building, I don't see anyone I recognize. That's both good and bad.

I wasn't going to show up here this morning. I made plans to meet Delaney for brunch just so I wouldn't. But when I woke up at six, I changed my mind.

I try to settle my nerves by reminding myself this is a means to an end. I'll sit through a short service, probably one my soul needs more than I care to admit, give the money I owe Walker to Peck, and then go back home and plot my escape from Illinois. Easy as pie. Except part of me wants to hear what Walker has to say.

Lying in bed last night, tossing and turning, I kept telling myself it didn't matter. My feelings are wounded, my pride is injured, so what do I care what he wanted to say?

Because what will it hurt?

The pastor stands by the front door step, shaking hands with each person as they enter. The air has a melody about it as the light breeze dusts across the steps. Laughs, stories about grandchildren, and talks about potluck dinners drift about, soothing my nerves like a warm balm.

My heels click against the steps, my hand guiding up the shiny black rail as I near the top. The pastor extends a hand, a warm, welcoming smile on his aged face.

"Welcome," he says, his voice passive and kind. "Are you new here?"

"I'm visiting for the day. A guest of . . . Nana? I'm sorry. I'm not even sure what her name is. How awful is that?"

"Quite the opposite, actually."

"How do you figure?" I take his hand and give it a shake.

"Well, you know her as Nana, a very important title. That tells me you met her through a memorable experience that left an impression on both of you."

"I don't know about that."

He pats the top of my hand before steering me inside. "We're glad to have you today. Please, make yourself at home."

"Thank you."

Stepping inside the sanctuary, most of the patrons are sitting in wooden pews. They form two rows with a walkway in the center that leads to an altar and an elevated platform behind it with a plain podium. A vintage piano sits in the corner and a lady with silver hair sits at the keys, playing an old hymn I remember as one of my grandfather's favorites.

Tucking my clutch under my arm, I scan the pews. My mouth is dry and I sidestep people, feeling like I'm just in the way of their normal weekly routine. Like I don't belong. Like I should just go home.

Left to right, I glaze over old folks, babies, toddlers, and middle-aged men and women all chatting softly until I get close to the front on the right.

Walker sits between Machlan and another guy, the one I saw with them the night of the bat-to-truck fiasco. A navy and brown plaid shirt stretches across Walker's wide shoulders, his dark hair combed to the side and shining in the bright morning sunlight streaming in through the windows. Machlan and the other guy chat around him, leaning behind so that Peck, who's sitting in the pew behind them next to Nana, can join in.

My feet want to march their way to Walker, to stand in front of him and try to gauge how he's feeling. Not that I should care. I shouldn't even give a crap but there's something about the man that I want to break open, to hold, to fix whatever it is that's so tarnished in him that he can't even smile a true smile without feeling guilty. That has to always keep everyone at arm's length. That he has to be so miserable.

Sucking in a breath, I head towards them, pausing every now and then to thank different parishioners as they welcome me to the service. With each step, I second guess why I'm here and wonder if I could just slip the money to Peck and bolt.

The journey to their position in the church takes exorbitantly longer than it should. Everyone wants to introduce themselves, say hello, ask me if I want a coffee or donut from the lobby. As considerate as they all are, as grateful as I am for the warm reception, each second that goes by is another opportunity for my nerves to warp into a tighter, more confounding knot.

"Good morning," I say, gripping the edge of the pew to keep from falling over as Walker's cologne whips me in the face. It's not that it's strong or that he's the only one fresh out of the shower. It's that his is the only one that I pick up out of all the body washes and aftershaves on this Sunday morning.

At the sound of my voice, all heads in the Gibson clan turn to me. Walker's eyes are wide and a little bloodshot and I wrangle mine away before he can see inside them. Plus, I'm not sure now I'm here that I want to see inside his.

Machlan smirks, exchanging a glance with the man on the other side of Walker. He's a lighter, thinner version of Walker but with a self-assuredness I can recognize as something I usually see in myself. Not today.

Peck stands from his seat behind them, effectively blocking me from Walker's line of sight. "Good morning," he says. "I was starting to think you weren't coming."

"I probably shouldn't have," I say, feeling a little relief in his simple smile.

There's something about the way he's looking at me—head cocked to the side, playful grin painted on his lips—that has me curious. As if to drive the point home, whatever point he's trying to make, he lobs me a wink before turning to Nana. "Look what we have here."

"Well, good morning, Sienna," she says, nudging the man next to her to move down a bit. "Here. Grab a seat by me."

"Peck's sitting there," I say, the collar of my dress feeling tight, as I avoid Walker's stare. "I can just sit in the back. It's not a problem."

"Nonsense. There's room for all of us. Patrick will move down, won't you, hon?" She glances beside her as the old man wearing a ruby-colored tie makes room. "Here. Sit right here."

Peck moves so I can pass him and take the spot between him and Nana. Walker is turned in his seat, his cuffs rolled to his elbows, and watches me like he might blink and I'll be gone.

"Have you met all my handsome grandsons?" Nana asks. "That's Machlan, of course you know Walker. That's Lance and Peck. They're all good boys," she says, patting my leg. "And so is their sister, but she's outgrown us by now."

Walker's gaze follows her hand to my thigh, letting it linger, before he blazes a trail back to my eyes. "Mornin'."

"Good morning," I say, shifting in my seat. My heart thumps so loud I think Nana can hear it as she rambles to Patrick about her morning glories.

Squirming in my seat, I situate my purse on my lap. Peck nudges me with his shoulder and I nudge him back, a playfulness between the two of us that takes the edge off my nerves.

"I've heard a lot about you." The man I know now as Lance settles against the back of the pew, a smirk playing across his features. He resembles his brothers handily, his face clean-shaven though, instead of the scruff Walker and Machlan sport. There's an air of refinement about him that's a stark dichotomy to the almost barbarianism that swims just below the surface of his striking hazel eyes. "I'm Lance."

"Nice to meet you," I say politely, noting the scowl on Walker's face out of the corner of my eye that might include a twinge of jealousy. "Walker and Peck have Crank, Machlan, Crave. What do you do?"

"I teach history at the high school in Carlisle."

"He's the resident nerd," Peck jokes.

"I love history, actually," I tell them. "American history, mostly, but I had classes on European history and Russian culture in college."

He seems impressed. "Meeting a woman who likes history doesn't happen often."

Walker fidgets in his seat, catching Lance's attention. He glances at Walker, his smirk deepening. "What's your story, Sienna?"

"She doesn't have one," Walker almost growls. I look at him, his gaze capturing it immediately and holding it hostage. It freezes me to my seat, causes a bead of sweat to line the back of my neck. I could easily sit quietly and just have this silent conversation, the one that makes me feel like no one else is in the room, but I don't. Because that's what he wants.

Clearing my throat, I tear my gaze away from Walker and settle it on Lance. I think, if not seated by his brother's side, Lance would be hard to look away from.

"How sweet of Walker to speak for me," I say sweetly. "Actually, I don't have much to share that wouldn't bore you to death."

"I doubt that," Lance mutters. "I seriously fucking doubt that."

Nana leans forward, swatting Lance in the side of the head. "Don't you think about using that language in here, Lance Miller Gibson."

"Sorry, Nana. Won't let it happen again."

"Better not let it happen again," Walker warns him, his tone so low that I find myself gulping. Lance doesn't seem fazed, just laughs. But he does turn back around towards the front.

The pastor taps the mic attached to the podium. Walker's eyes drag over me, leaving a scorched trail in their wake, before he, too, faces forward.

Shuddering in my seat, trying to remain unaffected, I feel a nudge at my rib. Looking at Peck, I'm met with a set of twinkling blue eyes. "Thanks for coming," he whispers. "He was an ass all night."

"Walker?" I whisper back as the pastor begins to speak.

"Who else? Did you see his eyes? Drinkin' like a fool since you drove off."

Staring at the back of his head, I wonder if he's trying to forget what happened. Trying to forget me. The idea causes my heart to ruffle in my chest. Turning back to Peck, I whisper, "I shouldn't be here."

"Hell yeah, you should. Listen," he says, leaning his head so he's almost whispering straight into my ear, "I know it doesn't seem like it right now, but he needs this."

"Needs what?"

"Please stand and join us in the singing of Amazing Grace," the pastor says. A piano strikes the first notes of the beloved tune. I join the others in singing from memory.

Nana's voice is soothing and I find myself relaxing into the lyrics. I make a concerted effort not to watch Walker, to block out the whiffs of his cologne and the way my body feels a tingle every time I hear his voice cut through the others.

"Do you trust me?" Peck interjects as we take a breath before going into the second stanza.

"No, I don't trust you," I hiss. "I don't know you."

"That's your second mistake," he chuckles.

"What's the first?"

"This is a house of God, Sienna . . ."

I can't help but giggle at the look on his face, a move that gains me a glance over the shoulder from Walker as we take our seats. I flash him a forced smile, a move that seems to confuse him more than anything. Machlan bends and whispers something in his ear. Whatever it is causes Walker's scowl to come parading back and Nana to swat at Machlan.

He doesn't look at me for the rest of the service. I just stare at the back of his head and feel my anxiety creep up with every tick of the clock. I replay things in my mind that should require some sort of Confession, but all done in the spirit of trying to figure out what happened with Walker.

As the pastor has us stand for a final prayer, I hang my head and say a prayer of my own for guidance. When I open my eyes again, as the entire room says a somber "Amen," Nana switches gears.

"Dinner is at two at my house," she says, picking up her pocketbook that looks like it could hold an entire casserole. "The boys usually come on over after church and you're more than welcome to drive over—"

"Oh, Nana, no," I say, placing a hand on her arm. "That's not necessary."

"Yeah, she's riding with me." Peck takes my elbow. "We'll be over in a second."

Nana readily accepts this bit of information and engages Patrick in a conversation about the library.

"Say that again?" Walker is facing us completely, his hands wrapped along the back of the pew.

His tone skirts over my skin, like a shot of adrenaline being injected in to my veins. My mouth opens slightly to keep from losing air as I look up at Peck.

"She and I will be at Nana's," he says easily, like he's completely unaware that Walker wants to rip his throat out. "Just letting Nana know."

The pastor comes up to Walker, Machlan, and Lance, forcing Walker to turn away but not without a final look planted straight on me.

"I'm what?" I ask, following Peck into the aisle. "Are you crazy? I'm not going with you."

"Shh," he whispers, looking to see if Walker is listening. "Trust me."

"I thought we went over this?"

He rolls his eyes and sighs. "Answer one question."

"Fine."

"Do you like him?"

"Like who?" I ask like I don't know.

"Walker," he scoffs. "Do you like him? If he wasn't a complete dick, would you like him?"

His tone sends a note straight to my heart, the goofiness of Peck gone and replaced with a sincerity that's beyond sweet.

"That's answer enough," he notes. "Give me this afternoon."

"Whether I like him or not doesn't matter, and for the record, I don't," I tell him. "Not anymore."

"Don't lie in church. We aren't Catholic. You just can't head to Confession and be absolved of your sins."

Blowing out a breath, I change tactics. "I'm not going to your Nana's and making a scene. It's Walker's grandma's house, Peck. Not mine. I have no business being there."

"Except she invited ya," he points out.

"Not knowing her grandson fuc . . ." I clear my throat. "Not being apprised of all the facts."

"Do you want to go home alone?" he asks.

"That has nothing to do with it."

"Come to dinner with me," he almost begs. "Hang out with my cousins. Have some good food. When's the last time you had a home-cooked meal?"

"Peck . . ." I whine.

He leans in, his eyes searching mine. "Walker is coming this way. Just go with me, Sienna. You can leave if you hate it. I'll even take you, but . . . *trust me.*"

As Walker walks by, not stopping to chat or even glancing at me, his fingertips brush my hip. That's all it takes. That simple contact not lasting more than a microsecond is all it takes to pull the trigger on the flood of emotion ripping through my veins.

To anyone looking, it would seem like an accidental brush, if they noticed at all. To me, I felt what he was saying. I just don't understand it.

"Fine," I say, heading towards the door. "But if he's an ass, I'm leaving and you're going with me."

"Fair enough, Slugger. Fair enough."

chapter
Eighteen

Sienna

"THIS IS THE WORST IDEA I've ever gone along with," I say, cringing as Peck's truck goes airborne over a set of railroad tracks and drops back onto the pavement. "Take it easy."

He looks at me out of the corner of his eye, his easy grin painted on his face. "What's the fun in that?"

"I don't know. Living?"

"You only live once."

"And here I didn't peg you as a YOLO kind of guy," I tease, grabbing the door handle as we take a curve on two wheels.

"What's YOLO?"

"Forget it."

He straightens the truck out, barely controlling the slide onto the gravel road just outside of city limits. Dust barrels behind us, whipping away into the cornfields lining both sides of the road.

With every mile we get away from my car and the church, it seems like we are a little further away from all sense and sensibility.

The cardboard pine tree hanging from the rearview mirror twirls in the afternoon sunlight. I focus on it and not on the way my brain is screaming at me to have Peck turn back. When I open my mouth to comment on how New Car Scent doesn't smell like a new car at all, something altogether different comes out.

"Are you sure about this?"

"Absolutely." He eases up on the accelerator, the truck slowing its roll so I can actually make out stalks of corn and not a yellow blur. "I wasn't kidding when I said he was a mess this weekend."

My skin feeling like it's too small for my body, I grab at my collar. "Why?"

"I'm not sure. Just that it has to do with you."

If I wasn't strapped in with a seat belt, I'd sag against the door. Instead, I rest my head on the glass and watch the country out of the windshield. "I really think we should scrap this, Peck."

"Hell fucking no," he laughs.

"This isn't funny."

"Look," he says, re-gripping the steering wheel, "I don't think y'all are gonna get married and have babies. I mean, if you do, great. Fine. I don't really give a shit. Molly McCarter will have my babies someday. But you seem to like him in a way most women don't."

"I don't like him at all."

"Mm-hmm . . ." he says, taking us around another corner on two wheels. "I think what's different is that you came into town not knowing anyone. Like, you don't know the gossip or the history or who's fucking who and who's getting fat, you know?"

"Oh my God," I snort. "That's terrible!"

"Yeah, small towns. It's true. Anyway," he continues on, "you just slugged your way in here and saw things for what they are. Not what they were or what they were supposed to be."

"First off, don't think I didn't get that jab you webbed in there for me . . ."

He grins, lifting his shoulders in a lazy shrug.

"Second," I continue, "are you saying Walker is not what he was? Does he have some crazy past?" Squirming now, blood racing, I demand answers. "Tell me, Peck. You wouldn't bring me around like this if he's a weirdo, right? Oh my God. I can't trust you, can I?"

He finds my near-panic hysterical and laughs like he's watching a comedy. "No, Slugger. He doesn't have a crazy past. He does, however, have a past, like we all do," he adds to stall my objection. "In a small town, that shades what people think of you and how they treat you and interact with you. Like, whatever you were deemed in third grade is what people expect."

Letting that marinate, I relax back into the seat. It's true—people do expect you to be a certain way. It's partially what I'm fighting in my own life when I look at it.

As a Landry, I'm expected to toe the family line. I've never been able to just spew what I'm thinking, lest it hurt someone's political career. I have to watch who I'm seen with in case a photographer is around. My parents, although pleasantly accepting of my pseudo-rebellion, would, without a doubt, prefer me in expensive heels and a pretty dress and leading a charity event to end childhood hunger.

"I get that," I concede. "But what was Walker 'supposed' to be?"

A small white house with the cutest front porch comes into view. There's an old-fashioned laundry line stretching behind, parallel to a small garden. A garage sits next to it, the doors open and an SUV and a car parked in front.

"Walker was supposed to be a college football star, even though I'm not sure he ever really liked the sport. He was just naturally good at it, I guess. He even got a scholarship for it," he tells me. "He dated a girl all through high school and everyone thought they'd have a shitload of babies to toughen up the Linton football program by now."

"What happened?"

Peck forces a swallow as he pulls into the driveway behind a dark purple Dodge Charger. "Life. Life happened."

"That's not an answer," I say hurriedly as he grabs for the door handle. "You can't give me that."

"Well, he didn't take the scholarship for starters."

"Why?" I ask, wondering why anyone would pass up free college tuition. I've heard people talk about how expensive it is and how families go broke, wrapping themselves up in debt for decades, just to pay for it. "Why wouldn't he take it?"

"His dad was sick, something they never really figured out before he died. I think Walker was the only one who knew. Lance and Blaire were gone by then, off doing their thing. Machlan was tearing shit up with Cross, being Machlan, and Walker stumbled into the news, I think." Peck's gaze settles into the distance. "He was really close with his dad. Thick as thieves. Walker was devastated. I only know that because he got drunk one night and kind of broke down about it. Otherwise, he would've held it in. It's what he does."

My shoulders fall as I think back on the picture Camilla posted of Dad and I imagine what it would be like to find out he was sick. To imagine he only has days, weeks, or months left. To have to watch him suffer and know the end is coming.

"Is that why he's so closed off?" I ask quietly.

"Part of it."

Before he can say any more, the door to his truck is jerked open. Peck gasps, grabbing the steering wheel as he almost falls out. Walker doesn't break stride, just keeps walking, tossing a glare Peck's way as he rounds the front.

My breath hitches, holding tight in my lungs, as I wait to see if he's going to come my way.

He's unbuttoned the two top buttons on his shirt, the ends hanging out and hitting him in the middle of his ass.

He looks up at me just before turning towards the house. Something pools in his eyes, a concentration of emotion that both lures me in and pushes me away. Before I can make sense of it, he's taking the steps to the back door, the tail of his shirt billowing in the breeze.

"What's that all about?" I ask, my voice squeaking a bit against my parched throat.

Peck climbs out of the truck then stops. Leaning inside, his arms against the top, he gives me his relaxed everything-is-gonna-be-great grin. "Things are gonna be a little awkward for a bit. He's gonna be pissy and dumb, but you've seen him like that before. Just give him a minute, okay?"

"Fine," I grumble opening my door.

"Sienna?"

"Yeah?"

"I also think he's really good for you. This isn't about just him, you know?"

Twisting in my seat, I look at him over my shoulder. I don't know what to say to that.

"One more thing," he says, shoving off the door and shutting it. "If he kills me or seriously injures me, have them take me to Linton General and tell them I requested Nurse Shelby."

"Oh my God . . ."

———

NANA'S HOUSE IS EVERYTHING I imagined it would be. Neat as a pin, smelling of roast beef and sugar, with pictures everywhere in adorable frames, it's as cozy and inviting as only Nana's house could be.

A blue apron wrapped around her middle, she pulls open the oven door as Peck and I walk in. "Peck," she says instantly, "go in the laundry room and grab a towel. I need to set these pies on something and I'm out of potholders."

"Sure, Nana."

Peck disappears around the corner, leaving me standing in the middle of the kitchen. As inviting as it is and as invited as I was to be here, I still can't help but feel awkward. Although it's homey, there's nothing familiar. No spoons from vacations we took as kids, no memories of my family sitting around eating breakfast in the mornings. Even Nana, as sweet as sugar, isn't mine. She's Walker's. And he's not mine either.

Looking around, wondering where he went, I know I need to say something in order to calm down before I all-out panic and make a mess of myself.

"Um, do you need some help?" I ask, figuring it to be the best way to break the weirdness. "I'm not a great cook, but I can do menial labor in the kitchen with the best of them."

Nana laughs, lifting a pie out of the oven. "Grab a spoon and stir the potatoes. I don't want them sticking to the bottom. That pot isn't my favorite, but it's the only one I have big enough to feed all the boys on Sundays."

"Where are they?" Peck asks, coming around the corner. He lays a red towel folded in half on the middle of the table.

"Not sure," Nana says with a nod to a doorway between the refrigerator and sink. "He came in and muttered hello and took off that way. Machlan and Lance are in the family room watching one of those games y'all watch. I made a cheese ball and Machlan swiped it up and carried it off when I wasn't looking."

"You let him have the whole thing?" Peck whines.

"No, I didn't let him have the whole thing. He took it when I was rolling out a pie crust."

"Well, go get it."

"I'm not going to go get it," she laughs. "You go get it. You're a big boy."

Peck looks at me and sticks out his bottom lip. "It's the best cheese ball ever. She puts bacon bits on the outside."

A rustle comes from the doorway next to the kitchen and my heart comes to a screeching halt before roaring to life again. "I do love me some bacon," I mumble, my eyes on the door. "I'll go get it. Where's the family room?"

Nana gives me instructions and I head that way. Down a short hallway with images of what has to be Walker and his brothers hanging side by side, I spy Machlan and Lance at the room on the end. There's blue carpeting, white walls, and brown leather furniture. The boys are sprawled out, reclined back, and look up as I enter.

"Hey," I say, stepping into the room and then off to the side so you can't see me from the hallway. "What are you watching?"

Machlan gets a big scoop of cheese ball nestled on a cracker and shoves the whole thing into his mouth. "Baseball," he says over the snack.

"It's the Tennessee Arrows against the Wisconsin Bucks," Lance chimes in, settling himself sideways to see me. "Wanna watch with us?"

I watch as the pitcher throws a fastball on the outside, just enough for the Arrows' first baseman to get a poke at it. He sends it flying into right field, over the fence, and into the stands.

"Yodeski is an animal," I note. "Never throw a fastball outside to him on a full count. He'll jack it every time."

"What the hell do you know about baseball?" Machlan says, picking up a glass of tea in the cup holder between him and his brother.

Leaving out the fact that my brother played for the Arrows for his entire career, I let them think I'm just some kind of baseball fanatic. "I know a little," I grin. "I know a lot about the Arrows. They were my team for a while."

"You like baseball and history?" Lance asks. "Fuck Walker. Wanna blow this joint and go home with me?"

Machlan and I laugh as Lance shakes his head and takes a cracker off the tray.

"What else do you know?" Machlan raises a brow. "Pretty eclectic lady, aren't you?"

"I have a lot of brothers," I say, trying to play it off.

"So, what do you know?" he presses.

"Well," I say, trying to not seem disinterested, "I know a little about politics. Some business stuff but that's pretty dry. I know a few things about the military, being a twin, fashion, California, and Southern culture, and that I hate Illinois winters." I tap a finger to my chin. "I think that's it."

"She knows more than the two of us put together," Machlan says to Lance.

I laugh, feeling myself relax. "I was sent in here to collect the cheese ball. Fork it over."

"Not a chance," Machlan laughs. "This is my favorite thing ever."

"Well, it's apparently Peck's too, and Nana said to come get it."

"You tell him to come get it." His eyes darken and a slow smirk spreads on his face. "But if you'd like to fight for it, I'm open to that."

"What's going on in here?" Walker is standing in the doorway, looking pointedly at Machlan. His hands are digging into the doorframe above his head, his forearms thick and roped and on display. His shirt comes up just a little above the top of his jeans and I have to force myself not to stare at the lines carved from his hips to his cock.

"Just chatting with Sienna," Lance grins. "I have her almost ready to go home with me. Right, Sienna?"

"You are handsome," I note. "And pretty sweet. And you say nice things to me, which is a plus." Moving towards Machlan, my heart beating in my throat, I hold out a hand. "Gimme."

"I thought you'd never ask," Machlan winks.

Lance chuckles, his gaze shooting over me and towards the door. I don't follow it. I can't. I have to stay focused on the task at hand and getting the hell out of here.

Reaching down, I grab the plate with one hand. "I'm taking this."

"I beg to differ."

"Machlan, you're not a little boy. Stop acting like one."

"Yeah," Lance chimes in as Machlan lets go of the plate.

"Thank you," I say, smiling sweetly. For good measure, I pat him on the head as I walk by, much to Lance's amusement. Really, it's for my distraction. I have to get past Walker before I can leave the room.

Forcing a swallow, the cheese ball topsy-turvy on the plate thanks to Machlan's digging, I look up to see Walker not there. I hold my breath as I step into the hall, wondering if this is what it felt like for the gladiators to step into the Colosseum. Like their death is imminent, facing the battle for their lives.

I no more than get both feet on the hardwood floor of the hallway before my back is pressed against the wall. Walker is in front of me, his eyes blazing. Yet just beneath the ferocity lies something that makes me want to reach out and pull myself into his chest. But I don't. Because fuck that.

"What are you doing here?" he asks, his voice just loud enough for me to hear.

"I was invited."

Looking him right in the eye, my words much steadier than I anticipated, I try not to focus on his lips and how close they are as he leans over me, his breath hot and cinnamon-y against my face.

"No. Why are you *really* here?"

"Why do you think I'm here?" I volley, giving him an opening to make this conversation easier.

"It sure as hell ain't for Peck."

His assuredness irritates me, but it's his insinuation that I'm so pathetic I'd chase him to his Nana's house that incenses me. I can feel my face get hot, my exhales vibrating as they roll out of my body.

"What do you want me to say?" I hiss, gripping the plate. "That I'm here for you? That I wanted to give you a chance to say whatever you were going to say yesterday?"

He does that thing where I think he's going to smile, but he doesn't. Instead, he plants a cocky smirk on those kissable lips that I now want to bite and storm away.

"For the record, I am here with Peck. You want to know why? Because he asked me," I say, the cheese ball sliding to the side. "Because your grandmother asked me." I search his eyes for something to quell my rising anger, but there's nothing to grab onto. "Because they aren't complete assholes."

I start to step around him, but he steps in my path. "So you don't want to hear me out?"

"Yes. No," I contradict myself. "I don't know. That's the problem, Walker. I don't know what to do with you. I've tried to be nice. I've liked you enough to have sex with you, because believe it or not, I don't do that with everyone," I say, tilting the platter so the cheese ball centers again, never taking my eyes off him. "But the deeper I get with you, the farther you pull away. So, fine. Retreat back into your little world. But I'll tell you one thing, I may regret hitting your truck with that bat, but I don't regret being with you because I honestly liked you. I'm sorry you feel I was such a mistake. I promise I won't get in your way again."

Hitting him in the arm with my shoulder as I step out from between him and the wall, I walk towards the kitchen. He doesn't call out for me. He doesn't even say my name.

chapter
Nineteen

Sienna

"HERE YOU GO," I SAY, setting the platter down. It clatters against the table, causing both Nana and Peck to look up from the sink. "Cheese ball."

"You got it away from Machlan?" Nana asks, wiping her hands on her apron. "I'm impressed."

"Peck. Outside," Walker barks, storming behind me and making a beeline for the door.

"Now it's time to eat," Nana says. "Peck and I have everything in the dining room."

"It'll only take a minute."

Pecks flashes me a look. "Remember. Nurse Shelby," he whispers as he follows Walker out the door.

Instinctively, my heart in my throat, I follow him and stop at the glass. They stand at the edge of the house, the vein in Walker's temple throbbing, his finger in Peck's chest. Peck's hands are up in the air in a "don't shoot" stance, his back to the house. The rumble of Walker's voice trickles through the door and I can hear the emphatics in his tone, but Peck's climbs louder, over the shouts of his cousin.

"What's going on out there?" Lance asks, coming up behind me. "Oh, fuck."

"It's not Peck's fault," I whisper. "Do something."

Lance claps a hand on my shoulder, the feeling strangely comforting. "Don't worry about it. Walker knows this has nothing to do with Peck too. Peck's just the one he can . . . vent to."

"That's venting?"

"In Walker's way, yeah. It's therapy."

"I can assure you he doesn't pay Peck enough for that."

Lance laughs, squeezing my shoulder. "Peck can handle himself, Slugger."

Glancing up and behind me, I take in his hazel eyes. "Not you too."

He winks before flicking his gaze back outside. "They'll be fine. Let's go eat."

"I don't know . . ." I mutter, watching Walker get right into Peck's face. "He said to take him to Linton General and ask for Shelby."

"Oh, I bet he did," he chuckles. "Come on. Let's go."

Spinning around, I look at him in disbelief. "We can't leave them out there like that."

"I thought you had brothers? You should know how this works."

"My mom would've killed them had they acted like this," I say, jabbing a finger towards the door. "My brothers just exchange barbs until Ford gets them down and makes them submit."

"Ford sounds like my kinda guy," Machlan teases as he walks by with a pitcher of tea. "Now come on. The sideshow is wrapping up and Nana's gonna have a fit if we don't get to the table."

Lance follows Machlan, their conversation making a one-eighty shifting to baseball as the door behind me opens. Startled, I turn around to see Peck. He's not grinning his usual goofy smile, but he's not bleeding either.

"You okay?" I ask.

"I'm fine," he says, blowing me off.

"Where is he?"

"Peck? Sienna? Get in here. Time to eat!" Nana calls from the dining room.

"You heard her," Peck says, motioning towards the doorway.

Not knowing what else to do but knowing one hundred percent that this conversation is over, I put one foot in front of the other and make my way to the table. Continuously looking behind me and out the window, I don't see Walker. I want to ask, but there's no way to do that without everyone hearing me.

The table is lined with a dozen platters of meat, potatoes, salads, and sides. It reminds me of Savannah. If I closed my eyes, I could open them to see my family at the table, waiting to dig in. Instead, I rest my sights on the Gibson boys and their Nana, all waiting for me to take the seat Peck has pulled out for me.

"Thank you," I say, feeling flushed. "This looks great, Nana."

"Thank you," she says, fanning her face with a napkin. "Where's Walker?"

The boys glance around the table. It's a scene I know well from having a large family. They're silently conspiring, covering for one of their own. As terrible as I feel for being the cause of this situation, my heart also warms at their camaraderie for Walker despite his being as ass.

"He had to chop wood," Peck rushes, his eyes bulging when he realizes the stupidity of his words in the middle of summer. "I mean . . ."

"He had to take a call. Something about the shop." Machlan rearranges his silverware and pointedly doesn't meet Nana's gaze. "He'll be back. He just needs a few minutes."

"That boy," she huffs, instructing Lance to lead the family in prayer.

We bow our heads, Lance giving thanks for the meal in front of us and family around us, before closing it out with an "Amen." When I look up, Machlan is grinning at me.

"What?" I ask, taking the bowl of mashed potatoes he offers.

"Nothing."

"Don't be rude," I say in the same tone I'd use with my brothers. "Say what you want to say or stop insinuating you want to say it."

"Exactly," Nana cuts in. "I like the way you put that, Sienna. You handle these boys well."

"I don't know about that," I say, thinking of Walker and how I haven't handled him at all. "You have any tips for me?"

"For these rascals?" she sighs. "Well . . ."

"I could give you some tips," Lance jokes.

"You will not. Not with that tone." Nana looks at him over the rim of her glass of tea.

"You don't even know what I was going to say," Lance says.

"I can imagine." She sets her glass down and looks at me. "I always think intention is more important than action. Take, for example, the time Peck wrecked my town car."

Peck drops his fork. "I didn't wreck it. I hit the gear shift with the hose while I was cleaning it out."

"You took out an entire shed," Machlan cackles. "You wrecked it."

"The important thing," Nana says, giving Machlan a stern look, "is that he was trying to do good. Or, since you are so ready to jump into this conversation, Machlan, take the time you shorted out half the house with a bobby pin."

Lance bursts out laughing, much to Machlan's dismay. "I'll never forget that as long as I live."

"Fuck you," Machlan mutters.

"Excuse me?" Nana looks at him. "At my table, sir?"

"Sorry."

She turns her attention to me. "Actions have emotions incorporated in them. Other people and things can factor in too. I've always been an advocate of looking into someone's intentions as opposed to how those actually turn out. I think it tells you a lot more about the person than their results. Does that make sense?"

"Yes," I gulp, the squeak of the back door flooding my ears. I sense him walking into the room, smell his cologne way before I see him. His energy hits me like a seismic wave, rolling over me and demanding me to pay attention.

Looking up, I'm not a bit surprised he's looking at me, but I am surprised at how. The fury is gone, the tightness in his jaw eased. Instead, there are lines furrowed in his forehead and his hands are tucked into the pockets of his jeans.

"Sit down and make a plate," Nana says, motioning towards the seat at the other end of the table.

He studies me intently before rocking back on his heels and moving his gaze to Nana. "I know I promised you I'd be here today. But, um, would it be okay if I miss dinner?"

She rests her fork against her plate and folds her hands on her lap. "Go ahead. I can tell it's important."

Walker looks down. Taking a deep breath, one that we all watch him take, he finally blows it out as his head turns to me. "Would you mind going with me?"

I forget to answer. The words just dangle in the back of my throat, mixed up in the emotion that's drifting from Walker's face to mine. Finally, Peck elbows me in the side.

"Um, sure," I croak. "Would that offend you, Nana? If I went with him?"

"It would me," Lance offers, getting a chuckle from Machlan.

"It's the intent," Nana smiles softly. "Go. I'll pack a meal for you to take home with you when you get back."

"Thank you, Ms. Gibson."

She starts to correct me, but thinks better of it. "See you soon. Boys, get back to your dinner before it gets cold."

Scooting my chair back, I give Peck a squeeze on the shoulder.

"Go get him, Slugger," he whispers loud enough for only me to hear.

Heading to the doorway, Walker steps to the side to let me through. Not sure what to do or what to say, I keep walking until I'm out the door.

chapter
Twenty

Sienna

"WHERE ARE WE GOING?" I ask as he passes me. The gravel crunches beneath his feet as he passes the front of Peck's truck. "Walker?"

He draws a line across the top of the Charger with the tip of his finger as he all but storms past, my legs struggling to keep up in the low heels I stupidly decided to wear for church. Stopping and leaning against the car, I take them off and carry them as I feel the gravel turn to soft earth beneath my bare feet.

He's halfway to a tree line, still not looking back.

"Damn it, Walker," I yell after him. "Answer me."

I want to take a shoe and throw it at his head, both as a way to get his attention and to ease some of the frustration that's causing my teeth to grind together.

There's nothing worse than being ignored, except when that person asks for your attention and then flips it back around like you're begging them.

To hell with that.

"Screw it. I'm going back."

His feet plant just inches from the trees. The shirt, the first time I think I've ever seen him in anything but black, stretches across his wide shoulders, the pockets of his jeans hugging his ass. Strands of hair hit the top of his collar and I want to run my fingers through them and ask him why he's hell-bent on driving me nuts, but I don't because he's still not looking at me.

Flying him the bird, an un-ladylike gesture that feels like a huge moment of rebellion, I take a step back towards the house when I hear him speak.

"I didn't say I regretted anything."

Our positions now flip-flopped—him looking at my back, me refusing to look his way—I focus on the back of the old barn bearing a few streaks of paint leftover from an old tobacco ad.

"Sometimes you don't have to say things to have them understood." My voice is clear over the bright green grass, floating across the bunny that's standing on its hind legs watching us, and through the band of evergreens. "I think you're the master at not having to say what you mean to get your point across."

The sun hits my face and I feel all the mixed emotions of the last few days just kind of lump together and fall, sinking in the warm afternoon. I'm almost numb, not really feeling any certain way. I stand at the back of the yard, my face to the sky, and wonder what I should do. Then again, I wonder if it's even worth my energy.

I have a phone full of numbers, social media accounts brimming with contacts, of men I could call up and go out with. Handsome men, charming ones, guys who would wine and dine me senseless. Some of them have names every household in America would recognize, some have faces every female in the country could name.

Yet, none of them have the appeal of Walker Gibson. That's something I don't understand.

I've always known I wasn't cut out to be arm candy for some trust fund baby. I've dated my fair share and being expected to not have an opinion, to look the other way, to have my hair, nails, and eyebrows ready to go at all times is not my idea of a good time. It actually makes me want to punch people in the face. But that doesn't mean I have to go polar opposite with work boots and grease, does it?

His shadow creeps up beside me, stretching much longer than mine. Even it keeps a distance.

"I mean it." His voice rushes across my skin, the genuineness in his tone a balm to some of my aches. "I don't regret it. I never said I did. That was you putting words in my mouth."

"That was me drawing lines between what you were saying and doing."

"Fair enough."

Surprised that he's giving in that easily, I ease up on the clench of my fingers around the straps of my heels. Blood rushes back into my digits, divots dug into my palms.

"I'm glad you came today," he says. "I mean, I know it probably doesn't seem like it, but . . ."

"It doesn't seem like it," I say, my voice struggling against the tightness in my throat. "It seems like you think I'm out to make your life miserable. I assure you I'm not."

"Could've fooled me," he mumbles under his breath.

Not sure I was supposed to have heard that, I did, and I'm not about to let him get away with it. I practice the art of the fake smile as I rein in my annoyance. "Fooling anyone isn't in my plans. A big 'screw you' for even insinuating that."

"Sienna." The way he says my name, like he's wrapped everything he has around the three syllables, makes my knees weak despite my anger. "I didn't mean it like that."

"Then how did you mean it, Walker? Because I'll be honest—I'm exhausted from trying to figure you out. I'm sick of doing this with you."

A storm crosses his face, a steeliness settling on the hard lines of his jaw.

"That. Right there," I say, pointing a finger at him. "That's what I'm talking about."

"What?" There's a sharpness to his tone, a bite that seems to warn me off of prodding. Most days this would work. I'd stop and just let him go on about his day. Today is not most days. Today I'm tired of it.

I'm not sure it even matters and I'd put my money on the fact that it doesn't. Even so, there's an exhaustion in my shoulders from carrying around all of the guesses I put together about why he acts the way he does and an acute sense of curiosity as to what's real—his verbal spars or the zing of his touch that says otherwise.

"One minute, you and I are having a conversation and teasing each other and laughing—well, I'm laughing. I'm not sure you'd do such a thing," I say, rolling my eyes. "And the next minute you're dismissing me like some woman you can't shake. Like a bad habit. Like a quick fuck," I eke out. "Yet you give me just enough rope to hang myself."

"That's not true."

"Could've fooled me." I give his words back to him, a little salt dashed on top as I throw them back his way. "I've never met a man who twists me up like you do. Like you get some thrill out of keeping me flailing around, unsure if you like me or hate me."

"Stop it," he growls.

"I'm not going to stop it," I shoot back. "I'm done with this shit. If you want to string some woman along, fine. Go ahead. But it won't be me."

"I don't want it to be you. I mean," he roughs a hand against his head, looking anywhere but at me with a scowl. "Damn it. What I mean is, that's not true."

"Oh, it's true and you know it."

Refusing to back down, I meet him glare for glare. He stands taller; so do I. He angles his head and I do the exact same thing. I won't budge an inch.

"You wanna know what's fucking true?" He takes a step towards me, his hands coming out of his pockets in a quick rush. "Here's what's true—you're making my life so goddamn miserable I can't see straight. I can't sleep. I can't think. I say shit I don't mean on purpose because pushing you away feels like saving you from myself. I can't work on an engine without smashing my knuckles off the side like some rookie."

He flashes the back of his hand my way. It's cut across the top, the skin sliced and rough.

"All because of you." His boot sinks into the grass as he gets closer, his Adam's apple bobbing in his throat. "I've not been able to stop thinking about you since I saw you on the sidewalk trying to hide that bat behind you."

His gaze peers into me like there's nothing else in the world to look at. Like the entire world has stopped—the axis stopped turning, governments paused work, people suspended mid-whatever, just so Walker can concentrate on me.

"I'm sorry, Sienna."

"What are you sorry for?"

Shifting my weight, my feet feeling the coolness of the ground, I try to find my center in the midst of the chaos playing through every cell of my body.

"I thought you'd be out of here by now," he says, his voice having lost the grit from earlier. "I figured I could push you away and you'd just go."

"Just maybe I am hardheaded."

"Um, no doubt," he chuckles. "But I am sorry for a lot of things, but mostly for what I said to you Friday night. And the way I made you feel. For the record, I wanted to pick you up and carry you to my truck and take you home with me."

My heart zips in my chest as I struggle to process that. "I don't understand."

"I didn't expect you to still be here." He takes a deep breath. "I thought we could kind of fuck it out and you'd be over it. But here you are."

"Is that okay?" I whisper. "That I'm here?"

"I'm so glad you are."

Taking my shoes from my hand, he rubs his thumb across my knuckle. He watches each stroke, his eyes glued to the movement as he speaks. "Nana talked about you last night. I was over here helping her fix her sink drain. She waited until I was on my back and under the sink before peppering me with a million questions."

"What did you tell her?" I ask, trying desperately to keep my voice steady.

His thumb stops moving. Looking up and into my eyes, there's a softness there that, if he weren't holding my hand, would catapult me over.

"I didn't tell her anything she didn't already know."

His thumb stills, pressing into the top of my hand. I can feel his struggle, the war within himself, at saying that aloud. He didn't say anything.

Not really. But in typical Walker fashion, he didn't have to.

As my heart flutters in my chest, a shaky sigh quietly passing my lips, I try to give him a soft spot to land after that semi-admission. Even though I don't know concretely what Nana already knew, I have an idea, and it wasn't that I bake great muffins. It would explain the way his palms are dampening. It would make sense as to why he seems unable to find words to follow. And even though I'm still angry, it's a feeling that's becoming harder to maintain.

"Hey," I say, scrambling for a way to give him some space. Over his shoulder, just a couple of rows in front of the forest, is a little structure up in a tree. "Is that a treehouse?"

The relief is evident in the way his shoulders sag. "Yeah."

"Is it solid? I mean, can we go up?"

He squeezes my hand, his thick and calloused skin rough against my own, before dropping it to the side. Chuckling, he shrugs. "You want to?"

"Can we? I know it's random, but it's the one thing in my life I've always wanted and never had."

He turns towards the trees. "I didn't have you pegged for a treehouse kind of girl."

"My father didn't either," I admit, just a few steps behind him. "I asked for one every year for Christmas for about four years straight. One of my brothers fell out of one when they were younger and Dad had some big machine there in the morning to rip it down. He refused to let my sister and I have one. It was the only thing we couldn't have."

"That explains a lot."

"What's that supposed to mean?" I laugh.

He stops at the base of the tree and plants one hand on the bark. Leaning against it, his eyes the color of the dark soil beneath our feet, he considers his words. "You seem like a girl who gets what she wants."

"Most of the time," I say, my chest clenching under his gaze. "I just need to be more careful with what I decide I want."

"Yeah. Some things look all right on the outside, but there's nothing on the inside."

"True," I say, unable to take my eyes away from his. "But sometimes that just means it's there to be filled up."

He presses off the tree, switching his gaze up the tree. "Let's go, country girl. I'll follow in case you fall."

"I'm not going first. I have on a dress. I'm a lady."

He bites back a smile. Leaning forward, his lips brushing against the shell of my ear. There's no way to control the shiver that rips across my skin and flips on my libido in an instant.

"Have you forgotten already?" he whispers.

"Forgotten what?"

"That I've been inside you."

I grip the wooden rung screwed into the tree as if I'm ready to climb. It's really so I don't sag against him. His words fire through my veins and singe my vessels, landing in one contorted mass at the apex of my thighs.

"And we saw what happened after that," I volley back.

He bristles beside me. Clean, un-Walker-filled air swallows my personal space and I instantly hate it. My body begs to fall back towards him, to feel the energy that buzzes between us when he's near, but I don't dare.

Instead, I put one foot on the bottom rung and look at him over my shoulder. He's watching me with intense, broody eyes, his bottom lip pinched between his teeth.

"Close your eyes, Gibson. I'd hate for you to see what you've been missing."

With a light head and clattering heart, I work my way up the pseudo-ladder. I don't look down. I show no fear. And even more importantly, I show no weakness.

———

THE LADDER OPENS INTO A makeshift treehouse complete with a trap door. I can stand up, only having to crouch a bit as I scurry away from the ladder so Walker can make it up too.

There are windows on two of the sides with short camouflage curtains that look like they've seen better days. There's a checkerboard sitting on a mini-card table under one window with some of the pieces strewn about on the floor. A couple of pocket knives, notebooks, and a red and blue striped blanket dot a slapdash couch made out of egg cartons and cardboard.

It's not as dusty as I imagined it would be. There are cobwebs in the corners and it could use a good cleaning, but it looks like it's been occupied recently.

"Well, is it everything you hoped for?" Walker looks up at me from the ladder.

"It's cleaner than I expected."

"I think Sawyer was up here not too long ago," he says, his palms setting on the floor. He lifts himself up into the room with me. "Peck has a brother named Vincent. Sawyer is his boy. They live an hour or so away, so we don't see them too much. Just when Nana puts her foot down."

Spinning in a circle, I take in the nuances of an area that's definitely all boy. There are three folding chairs lined up neatly along one wall with a sign that reads, "Gibson Boys—Stay Out Blaire".

"Who's Blaire?" I ask as Walker gets to the top.

He groans as he unfolds as far as he can into the tight space. Hunkered over, he doesn't hesitate to take a seat in one of the chairs. "Blaire's my sister."

"I think Nana mentioned her." Still looking around, I take in the carvings in the wood and the candy wrappers piled into a mound on the floor. It's the perfect little boy hangout. It brings a smile to my cheeks.

"What are you grinning about?" he asks.

"This is everything I always wanted, except maybe purple curtains and not the pocket knives," I laugh. "It's adorable."

"I spent half my childhood up here, I bet. Carving twigs, eating the cake we stole from Nana's that was supposed to wait until after dinner, making plans for world domination." He rests his elbows on his knees. "It was an easier time of my life."

"Would you go back?"

His head falls to the side as he ponders my question. "Probably. You?"

"No. I had a great childhood and all that, but growing pains were hard."

"I can't imagine anything being hard for you. You just go with the flow and fix shit. It seems like it's ingrained in you."

Grabbing a chair and scooting it a few feet away from him, I get situated on the cool metal seat. "Sometimes I feel like everything is hard for me," I admit. "I know that's not true. My life is pretty charmed. But for whatever reason, it seems like I can't figure anything out."

The air shifts between us and I know what he's going to say before he says it. "Are you talking about me?"

"I wasn't," I say truthfully. "But it applies, I guess."

His head drops, hanging between his two muscled biceps. My breathing shallows as I watch him absorb my admission.

"Tell me about Blaire," I redirect, not wanting to get into another pissing match with him. "She doesn't come around?"

"She lives in Chicago," he says, his voice ragged like its slipping past a parched throat. "She's an attorney. Kind of a big deal."

"That's awesome."

"She thinks so," he grins. "She's super fucking smart and a black belt in some random martial art. We don't get to see her much these days."

"Do you miss her?"

"Eh," he shrugs.

There's a purposeful playoff to my question that leads me to believe he misses her more than he's letting on. "What about your parents? Do you see them often?"

His hands twist in front of him. "My parents passed away a few years back."

A lump the size of an egg lodges in my throat as I watch a swath of pain wash across his face. I try for a moment to imagine what it would feel like not to have my parents. Just the thought chips a giant hole in my heart big enough that I find myself placing a hand over the organ as if the piercing pain is real. "Oh, Walker. I'm sorry."

"It was an accident. On a boat on the Fourth of July. Shit happens, you know?"

"I can't imagine."

He half-shrugs, half-nods, and seems to kind of fall away into his head for a moment. Watching him makes me wonder how lonely he is without his parents and sister.

"What do you do for fun?" I ask, hoping to see his smile again. I do.

"What kind of question is that?"

"One people ask when they're curious. Do you hunt? Fish? Date a lot?"

"No."

Tilting my head to the ceiling, I make a point of ensuring he hears my exasperated sigh. He makes sure I hear his chuckle in response. Lowering my face, I give him a playful look. "Don't get too in depth there, Walker. I'd hate for you to run out of words."

"What?" he laughs. "I don't hunt. I do fish some, but not a lot. And I don't date a lot."

"You could probably find more dates if you'd stop being such an ass," I joke.

"I don't not date from a lack of opportunities, Slugger," he says, lifting a brow.

"Then why don't you?" I ask, a little relieved that he isn't some playboy that just doesn't want to not date me. "Why would you want to be alone all the time?"

He strokes his chin, his elbow propped up on his knee. He watches me intently, like he's trying to weed out any unforeseen insinuations. "You know how you said sometimes you can't figure anything out?"

"Yeah."

"That."

"You don't know how to date?" I tease. "It's really pretty simple."

"No, smartass, I know how to date. I just . . ." He looks at me for help. When I don't give him any, he shrugs. "I guess I find it a hassle that doesn't usually seem worth it."

"Strangely, I get that. Although I do go into them sometimes and know it's a one-time thing. A guy will ask me to dinner or an event and I'll go with him, even though there's no hope of really seeing him after."

"So like one-night stands?"

My cheeks warming, I shake my head. "No. I actually don't sleep with many men."

"I didn't mean to insinuate that you did."

"I know. It's just I did with you, so of course you might think that."

There's something he wants to say. He opens his mouth, but the words don't come. Scratching at the back of his neck, he seems to change his mind.

"Do you date a lot?" he asks instead.

There's a slight change in his tone, a barely perceptible chill iced on each word that the average person listening in wouldn't catch, but I do. To me, it's unmistakable. And when I pair it with the intensity of his gaze, I could shudder despite the warm afternoon temperature.

"Sometimes," I answer.

"Are you dating anyone now?"

"Not regularly."

"What's that supposed to mean?"

Laughing at his reaction, the way he's sitting upright all of a sudden, I shrug. "It means I'm not seeing anyone exclusively."

"But you're seeing someone?"

"I went to dinner with a guy a couple of weeks ago. It was nice, but nothing I'd like to do again. There are a couple of guys in Savannah that I see when I go home off and on, but no one I call to chat with or that sends me flowers, if that's what you mean."

"I don't know what I fucking mean," he groans. "It's none of my business."

"No, it's not."

He fiddles with his hands again, taking in a deep, lazy breath that fills his solid chest. I find myself mirroring his action, the oxygen seeping in to my lungs and helping to steady my heartbeat as we blow out the air in unison.

"I'm just gonna toss some shit out there and you can take it or leave it or make fun of me . . ." he says, refusing, still, to look my way.

"Probably the latter, but go on," I tease. Anticipation of what he's about to say grabs hold of my hopes and emotions and pulls them up and up until I feel like I'm actually standing on the edge of a cliff, waiting to be pushed over or pulled back into his arms.

He lifts his eyes. They're crystal clear, the brown pools bared for me to see there's no bullshit, no ulterior motives behind whatever it is he's going to say.

"I don't know what to do with you," he says softly.

"I've seen you know exactly what to do with me," I say, my words falling right where I intended.

The corner of his mouth curls into a smile, but he doesn't let himself run with it. Instead, he cinches down, clears his throat, and continues on. "You bashed my truck with a baseball bat."

"Oh, Lord. Are we going back to that again?"

"Who does that, Sienna?"

"Me, all right?" I laugh. "I did that. I do that."

"Exactly. You do that. But you also bake muffins for Peck and I for breakfast," he says, the laughter falling from his voice. "You come back to the shop to bring me dinner when you know I'm working late and you pretend to know about tools when you don't know jack shit."

"I know how to navigate a search engine."

"But who takes the time to do that?" he sighs. "Who spends their evening in a dirty mechanic's shop and lies their way into helping someone else?"

I shrug. "Someone crazy."

"Yeah. You," he says. "And you make friends with my Nana and put my brothers in check and you're still sitting in a treehouse talking to me when I was pretty nasty to you." He shakes his head like he's been stumped. "You're the craziest person I've ever met."

He shifts in his seat, like he's just getting comfortable with the words slipping off his tongue. "Women will pretend to be sweet. I've seen it a million fucking times. But when the going gets tough, they'll back off and go somewhere easier. Every. Fucking. Time. Until now."

Biting the inside of my lip, I try to keep my mouth shut so as not to ruin his flow. He's softer than I've ever seen. More vulnerable. More real. And despite the overwhelming urge to plant my lips against his, I don't. If I do, I'm not sure when, or if, I'd ever get him to this point again.

"You know, the day you paid for Dave and MaryAnn's cars, I almost told you to just go."

"I thought you were going to."

"I remember that afternoon, after you left, Peck looking at me and asking me what I was going to do." He forces a swallow. "We both knew he wasn't referring to the money."

Squirming in my seat, my chest rising and falling so fast I quickly run the odds of passing out, I try to focus on staying present and not letting my thoughts get carried away. "What was he talking about, Walker?"

"He knew I was already in over my head."

I'm not sure if I reach for his hand or if he reaches for mine. Regardless, our hands are locked, his easily encompassing mine, somewhere in the middle of the room between us. With a gentle pull, he gets me to my feet and over to him.

My heart races as I sit on his knee and he locks his hands around my waist. It's not the closest we've ever been, nor is it the most intimate. But there's something so tender, so private, in this moment between us that I can't recall ever feeling so close to a man in my entire life.

Tilting his head back, dragging me closer to his torso, he looks at me unguarded for the first time. "I want to apologize for ever making you upset or confused or that you felt like I counted you as a mistake."

"For what it's worth," I tell him, "I knew you were wrong."

He rolls his eyes, a sweet grin playing on his lips. I love this look on him. It's what someone like Walker should look like—young and happy and carefree.

"I know you're leaving . . ." He unwraps and rewraps his hands at my waist, his Adam's apple bobbing as he swallows.

"I don't *have* to do anything," I say, running my finger along his bottom lip. "I kind of do things on my time, if you haven't figured that out by now."

He snaps my finger between his teeth before I see it coming. Yelping, I instinctively try to pull it away, but he holds firm. It's only when I give up and stop fighting that he wraps his lips around it and lets me slide it from his mouth.

The feeling sends a shot straight to my core. It's heightened by the look of pure, unadulterated lust coming from Walker.

"I need a minute," he says, running a hand through my hair. "I don't know what's happening here. I have shit to deal with. I—"

"Stop talking," I say, pressing a sweet, simple kiss to his lips. "You can have a minute. You can have an hour or a week or a month or a year. Hell, I might not even like you two minutes from now—Walker!"

In one quick, seamless motion, he stands, picks me up, and lays me on my back on the floor of the treehouse. Hovering over me, his forearms nestled on either side of my head, he grins down. "If you might not like me in two minutes, I better get to work winning you over now, hadn't I?"

Caressing his face in my hands, his stubble scratching at my palms, I look in to his eyes and find what I've been looking for: peace.

"Better hurry," I whisper. "You're down to a minute and a half."

My legs wrap around his waist as he lowers himself to me, his sweet lips finding mine. He kisses me this time not with a sense of urgency, not out of lust, but out of something else. Something that tickles the back of my brain to pay attention, but I don't. I'm too caught up in the moment.

chapter
Twenty One

Sienna

NANA'S CARE PACKAGE NESTLED SAFELY on my lap, I pick at the edges of the grocery bag housing the leftovers. Walker rolls the truck to a stop next to my car parked outside the church. He kills the engine, his elbow resting against the middle console.

"Thanks for the ride," I tell him, arranging myself in my seat so I can see him without craning.

He looks different this afternoon. His frown lines aren't dug as deep, his jaw relaxed instead of looking like it was grinding his teeth into oblivion. Even as his family gave him boatloads of crap as we left Nana's, he didn't seem as ready to kill any of them.

"It was on my way," he notes.

"Seriously, Walker?"

"What?"

"It's okay for you to admit you wanted to drive me to my car," I prod. "It won't make you less of a man."

"It *was* on my way," he insists. "I'm not saying I wouldn't have volunteered if it wasn't."

"I could've ridden home with Peck. And both of your brothers offered."

He snorts, shaking his head. "Oh, I bet those fuckers did."

"I was leaning towards Machlan, but Lance seems a little gentler," I grin.

"It's the glasses and it's a ruse," he laughs. "Lance is as rough as any of us. He was actually the only one to get thrown out of school before we hit high school."

"Lance?" I laugh. "For what? Charming the pants off his teacher?"

"It had to do with pants, but there wasn't much charm involved," he chuckles.

Our laughter mixes in the air, my high, feminine sound swirled with the bite of his rasp. The leaves blowing in the breeze outside the truck window, the sun pouring in the glass, it's a moment I could fall in absolute love with. Maybe a man I could fall in love with too, if I tried.

He fiddles with the button on the cuff of his shirt. "I know you said you weren't coming in to Crank anymore . . ."

"I say a lot of things. Besides, Delaney is basically gone, and other than mostly being on hiatus for a little while anyway, I do most of my design work at night. My creativity comes out after dark."

"I'll remember that," he winks.

The plastic bag rattles as I wind the top around my finger.

I look at Walker. There's a level of uncertainty mixed with the way he's twisting his lips together that sparks something inside me. Not roots, not that at all. But maybe a branch extending to him that I want to see if he takes. If he holds on. If it breaks.

"I don't really have any plans for what to do now," I tell him, gulping back a hot swallow. "Maybe I could help you out until I get my life sorted? I'm going to have to switch some gears around now that I'll be working by myself and I need some time to wrap my brain around that."

His brows lift to the sky, his hand stalling against the sleeve of his shirt. "You don't have to, Sienna. Really."

"What if I want to, Walker?"

It takes a full five seconds for the grin trying to spread across his lips to actually form. But once it does, he lets it go and I realize—I've never seen a full smile from him before.

My heart hiccups, skipping a couple of beats, as I absorb the warmth radiating off him. He lays his arm on the console and rolls his palm over so it's facing up. Like a rip current drawing things its way, my hand drops into his immediately.

"You're so weird," he laughs.

"Me? How do you figure?"

He laces our fingers together, watching them intertwine. My pink fingernails look odd against his torn knuckles, my ivory skin almost unreal against the dark, stained, almost olive-y hued tone of his. He works them back and forth, taking them in from every direction like it's some kind of anomaly.

Ignoring my question, he squeezes my hand one final time before resting them on the console. "Does this mean you're coming by tomorrow?"

"I'm still not cleaning the bathroom."

"I can deal with that."

There's an unsteadiness to his eye, something that makes me think maybe he's gone too far in one day.

Blowing out a breath, I squeeze his hand before slipping mine from his. "I better get going. I have a lot of things to think about."

"Anything I can do?"

"Besides be a distraction?" I laugh, reaching for the handle.

The door is partially open, the scent of evergreens whispering through the air, when he speaks.

"Sienna?"

"Yeah?"

Looking over my shoulder, I can see the uncertainty in his eyes. He stills for a split second before leaning across the console. I meet him somewhere near halfway.

He takes my face in his hands and presses a sweet, simple kiss that dizzies me as much as if he deprived me of oxygen for days. When he pulls back, he's no more certain but seems resolved.

"See you tomorrow," I whisper.

"Yeah. See you tomorrow."

I slip out the door and into my car without breathing or looking back. The light is brighter, the birds happier, the colors in the stained glass of the church more vivid as I buckle myself in and start the engine.

Walker watches me, one arm over the steering wheel. I wave. He holds his hand in the air in some guy version of goodbye, the engine ripping alive before he pulls out of the parking lot and heads in the opposite direction of my house.

I sit for a few minutes, trying to get my bearings. I can still smell his cologne on my skin. The deep, dark tones linger and I take a deep breath and hope they stick around for a while.

Putting my car in reverse, I pull out of the lot and onto the street and head to the left. Disappointment flickers when I don't see him in my rearview mirror.

A loud ring belts from my bag. Stopping at a stop sign at the end of the block, I fish around until it vibrates in my hand. "Hey, Delaney."

"I was just checking on you. Making sure those Gibson boys didn't have you for breakfast . . . although I can't say that would be a bad thing necessarily."

Sighing happily into the phone, I pull away from the stop sign. "I think we had a breakthrough today."

"Tell me more," she laughs.

"I don't know what happened. He was mad as hell that I was at church and even madder that I went with Peck over to their Nana's for dinner."

"You little rebel!"

"It's not like that."

"Yes, it is. You flaunted that right in his face like a good girl."

I roll my eyes hard as I take a left on the road to take me to Merom. "Hardly. I told Nana I'd go and then Peck was insistent and I kind of wanted to give him an opportunity to say whatever he had to say. He did come out to get me yesterday," I shrug.

"Peck's hot. He can insist whatever he wants with me and I'll play along."

Laughing, I picture Peck with his hands in dishwater as Walker and I left Nana's. "He's hot if you like that tall, lanky, blond, loves-his-grandma kind of thing."

"I do. Sign me up," she giggles. "So back to Walker. What happened with him?"

"I'm not sure . . ." Taking a deep breath, letting the spicy signature of his cologne soothe me, I work out how to explain something I don't really understand. "I don't know what happened, Delaney. We went outside and I told him I was tired of the way he's so hot and cold. There was a treehouse . . ."

"And you got hot and dirty in the treehouse, didn't you, you little minx?" she rushes. "I didn't know you had it in you, but damn it, I'm so proud."

"I didn't have sex with him in his childhood treehouse," I laugh. "He kissed me and whatever it is that drives him to be so wishy-washy came roaring back. But he communicated that with words and not scowls per usual."

"What do you think it is? Guys go gaga over you, Sienna. I can't take you anywhere without at least one date offer. I think it's so odd that he fights himself about you."

It's the exact same question that's been rolling around in my brain for days now. A question I wish I had an answer for.

"Maybe he's had his heart broken," I offer. "Maybe he didn't like me at first."

"Nah, it's more than that. It has to be, doesn't it?"

Shrugging, my buzz from the afternoon evaporating like a puddle of water in the desert, I sigh. "I don't know, Delaney. Maybe I'll figure it out after a shower and pie."

"Okay. I gotta go anyway," she says, reading my need to stop talking about it. "Talk to you later."

"Bye."

My phone lands on the passenger seat with a thud.

Walker

WHY DIDN'T I THINK OF this before?

A dog would cure not all, but a lot of my problems.

They're loyal. Don't complain about anything as long as you feed them and give them some attention. They don't ask for much or have unrealistic expectations and when you let them out to piss, they always come back.

"Yeah, but so does Peck." Running a hand through my hair still wet from the shower, I pad through the dark house until I hit the kitchen. The light comes on, shining brightly across the room that I need to remodel first. When I get to it.

The thought irks me and I shove it out of my mind and focus on the good. It's not often I have good to even think about, and today is about as good as it can get. Sienna's beautiful face takes the place of the dingy linoleum in my mind's eye and I find myself grinning as I take out a mug and pour a glass of root beer from a two-liter bottle.

There's no ice because I forgot to buy it on my way home from Nana's, and I'm too lazy to go back to the gas station to get it. It's times like these that make me think I should just sell this place on the edge of town and move to a city that at least has a grocery store.

Sipping the room temperature pop, I lean against the counter. For a moment, I consider packing all my shit. I think about what it would be like to start all over again in a new space, maybe even a new zip code, and just leaving everything behind. I only consider it for a second, though, because I know as much as I tell myself it's what I should do, I can't.

What would happen to Nana? Who would make sure Machlan remembers to mow around Mom's mums in the front yard of his house? Who would listen to Lance's stories from the trenches of dating women he meets online? Who would keep Peck in a job?

As great as starting all over again sounds, I know I couldn't leave. Every morning I stop at Goodman's and get a cup of coffee just like Dad did. It's stupid as hell; that's not lost on me. But there's something about the routine of it, the carrying out a tradition of the old man, that seems like in some ridiculous way it keeps his memory alive. Some mornings I see Dad's old buddies and we stop and shoot the shit. Sometimes I'll hold the door open for a woman Mom sang in the church choir with, and she'll tell me how much I look like my father and that my mother had the best voice this side of the Mississippi.

Finishing the drink, I rinse the glass and set it on a towel by the sink. Some of the water splashes against my bare chest. Swiping a towel from a drawer next to the stove, I run the towel across my skin and remember what it was like to have Sienna's hands on my body and the way she didn't seem to give a damn about anything other than enjoying the moment with me.

With me.

My mind goes into overdrive at those two little words. What would it be like to be with a woman who is *with me*? Who doesn't think Crank is a waste of time and energy? Who doesn't look at a relationship like a one-sided event? Who gets along with my family, doesn't mind Nana's demands for Sunday dinner, doesn't find Peck to be an annoying weight on their existence?

I still think, after all these years, that's why Tabby left.

If Sienna is a blessing or a curse, I haven't figured out, but pushing her away is pointless. It's like pushing a ball up a hill and thinking it'll stay. It won't. Gravity doesn't care you want the round ball to sit on an incline and it doesn't care that I need Sienna to stay away.

The grandfather clock in the living room chimes, sending a chill down my spine. I toss the towel in the sink and head to bed.

chapter
Twenty Two

Sienna

I'T'S THE SAME CRUNCH OF gravel. The same parking spot. The same hour in the morning, more or less, that I've pulled into Crank to start the day every time since I've come by to pay off Daisy.

The thought of that night widens my grin as I pull into the spot to the left of the front door and kill the engine. Walker is in the lobby, working at the desk, and doesn't look up.

He's wearing a grey t-shirt and navy baseball cap as he sits at the desk. Instead of flicking a pen between two fingers impatiently, as is his custom, he sits with his face cupped in his hand. Every now and then he writes something down before resuming his position staring at the screen.

I sit and watch. The longer I do, the more all the stress about what to do and where to go fizzles away. Sitting in the warm sun, wearing ripped jeans and an old Arrows t-shirt, the smell of grease permeating the air, I can't believe I feel *happy*. Unrushed. Okay with the way things are right now.

It's not something I feel a lot. There's always a need to go, do, find, create, discover . . . keep up. My siblings conquer new parts of the world every day, it seems, whether it's making business deals, saving people's lives, or having babies. Even Camilla has bought into the madness by settling down with Dominic and helping chair events alongside our mother. Me? I can't keep up. Hell, I can't even join the fray because I don't know where my starting point is, but I can't deny that I don't feel compelled to get on a plane and start fresh. Yet.

Grabbing my phone that fell onto the floorboard, I swipe it on and go to the texts app. A smile tickles my lips as I open the top message and read through the exchange with Walker from last night.

WALKER: *Hey.*

ME: *Hi.*

WALKER: *Just making sure you made it home.*

ME: *Well, if I hadn't, the murderer that abducted me would've had a huge head start. LOL I got home hours ago.*

WALKER: *Yeah. Good. Glad you made it.*

ME: *Admit it. You wanted to say hi. ;)*

WALKER: *You're impossible.*

ME: *Impossibly right. Ha. So, what are you doing?*

WALKER: *Thinking about flooring options.*

ME: *At eleven at night?*

WALKER: *Does eleven in the morning sound more reasonable? I don't see the difference.*

ME: *I like a good hardwood, if you're asking my opinion. Nothing too dark because it shows all the dirt. If hardwood is out, do tile but not in the living room because that's just not cozy. I guess carpet in there or if it's a bedroom. Nothing too thick or light colored.*

WALKER: *Wow. Okay.*

ME: *You asked.*

WALKER: *I didn't, actually.*

ME: *No, you did. You always ask without asking. It's part of your charm, I'm beginning to see.*

WALKER: *No one has ever said I'm charming.*

ME: *I didn't either. ;)*

WALKER: *Go back to doing what you were doing. I'm going to bed. You exhaust me.*

ME: *Must've been all those dirty thoughts you've been thinking about me all evening.*

WALKER: *Maybe.*

ME: *See? That's a yes.*

WALKER: *I had fun with you today.*

ME: *I had fun playing in your treehouse.*

WALKER: *I'm not about to touch that. See you tomorrow, Slugger.*

ME: *Night.*

Giggling out loud, I can't remember feeling this dopey over a boy since high school. Jake McGowan was the love of my life at fifteen and when he'd slip me a folded note between biology and algebra, this is how

I would feel. Giddy.

"What's wrong with me?" I sigh. Grabbing my purse, I turn to leave the car when I look up and melt right back down into the seat.

Walker is looking at me, a shy smile gracing his handsome face. I wonder how long he's been watching me and what stupid faces I made and how fast I can get in the building to see him.

I'm out of the car and almost to the door when my phone rings in my hand. When I look down, it's my brother, Graham. It takes all of three seconds to know I have to answer it. Graham never calls unless it's important.

"Hey," I say, waving at Walker through the door so he knows why I didn't come in, then stepping off to the side. "What's up?"

"Good morning to you too."

"I'm sorry. Good morning, G," I say as sweetly as I can muster. "How are you, big brother? Are things well at the homestead?"

"Homestead? What has Illinois done to you?" he chuckles.

"More than you want to know."

The sound of his chair rolling around the floor of his office can be heard in the background. "Noted. What's the plan? Camilla said you were wrapping up things there soon."

"Delaney is getting the last of her stuff out of the house today. She finished her last project a couple of days ago, so it's just me in charge. Does that scare you?"

"A little." He pauses just like our father does before he changes the subject. "What's happening with you? Are you coming back to Savannah?"

It's a loaded question. I can hear the follow-ups now if I answer it truthfully and I don't want to get into all of that today, standing outside of Crank.

"I'm not sure."

"What are you not sure about?" he asks.

"I might stay up here for a little while, actually."

"For what?" He says it like it's the most ridiculous thing anyone has ever said.

"Because I want to."

"Well, Dad and I were talking . . ." He clears his throat. "What would you think about coming home and getting your feet wet at Landry Holdings?"

The question stuns me so much I can't move. "What?"

"I know it sounds a little random—"

"A little random?" I laugh. "You won't even free up enough of my trust fund to let me start my own real business doing what I know. Yet you are wanting me to come work with you?"

"You've done really well at managing things up there with what little you had to go on. Dad and I were going over your numbers and were impressed with your business aptitude, quite frankly."

"Whoa, wait up. Did you just say I impressed you?"

"Don't let it go to your head, Sienna."

"Say it again."

"Sienna," he grumbles.

"Say it again," I insist.

"Your numbers were strong. The profit was lagging, but that's typical for a small business not yet off the ground. You budgeted very, very well, had interesting marketing concepts. I really think, as dumb of an idea as this design company was to start with, you could build something out of it had you not located it in a soybean field."

My cheeks ache from smiling so big at Graham's compliment, something that doesn't happen often. If ever. "G, I don't know what to say."

"Just think about it. I really think you could be an asset around here and you know how I like Landry's to be involved in Landry businesses. I think it sets a good example, keeps us strong."

"I . . . Wow. What a start to the day," I laugh. "I'm . . . I don't know what to say. Yeah, I'll think about it. When do you need to know?"

"You're always welcome here, obviously. But we're expanding the Operations Division right now with Landry Security booming. Ford has his hands full over there. I'd essentially like you on board when we go live with the new changes there. I expect that to happen in the next couple of weeks."

"You do know I know nothing traditionally about business, right? Or security. Or . . . anything."

"I do. But you learn fast and if what you were able to manage on a baby scale holds true, in five, maybe ten years, you could be doing a lot of things. Guess you listened to all those business talks at the dinner table growing up after all."

"Those were so boring," I chuckle.

"Hey, I have to go. The babies have a doctor's appointment this morning and I don't miss those for anyone."

"How are they? How's Mallory?"

"Everyone's good. Everything is really, really good."

"Tell Mallory I said hi and I miss her," I say, wishing I was there to snuggle with Graham's offspring. "Kiss the babies."

"Will do. Let me know what you decide as soon as you do, okay?"

"I will. Bye, G."

"Bye."

Laughing out loud as I shove the phone into my purse, I consider if that conversation just happened. Me? Working at Landry Security on invitation? I've quite possibly never felt so proud in my life. Getting kudos from Graham, the essential Chief Executive Officer of our family, is harder to get than from my parents. From any professor I ever had. From any client.

I feel stupid because I know I'm beaming, but I can't help it. It's not just because of Graham either; it's because maybe the struggle I felt with the first year in business wasn't a bad thing. Maybe it meant we were making it, that we were battling through better than I expected and I just couldn't see it.

"Hey."

I jump at the voice behind me, spinning around to see Walker's face poking out from around the door. He takes in the look on my face and relaxes when he realizes I'm fine.

"Sorry," I tell him. "That was my brother."

"Don't you have like six of them?" he asks, holding the door open.

"No, four," I say, entering the lobby. "That was Graham. He offered me a job." I turn to face him, but his back is already to me as he rounds the corner of the desk. "It's kind of a big deal for Graham to think you're capable."

"Does he not know you?" There's no tease in his tone, no levity. No grin waiting to be cracked either. Just a blank question that he waits for me to respond to.

"Graham's hard core," I explain. "He was saying he went over the stuff from my design business and was impressed."

Walker continues to wait, as if there's more. Some bomb to drop. Something else to explain my exuberance.

"It made me feel good." That's the best I can do to make my point known without him knowing my brother. I go to the back and put my purse into the cabinet, waiting for him to say something.

He clicks around on the computer before clearing his throat. "Are you going to take it?"

"I don't know. I don't know what I'm doing. I just think it's cool that he thought enough of me to ask me to work for him."

"Well, I thought enough of you already to let you work for me." He looks at me through his lashes. "Doesn't that count for anything?"

"I'm here, aren't I?" I say, letting my hand drop to his thigh. "What would you like me to do today?"

"That's a loaded question," he chuckles. "First thing, before I get another call and have to deal with it," he says, palming the back of my thigh with his hand, "is something really dumb, but I'd like to know."

"What?"

He twists his lips together, trying to hide his almost embarrassment. "What's your last name? I don't even know. It occurred to me this morning."

Scooting closer to him so that my torso is lined up with his, I try to concentrate on his words and not the way his fingers are deliciously close to my vagina.

"Landry," I breathe, rolling my hips as his fingers press into the denim of my jeans.

"Well, Miss Landry," he husks, his hand moving north, "it's a pleasure to meet you officially."

"Didn't we meet *officially* in the shop the other night?" I giggle.

"Nah, that was just us fucking."

Swatting his shoulder, I take a step back and out of his reach. I have to. Otherwise, I'm going to have to get out of these jeans and pull him into the shop bay with me again. "I love how eloquent you are, Mr. Gibson."

Rolling his eyes, he picks up a pen and twirls it between his fingers.

"Hey," I say, grabbing a rag and wiping down the edge of the desk. "I saw on the news this morning there's going to be a meteor shower tonight. Did you see that?"

"Nope."

"It was the top story."

"I don't watch the news. It's all bullshit."

"Then how do you know what's happening in the world?"

"Peck."

"Isn't he full of bullshit too? I don't understand your logic."

This gets a laugh out of Walker. He leans back in his chair, his eyes sparkling. "We need to get a few things straight before this day goes on any further."

Dropping the rag, I circle the desk and plop on top of it. Invoices and papers scatter, a pen rolls off the desk and hits the floor.

"A little respect for the workplace, why don't you?" he asks, wrapping his arms around me and locking them behind my waist. He sits in front of me, nestled between my knees, and lets me take off his hat.

My fingers run through the silky strands of his hair as I breathe him in. "Don't pretend you know what was where on here anyway."

"Maybe I did."

"Whatever," I say.

"I sure as fuck know what's on here now."

He tilts his head back, asking without asking for me to kiss him. So I do. He cups my ass cheeks in his hands, scooting me closer towards him as he takes over the kiss.

Despite my insistence, he moves us slowly against one another, the kiss long and leisurely. He takes his time, his tongue parting my lips in the slowest, most delicious way. He nibbles my lip, refusing to let me do anything back but lap up his attention and bask in the glow of being at the receiving end of his attention.

"Walker," I breathe, resting my forehead against his.

His breathing matches mine breath-for-breath as he pulls me into a straight-up hug. My head falls onto his shoulder, his heartbeat strumming steadily if not maybe a touch elevated. He's warm and strong and I close my eyes, wishing for the first time ever that the world would stop spinning and end with me right here, right now.

But it doesn't.

chapter
Twenty Three

Sienna

FLIPPING OFF THE LIGHT IN the bathroom, I make my way down the hall, my bare feet slapping against the old hardwood. I suspect its original to the house that has to have been built around the turn of the century. The thick trim, small, oddly-shaped rooms, are nothing like the houses I've lived in before.

Running my hand down the wall that was outfitted with a disastrously awful deep green and burgundy wallpaper, I see the holes and marks from the things that hung there previously. Some of them Delaney's.

I glance in her room as I pass, a heap of newspapers and leftover boxes in the middle of the floor. I asked her to leave them since I'll be moving soon. Still, the sight of them sitting where her bed used to sit, where we used to hang out with our laptops and build designs and dreams, makes my loneliness grow.

"This is good for me," I tell myself, shutting Delaney's door. "You've never lived alone. This will build character." Pivoting to my right, I see the half-emptied living room and frown. "Ugh. I have enough character."

My stomach rumbles, but most of the kitchen stuff was Delaney's and I don't have the energy to go figure out something to make with the little I have on hand. The idea of eating alone depresses me, a side effect of being a twin and from a large family, always having someone around in my formative years.

I flop onto the sofa, the one piece of furniture besides my bed that remains. Flip-flopping between going to sleep and going for takeout, I'm undecided when the doorbell rings.

My phone in one hand, a baseball bat in the other, I lament the fact that the door doesn't have a peephole. "Who is it?" I call.

"It's me."

"Walker?"

"Do you have other men swinging by at night?"

Grinning ear-to-ear, I set the phone and bat down and fiddle with both locks. It seems to take forever before I'm able to pull the door open and let my eyes rest on him.

He's dressed in a pair of jeans, a black shirt with blue writing, and a black hat. In his hand is a brown plastic bag.

"Hey," I say, rocking to my heels. "What are you doing here?"

"Well, Nana called and had me come over to check her oil. The warning light went on which means she could've waited until tomorrow, but . . ."

"But Nana's not waiting."

He grins. "Exactly. And she really shouldn't have to. It took fifteen minutes." Raising the bag, he shrugs. "And she made dinner."

"Of course she did," I say, stepping to the side and letting him in. "Don't mind the mess. Or lack of furniture. I'm kind of using this as a bachelor pad, I guess."

He doesn't blink at the reference, just looks around. "I think I'd know this was your place."

"Oh, God, I hope not," I laugh. "It's awful. There's so much I'd do to it if I were staying here."

"So you're not?" He looks at me, the bag crunching in his fingers.

"I mean if I were staying in this house permanently. No, I can't see having a family here someday."

"I see what you mean."

"What would make you think this was mine?"

He walks to the mantle, glancing over the pictures and figurines that are set off-kilter from having been moved when Delaney was taking her stuff. "It feels like you."

"I was just thinking how lonely it feels in here."

"I get that. But I'm talking about the pillows on the couch and picture frames and that blanket over there. It's all very particular. Pretty. Clean."

"You just like me for my organizational skills, don't you?" My stomach growls, reminding me I didn't figure out dinner. "I hope you plan on sharing that food because there's little chance you make it out of here alive with it."

"Actually," he says, shifting on his feet, "I was hoping you hadn't eaten yet."

"Wanna eat with me?" I ask, probably a little too excited for the cause but uncaring because this kills two, maybe even three, birds with one stone.

He heads to the coffee table and plops the bag on top. "We have cheeseburger casserole. Does that work for you?"

"Um," I say, shrugging. "I've never had it."

"You've never had it? Ever?"

"Never. What is it?"

"Perfection." He slips two Styrofoam containers from the bag and places them on the coffee table. Fishing around again, he retrieves two plastic forks and holds them up. "If you have drinks, we're good to go."

"I think I have something . . ." Making a face, I flash him a finger indicating to hang on and disappear into the kitchen. Popping open the refrigerator, I do a quick inventory. One small chocolate milk, three bottles of water, and two bottles of wine. "Ah!"

"Like wine much?"

Giggling, I lean back into his shoulder. "Not really. That was Delaney's. She must've forgotten it."

"You have no root beer."

"Is that what you like?" I ask, inhaling his cologne.

"Yup. But I guess it's water tonight. Unless you think wine and cheeseburger casserole is a good pair?"

I could stand here all night with no food and no drink, just leaning against Walker. "I don't know what it tastes like, so maybe we should stick with water?"

He buries his head in my hair. His hands cinch at my waist as I hold my breath and wait to see what he does. I exhale when he gently shoves away. "Water it is. Let's go."

Grabbing all three bottles, I kick the door shut and follow him back to the living room. He gets settled on one end of the couch and I on the other.

"I grew up eating this," he says, offering me a container. "It's hamburger, cheese, onion, biscuits . . . I don't know what else. But this is my ultimate comfort food."

Laughing, I take the container and pop it open. Scents of the hot meal waft through the air, making my stomach rumble harder. "I love that you used the words 'comfort food.'"

"Nah, Nana said that earlier. I just repeated it."

"Figures," I say, lifting a forkful of the casserole to my lips. Blowing softly, the motion catching Walker's attention, I wrap my lips around the end of the fork and slowly pull it out of my mouth. His eyes go wide ever-so-slightly as I lose myself in the taste of home-cooked food. "Oh my gosh."

"I hope it's half as good for you as this is for me."

"I can taste the onions and cheese and the sweetness from the biscuits," I groan, taking another bite. "This is delicious."

The garlic is subtle, a hint of pepper and a dash of heat that makes me wonder if she used hot sauce, I fall back on the couch cushion and savor it. Closing my eyes, the flavors remind me of my mother, the scents the same that fill the Farm when we all congregate for dinner.

When I open my eyes, Walker hasn't taken a bite. "What?" I ask, swallowing.

"Nothing." He swipes a forkful of casserole and shoves it into his mouth.

"You did that so you didn't have to talk to me."

He makes a face, stopping only to fill his mouth again.

"I guess I'll have to keep talking and then you will have a laundry list of things to answer when you stop eating," I shrug smugly.

Looking alarmed, he washes down his food with half a bottle of water. "I'm done. No need to back me up until tomorrow."

"That's what I thought," I giggle, dragging the fork through the food. "I'm happy you came over here."

"I was in town."

"Walker Gibson, you were not," I laugh. "Nana lives in the country. There's an entire town between her house and here."

"So?"

"So just admit you wanted to come see me," I say, setting my container on the coffee table.

"I . . . might have . . ." he says, messing with me.

"I . . . might have . . ." I mock, standing up. "Had a date tonight."

He sweeps me off my feet, settling me on his lap before I can stop him. Laughing as I get situated cross-ways over his body, I gaze up in to his face.

"Did you?" he asks.

"Did I what?"

"Did you have a date?" He peers down, a crinkle in his forehead, as he searches me for something that convinces him I'm telling the truth.

"If you consider a date with the drive-thru guy a date, then possibly," I wink.

He rests back, one hand flat against my stomach. I'm not sure he even knows he's doing it. It's like he's subconsciously asking me not to get up. I hate to tell him, but I'm perfectly comfortable right where I'm at.

"Pie or cake?" he asks out of nowhere.

I want to ask why he's asking me such randomness, but I don't want to spoil whatever it is he's thinking. "Pie."

"Pepper or salt?"

"Salt bloats. Pepper."

"Television or movies?"

"Depends who I'm with," I say, taunting him.

"Me?"

"Movies."

"Why?"

Clenching my stomach, his fingers flexing against me as I do, my brain immediately goes to the gutter. "They take longer. More cuddle time."

"You want to cuddle with me?" he asks carefully.

"Depends."

"On what?" he says, fighting a smile.

"Casserole or cobbler?"

His eyes light up. "Cobbler."

"But I thought cheeseburger casserole was your favorite comfort food?"

"Have you ever had cobbler?" he deadpans.

"Fair enough. Plane or truck?"

"Depends on where I'm going."

"Can you just answer a freaking question?" I laugh.

He laughs, taking off his hat. Running a hand through his hair, I can't help but notice how relaxed he looks. "Why do you dye your hair purple?"

"I don't know," I say, lifting a strand of colored locks. "Do you not like it?"

"I love it. I just wonder why purple?" He takes the strands from me and slips them between his fingers.

My heart falls a bit as I remember Carrie's face. "I had a friend in California. She was twenty-four and diagnosed with pancreatic cancer," I say softly. "It's a fatal disease and she passed away only nine months after she found out. She was so free-spirited and beautiful and kind and everything good. Purple is the color of that ribbon, so sometimes I just feel like it honors her in the dumbest way." I feel my face flush. "That seems so stupid, doesn't it?"

Instead of laughing or agreeing or ignoring the crack in my voice, he hugs me into his chest and holds me against him. I feel him press a soft kiss to the top of my head. There's something about the gesture, the super sweet way he holds me. There's nothing sexual about it, no overtones or indications this is anything but a man sensing my broken heart and wanting to try to ease it somehow.

We sit quietly on the sofa, wrapped in each other's arms. He draws small pictures on my side from the tip of my sweatpants to just beneath my bra. I can't tell what they are, but I love the way they feel.

"I didn't realize how much you love baseball," he says, the swirls stopping.

"What makes you say that?"

"The thing with Daisy and then there's an Arrows blanket over there and you knew a lot about baseball with Machlan and Lance. You had an Arrows shirt on today too."

"Very perceptive," I say, sitting up and stretching. "I really don't love baseball, but I was an Arrows fan."

"Was? Not anymore?"

Climbing off his lap, I start gathering our containers and putting them back into the bag. Chewing my bottom lip, trying to decide how to tell him Lincoln is my brother, I move to the other side of the coffee table.

I've never been in this situation before. Everyone in Savannah knows who my family is. My friends in California knew too. It's not that it's a big deal to me, but sometimes other people think it is and that makes things awkward. I don't want to do anything to destroy this serenity with Walker, but I can't lie to him either.

So, I go for nonchalance.

"My brother doesn't play for them anymore," I shrug, turning away towards the kitchen. "I don't have to like them now."

"Your brother what?" There's a tinge of disbelief on the end of the question, a rasp to his voice that makes me recenter before speaking or turning around.

After a deep breath, I explain. "My brother, Lincoln, played centerfield for them. I had to like them. Family rules."

Stopping and looking over my shoulder, I see Walker lean forward and balance his elbows on his knees. "Your brother is Lincoln Landry?"

"Yup."

"*The* Lincoln Landry?"

"The one and only," I say with a shrug. "I told you my last name."

"Yeah," he scoffs. "But I had no idea that you were from that family."

"*That family* is my family. It's not a big deal."

"So, that makes your other brother a senator or something?"

"Governor. For now," I add. "He's not running for reelection, so that's about over."

"That's a big deal. I . . ." He shakes his head, like he can't make sense of what I'm saying. "Why didn't you tell me?"

Resting the bag of trash on a stack of boxes near the doorway, I take a deep breath. "Would it have mattered?"

He ponders this, his eyes kind of glassing over as he lets this marinate. Finally, after what feels like a hundred years, he flips his gaze back to me again. "I guess not. But I wouldn't have fed you cheeseburger casserole, for fuck's sake."

"Why not?" I laugh. "It was amazing. Is there anything Nana can't make?"

"No," he agrees. "But you could've had . . ." He shakes his head again, harder this time. "You've been cleaning my fucking office and you're practically royalty."

"Oh, I am not," I huff. "That's tabloid bullshit."

"I'm a little shocked, okay?" he laughs. "This does explain a lot."

"Like what?"

"Like you just paying for MaryAnn and Dave's cars like it was nothing," he says slowly. "You could've just bought them new ones."

"I couldn't because Graham would ask way too many questions," I laugh. "But, yes, now you see why I didn't want you calling the police on me over Daisy. It could've been a big deal."

He nods, standing up. Wiping his palms down his jeans, he takes a deep, labored breath.

"This doesn't change anything," I tell him, panic starting to seep in my tone. "I just wanted to be honest."

"I'm glad you did. Honesty is the best policy, huh?"

Even though he's the one who said it, I have concerns that maybe he doesn't necessarily prescribe to that theory. There's a niggle in my stomach that worries me.

"I always go for honesty," I say. "So you can say goodnight or we can watch a movie. But I'm not discussing the Landry thing anymore."

"Good. Because I don't want to discuss it either. Let's go get some root beer and come back and watch a movie. That is, if you want to cuddle."

"Are you any good at cuddling?"

His eyes darken. "I'll let you be the judge of that."

chapter
Twenty Four

Sienna

"WELL," HE SAYS, STRETCHING HIS arms overhead. My body just moves along with his because I have no intention of getting up. He smells too good. Feels too sturdy against my cheek. Makes all the butterflies swarm like it's the first day of spring in my belly. "Am I a good cuddler or what?"

"The best."

"I was afraid I forgot how," he yawns, scooping me up into his arms again.

"How long has it been since you cuddled someone?"

He moves us side to side in a breezy kind of way, like we're on a hammock somewhere warm with no cares in the world. "I don't know."

"Last week? Month? Six months?" I prod. "Not that I care, just curious."

"I've been with women in the last six months. But no cuddling."

Burying my face in his shirt, I smile against his torso. He chuckles, his chest rumbling. "You like that?"

"Of course I like that," I giggle. "Can I ask you a question?"

"Sure."

"Why me?" I ask, pulling away.

He furrows a brow. "Why you what?"

"Why are you cuddling with me? If it's not your thing."

"I didn't say it wasn't my thing," he says, tilting his chin to the ceiling. "I just said I hadn't done it."

"So . . . why me?"

I think he's going to blow me off. If I poke too hard, he changes the subject or turns it around on me. This time, however, he seems to consider my question. "I don't really know. Whatever I say will make me sound like a pussy."

"I think you're a pussy anyway, so . . ."

He grins, cinching my waist and moving me so I'm straddling him. We face each other. "There was something about you from the night I met you. You were a little mouthy and I was a little mad, but there was this thing in your eyes that I couldn't stop thinking about."

"So it wasn't my ass? Peck said it was my ass."

Laughing, he digs his fingers deeper into my hips. "Your ass is perfect, but that's the thing—that's not what I was thinking about that night or the night after or the night after that. It was that *thing*. Like there was more to you than some drunk girl smashing my headlight out."

"Maybe there is, maybe there isn't," I tease.

"Oh, there is. I've seen it now. You're kind," he whispers, pressing a kiss to my sternum. "And thoughtful," he says, laying a series of kisses from my collarbone up to my ear. "And so fucking sexy."

The last words come out as a growl, making me tremble in his hands. He nips at my lobe, his breath hot against the sensitive flesh at the back of my neck.

"Are you trying to keep me from asking you more questions?" I breathe, melting into him.

"I'm trying to make you forget about whoever cuddled you last."

"Done." Moving my head to the side, allowing him all the access he wants, I rock back and forth as his cock grows beneath me. I can feel it moving, lengthening, the urgency of his kisses growing more frantic as he lets himself unwind. His tongue draws a line to my mouth, his eyes flashing open as our mouths meet in a slow, delicious union.

He kisses me with the ease of a man who knows what he's doing and with the hunger of a man who needs more. His hands roam my body—squeezing my ass, skirting up my shirt and pinching my nipples until they harden between his fingers, cupping my cheeks as he holds me still and kisses me like a cool drink of water on a hot day.

I'm drunk, doused in his spell, lit up with his attention and sated with his tenderness. It's dizzying, my brain befuddled with too many sensations fighting for attention.

"Walker," I moan, tipping my head back as he kisses down my neck. The ends of my hair tickle my waist, my breasts pushed forward as my shirt is lifted. They're freed from the constraints of my pink lacy bra, resting on top of the cups.

When I look up, my breathing ragged, he's smirking. "God, you're beautiful."

"You know what you are?"

"An asshole?"

Rubbing myself against his hardness, I lay a hand on each shoulder. "You can be. So much that I can't stand you," I say, kneading his muscles in my hands. "But you can be protective, like with Tommy at Crave. And caring like changing my oil, and even sweet like how you held me while we watched the movie," I say, trying to drive home my point by refusing to let him look away. "You make me feel good."

"I want to make you feel good, baby."

Before I can process it, his head bends to my chest and sucks a darkened nipple between his teeth. Instantly, I'm wet, my pussy clenching, begging, *throbbing* for contact. I grind against him, swirling my hips as his hands hold on and guide me in slow, small circles.

It's his turn to groan, biting the peak lightly before pulling back and looking at me like he's about to devour me.

"That feels beyond good," I moan, arching my back. My eyes fall closed, unable to hold open as my body switches to life.

"I told myself I was going to go slow," he pants. "Easy. Enjoy it. But damn it if you don't make it hard not to lose control."

Climbing off his lap, I peel my shirt off and toss it to the floor. Emboldened by his words, buoyed by the confidence he bestows by giving me every single ounce of his attention, I don't lose eye contact as I unbutton my jeans and tug the zipper down. In a couple of seconds, they're in my hand and dropped to the side.

There's a rush of breath, a blowing out of a lungful of air that accompanies his shirt flying through the air and landing near mine.

I'm almost naked, my bra and panties the only pieces of fabric still partially covering my body. I turn and face the wall. The sound of denim being discarded, shoes thudding against the floor, is the background music to the sound of blood whooshing by my ears.

I've never stood naked in front of someone before. Even now as I bend at the waist, sticking my ass out for his benefit, and peel the pink lace down my thighs, I wonder why in the world I'm not more self-conscious. I unsnap the back of my bra and feel it pool into my hands just beneath my breasts.

Flipping my head to the side, all my hair falling to one shoulder, I look at him over the other. He's standing, his eyes glued to me, one hand gripping his cock.

The sight of the dot of pre-cum at the head, gaining a little more each time he strokes his impressive length, my legs feel like I've run a mile.

"Can I suck you?" I rasp, not just wanting but *needing* to make him feel as wanted as he makes me feel.

"Don't say that," he growls, squeezing himself harder. "I'll come right now."

He watches me with the intensity of a cat ready to pounce. His eyes strike down my body and up again, leaving a trail of flames in their wake. My mouth goes dry as he takes a step towards me.

My breasts are pulled together, the bra dangling from my hand beneath them. I feel like a vixen, as sexy as a cover model on one of the magazines I used to find hidden in my boyfriends' rooms. I've never felt this way before; it's the most powerful thing I've ever experienced.

I let my hand drop, the bra falling to the floor right along with Walker's jaw. I take the remaining steps between us, and before he can pull away, wrap my mouth around the head of his cock and take him in as far as I can. His semen is warm and salty and coats my mouth before sliding down my throat.

He groans, his head falling back, his hips pressing forward towards my mouth. But as I take him deep a second time, he quickly pulls away.

"I can't," he croaks. "Don't make me come yet."

"Do I have that much control?" I tease, wiping my mouth with my hand.

"Woman, you're in total control. Don't you know that?"

My clit sends a zip of energy through my veins every time I move. My stomach is in knots, wetness streaking my thighs as I feel the desperation for him to be inside me compound to a point I can't control it.

"If that's the case," I tell him, walking over to the couch, spreading my legs a bit wider than shoulder width, and turning my body towards the couch but my head towards him, "Don't take it easy."

"My God," he hisses, walking up behind me. The lines of his abdomen ripple with every movement. The scars dotting his arms and chest from years of manual labor just turn me on more. "You don't want it easy, right?"

"Just fuck me," I beg, my ass popped in the air. "Get inside me and make me come all over you."

He swats my backside, the sound ricocheting through the room. I yelp, only because I'm surprised because the sting, a sweet, sinful kiss, only makes me drip faster down my own legs.

One hand digs into my hip, the other presses on the back of my head. "Head down, sweetheart."

I fold my torso down so I'm resting on my forearms, feeling the cool air hit my pussy. The tip of his cock lines up, only barely parting the lips of my vagina. I'm stretched around him, my body pulsing, trying to drag him in farther. I try to push back but it's met with another swat.

"Will you please fuc—" The rest comes out in a gush as he sinks inside my body in one long, heavy thrust. He hits the back, an explosion of colors lighting up my vision. A hand claws into my ass cheek before moving over and holding my other hip.

He sinks into me again. And again. And a third time, each movement nailing the spot on the back wall of my pussy.

"You're squeezing the fuck out of me," he grits. "Are you doing that on purpose?"

"No," I gasp, the force of him behind me all but taking my breath away. "Keep moving."

"Damn you."

Our skin slips by the other, our bodies slapping as he builds me up like an expert craftsman. My arms begin to go numb, my legs threatening to give out, as I fall forward into the cushions and use them to help keep me propped.

I know it's going to end soon; I can't continue much longer. Every part of me is worked into a luxurious dance of hums and screams as I rise to the point of no return.

"I have to stop," he groans, "or come. What will it be?"

"Keep. Going," I pant, my feet almost coming off the floor. "Right there, Walker. Right there!" I scream into the cushions as a shot of energy tries to shoot through the top of my head. My legs shake just like they describe in raunchy rap songs, pulsing to a tune I can't hear over the orgasm ripping through every cell of my body.

I hear him moaning behind me as he finds his own relief. Somewhere I register the burn of his hands in my hips. There's a part of me that picks up the sweat dripping down our bodies and the scent of sex that permeates the air.

He thrusts one final time before slowly removing his cock. I fall into the couch in one very un-ladylike fashion, unable to keep my eyes open.

"Hey," he whispers. His hand brushes a strand of damp hair out of my face. When I open my eyes, I see him kneeling beside me. "Are you okay?"

"Do I look okay?" I ask, my throat burning. "I look awful, huh?"

He presses a kiss to my forehead. I rest my head against his, relishing in the safety of being in his arms.

"You look prettier than I've ever seen you," he says. "Can I put you in the bath?"

"You don't have to do that," I tell him sleepily.

"I know. But I'd like to do it."

"On one condition."

He chuckles, standing back up. "Of course there's a condition."

"You have to take one with me."

I wait for his answer, but it doesn't come right away. Finally, I twist my head to see him. His face is somber.

"Well?" I ask.

He still doesn't answer. Instead, he bends down and lifts me up, cradling me in his arms. "Let's go, Slugger."

chapter
Twenty Five

Sienna

"F UCK."

The sound of a male voice next to me as I switch from dreaming to awake is startling. Convinced I'm ready to be murdered, I jump.

"Good morning." His voice is rougher than usual, indicative of the long night we spent having sex, laughing, talking, eating, and repeating all of it until our eyes got so sleepy we fell asleep in each other's arms as the sun began to rise.

He kept telling me he wouldn't stay, that he'd have to go at some point, but we'd get distracted by a tale of our youth or how many pieces of heat-up bacon we could eat or how soft our lips are against different parts of our bodies.

It was the best night of my life.

Walker is lying on my left, between me and the nightstand, his phone held up in the air over his head. He's not looking at the screen, though. He's looking at me.

"Don't," I groan, squeezing my eyes shut.

"Don't what?" he laughs.

"Don't look at me." I start to pull the covers over my head when he snatches them away and tosses them halfway down the bed. "You're a jerk."

"You've said that before. I'm also late to work."

"That rhymes. Late to work, you're a jerk," I yawn.

"This rhymes too. Give me a kiss, or I'll be pissed."

"That doesn't rhyme," I note, repeating it back to him. "See? Try this: I'll give you a lick, you give me dick."

He laughs, his phone dropping to his chest. "Sometimes you seem so cultured. Other times, you're a cavewoman."

"I don't hear many complaints."

"Okay, let's try this one. Let's go to dinner, make me a winner."

"Ooh," I say, kicking my feet until the blankets cover them. "I like that one. It makes it sound like I'm a prize."

"That," he says, groaning as he moves to kiss me, "is a fact."

Our lips touch in the simplest, sweetest way. There's no urgency this time, no desperation to connect in as many ways as possible. It's like that's been screwed out of our systems and now we're on the other side. What that means, I have no idea. But I love the way it's working out so far.

"Peck has a tractor coming in this morning. He just sent me a text," he says, rolling out of bed. "I have to run home first and grab some clean clothes." He slips on his jeans and shirt from last night before rummaging around under my bed for his hat. Sliding it on his head, pulling it snug, he holds his hands out in front of him. "You coming in later?"

"Maybe."

Shaking his head, he heads to the door but stops in the doorway. "I'll be there in about an hour."

"Just go in there like that," I say. "Your clothes look fine to me."

His eyes hood. "They smell like your pussy."

"Walker!" I exclaim, pulling the covers over my head.

The bed bounces as he jumps on it, locking me in with one hand on either side of my mummified body. His breath is hot against my cheeks from the other side of the blanket. "How can that embarrass you?"

"It just does."

"Well, for the record, I love the smell of your pussy." He exaggerates the word, his mouth forming every syllable against the fabric. "But

I wouldn't get anything done and God forbid Peck ask me why I was licking my shirt all day."

"Go on," I giggle, moving my body to encourage him to get up. "Get to work, slacker."

The blankets rip down again. We're face-to-face, his eyes twinkling. "Will you go on a date with me tonight? Like, to dinner or a movie or whatever it is people do on dates?"

"Are we going to Nana's?" I tease.

"If you want. She'd love that. But I'd rather take you to this place on the other side of Linton. I haven't been there in forever and I think you'd like it."

Leaning up, I wrap my arms around his neck and pull him to me. "I'd love to."

Like a little boy on Christmas morning, his cheeks split. "I'll be looking forward to it."

A kiss that smacks my cheek, a vibrating mattress as he leaps off, he's out the door and in his truck before I can say goodbye. It's just as well. If he would've stayed much longer, I probably wouldn't have let him leave at all.

Walker

"'BOUT TIME YOU SHOWED UP." Peck flips off the water and dries his hands off on a towel. "I got the tractor coming in any minute. They came for the SUV this morning and I got two more in and out already."

"Good deal."

I walk straight through the garage bay and make a beeline for the lobby, knowing the inquisition is coming and not wanting to face it yet. Whatever this is between Sienna and I is wild, like a truck on an incline with no brakes. I don't know how it's possible to keep it from running away and talking about it with Peck seems like the worst idea in the world.

As I expect, he chases after me like the pain in the ass he is.

"You know," he says, the door closing behind him, "I've worked here for four years or so and I don't think I've ever beat you to work once. Not

even the time you had pneumonia. I beat you today by two hours. *Hours.*
That's like a hundred and twenty minutes."

"Good job."

"Cut the shit, Walker," he laughs. "What's going on? Were you with
Sienna?"

"Is that really any of your business?"

"You're goddamn right it's my business," he says, bewildered. "I've
gone through a lot of shit with you. I've held your hand, gave you that
little push you needed to get her in here. Hell, I'm practically Cupid at
this point."

"Will you shut the fuck up?" I laugh, picking up a pen and throwing
it at him. He ducks, of course, and it misses him by a mile. He pops back
up and grins. "You aren't going to, are you?"

"Do you know how long it's been since you acted like this?"

"Like what?

"Like the world isn't ending. Like maybe you know how to smile.
Like maybe you are—dare I say it?—happy?"

Planting my hands on the desk, I sigh. "You're acting like a girl."

"Nah, I think you just have pussy on the brain."

I wait, telling myself to stop talking, but go ahead and do it anyway.
"Damn right I do."

Peck fist pumps around the lobby, doing the little dance he does at
Crave that promptly gets him ejected. I usually find it completely juvenile
but today it's entertaining.

The door opens and old man Dave comes in. Peck almost runs into
him in a variation of the Moonwalk, making Dave's face light up like the
sun.

"Well, what's happening in here?" he chuckles. "I haven't seen this
much activity in this place in years."

"Peck's about to lose his job," I joke, coming around the corner.
"How are you, Dave?"

"Good, good." He places a hand on the wall and braces himself. "Can
one of you run out and check my oil? Damn light keeps coming on and I
tried to check it this morning but didn't have any oil at the house anyway.
Ended up burning my arm on the radiator."

"I got it." Peck pats Dave on the shoulder and disappears into the parking lot.

"Need a seat?" I ask, dragging the chair from the desk around for him to sit. He falls into it with a thankful sigh. "How're things other than the oil?"

"Not bad. The wife had a good morning. We talked a few minutes about a dog we had back in the seventies," he laughs. "She can't remember me most times and doesn't remember Noodles, the dog we've had since Nellie died. But she remembers Nellie, a Reagan-era Pomeranian. So funny what people remember, isn't it?"

"I guess we remember the good times, right?" I offer. "Maybe Nellie was her favorite?"

"Oh, she was. Just like that girl in here is yours." He looks around the lobby and then back at me. "Where is she?"

"Who?"

"The cute one. Purple hair. Sweet as can be. You know who I mean," he cackles, patting my leg. "The one you can't take your eyes off of. I see you watching her. Even if I didn't, this whole place is changed in a way that only a woman can do."

I open my mouth to protest, to say his crazy assumption is as false as a three-dollar bill, but there's no use. He's been around enough to see through bullshit.

Taking a deep, battered breath, my arms tired from holding Sienna against the wall last night as I made her squirt all over me, I look at Dave. "She's not in this morning."

"But she's still here, right? Still working for ya?"

"Yeah. For now."

"Let me ask you a question, son. Are you in love with her?"

"What kind of question is that?" I snort, rising to my feet and putting distance between us.

"An important one."

"I haven't known her long enough to be in love with her."

I think back to how long we've known each other, how many days since she hit Daisy with the bat. It all becomes a tangled mess as her face keeps popping through the mental calendar, making me smile.

"Love isn't confined to time." He waits to continue until I look up. "Just like if someone passes, like your mother and father, that doesn't mean your love stops. Right?"

"Yeah."

"It goes on," he says, his arms moving through the air to illustrate his point. "Love starts the same way. People say love at first sight isn't real. How could it be? How could you love someone before you ever say a word?"

"It's bullshit," I say without the oomph behind it that would've told him, and me, that I believed that.

"Not when you get all scientific," he says, cringing as he readjusts himself on the chair. "Let's think of it this way—do you make a choice to love Nana? Or Blaire? Or even Peck? Even if you got mad at them, and I suppose you do from time to time, do you have to choose to love them?"

"No. They're my family."

"Exactly. That kind of love is born inside you. You're born with an energy that connects to someone else's, and for reasons we will never understand, you're brought together and it isn't a choice anymore. That's true love."

"I don't know about that," I say, forcing a swallow.

"I do. True love isn't something you pick; it's something the universe picks for you. It's like you're born knowing this woman can cook your sausage patties the way you like, will humor your Thursday night poker games, and will stand by your side as you fight whatever life throws you just because you're you. For no other reason. That," he says, jabbing a finger my way, "is true love."

A chill stirs in my stomach, forcing me to look away. All I can see is Sienna in her sleep and remember how I laid there all night wondering how I could capture the moment for the rest of my life, because as crazy as it sounds, it felt like the place I was meant to be.

I tried to picture her as someone else. I pretended to be home and alone. I thought about never seeing her again, never hearing her laugh, or watching her blush as I call her out on something. And all of that, every single thing, was unbearable.

My stomach roils, knowing she's said she might leave town. Every part of me objects. There's not a piece of me that would want to watch her go but I'm not in a place to ask her to stay.

"You've been through a lot," Dave says, bracing a hand on the wall and standing slowly. "Don't you think it's time to be happy? The woman before Sienna . . . I remember you with her. No good, Walker. No good."

"Yeah, well . . ." I shrug, not sure what to say and wishing she didn't exist in any capacity.

He looks around, a smile stretching across his lips. "I've haven't seen this place so bright and cheerful since your mother would come in the first week of the month and clean up after your father," he laughs. "I'd come in with some of the guys on Saturday morning and drink some coffee and shoot the breeze. Those were good days."

"I remember you all doing that," I recall.

Peck's voice sounds outside the door, and Dave turns to grab his wallet.

"Don't worry about it," I tell him. "It was just a quart of oil or so."

"Are you sure?"

"You kept Peck busy and out of my hair for five minutes. I really owe you."

We exchange a smile, a nod to a conversation we both know dug a lot deeper than either of us let on. He turns to go, his hand on the door, when I call out.

"Hey, Dave."

"Yeah?"

"Thanks."

With a final nod, he disappears into the parking lot as Peck walks back in.

"Just a quart and a half," he says, wiping his brow. "Getting warm out there."

Shuffling papers around, I think about what Dave said. I am happy right now. I didn't think I'd ever be, but damn it—I am. And I don't want to ever let it go.

"Do we still get a phone book?" I ask Peck. "They used to throw one at the door every six months or so. Do they still do that?"

"Fuck if I know. Why?"

My eyes close, my hands go still, as I force a swallow. I picture Sienna getting in her car and driving away, the guilt and hopelessness that swamps me is something I can't deal with even pretending.

"I think it's time I settle this shit," I say. "No, I know it is."

Peck nods, knowing exactly what I mean. "It's about fucking time."

"I don't know where to start. I mean, I haven't given a fuck about it in so long, God knows where to even look."

He pauses, his hand on his hip. "You could call Blaire. She'd drop anything to help with this. She might even come home to deal with this."

"I almost don't want to call her to give her the satisfaction," I laugh.

"Just do it," Peck says, watching the tractor pull into the parking lot. "You handle the problem, I'll handle the tractor."

He pops open the door and disappears in to the parking lot.

With Blaire's name staring at me on my phone, I sigh. "A tractor has never looked so easy."

chapter
Twenty Six

Sienna

WE PULL UP TO A little log cabin that isn't much bigger than a single-family home. The porch is oversized, probably half the size of the cabin itself, and stretches along the front. Whiskey barrels of flowers in all sorts of colors line the walkway to the steps that lead up to the porch, solar lights stuck inside the simple but cozy landscape that immaculately dresses up the front.

Walker shuts off the ignition and then grips both hands on the steering wheel. He takes in the surprising amount of cars lined up in rows.

"It's pretty busy," I note, hoping to ease his nerves if he didn't make reservations. "I'm always good with take-out, you know."

"We have a seat." He says it like it's silly to consider he didn't call ahead.

"Then what's the matter?"

"You want to sit here and ask questions?" he grins. "Or go in and eat?"

"You know me," I say, opening my door over his objection. "I'm always ready to eat."

His joke was a distraction, but from what I don't know. I push it away and take his hand as he comes to my side, ignoring his annoyance that

I opened my own car door, and step onto the gravel. He doesn't let go.

My hand enclosed in his palm, we walk along pots of daisies. His cologne is different tonight, more outdoorsy. It's more rugged than usual, and while I love it, I wish he hadn't worn it. It's hard enough to keep my hands off him.

A button-up shirt is tucked neatly into a pair of jeans, a pair of work boots free of grease on his feet. I've only seen men like this on television or in magazines growing up, and I get it now. There's something primal, something instinctive, about being with a man like him. Like he could catch a fish if I were hungry or fix my car if I were stranded. I'm no damsel in distress, my father ensured I'd always have the tools to take care of myself, but I can't deny how much I adore the feeling of being . . . safe.

As he looks at me over his shoulder, a private smile sliding across his lips in the same way Dominic looks at Camilla or Lincoln looks at his wife, I realize it may be something else too. Something deeper, something I wasn't sure I'd ever find.

A hostess is set up just outside the front door. She checks Walker's name and leads us inside. Candles glow everywhere, the lighting soft and sweet as we get situated at a table along the wall in the back.

"This place is adorable," I tell him, studying the fishing scene on the wall above us. "Thank you for bringing me here."

"This was my mom's favorite place. I haven't been here since she died. Didn't even know it was still open until I called this morning."

My heart melts at his words, that this is the place he'd choose to take me for dinner. A place that means something to him. "I'm honored."

"I hope you like meat and potatoes."

A waitress approaches, takes our drink orders and hands us menus. With a little too much attention placed on Walker for my liking, she struts away. He seems to notice my annoyance.

"She seems nice," he says, burying his head in the menu.

"I might have to walk her to her car if she keeps it up."

"Do you have a bat I don't know about?" he snickers.

"So funny," I say, rolling my eyes for effect. "What are you ordering? What's good?"

"Well, being that I haven't been here in forever, I'm going with the steak cooked medium and a baked potato with extra butter and no sour cream. You?"

"Probably the chicken breast. But if you like steak," I say, setting my menu down, "one of these days I'll take you to Hillary's House. They marinate them with kiwi, I think. Like they rub it on there and lets it sit overnight. It's delicious."

"Is that around here?"

"No," I blush, realizing what I'm doing—considering spending time with him in the future. "It's in Savannah."

He fidgets in his seat and I do the same in mine.

"I didn't mean to insinuate anything," I say. "I just . . ."

"Have you given more thought to your brother's offer?"

"Yeah. I'm still not sure." The struggle that sweeps through me every time I think I have the right answer to Graham's offer pelts me again. There's a wide swath of pride that makes me want to wear a sign that says he asked me, just so people know. Then there's reality.

Going to work for him would feel like a failure despite the victory it also carries. It means I gave up on my dream. It means I need him to be successful. It means I'd be stuck there for the rest of my life because I could never quit. I could never fail or bail on Graham.

There would be no more random travel, no more doing anything that's not on my schedule.

No more Walker.

"It's a pretty great offer," Walker notes, his words weighed carefully.

"Yeah, it is. I'm not totally sure it's the right choice for me."

Our drinks are placed in front of us, our orders sent to the kitchen. Walker pays no attention to anything but me.

"I took over my father's company," he says, stumbling through the sentence. "I remember a lot of people," he says, clearing his throat, "thought it was stupid to want to do it for a living. But there's a part of me that really likes being able to carry on that tradition."

"I get it." Those three words seem to mean something to him, his body actually softening as I watch. "I totally understand why you wanted to do that. Especially after he passed. It gives you a connection to your history. That's important. Your kids may even want to work it someday."

"I can't imagine that."

"I can," I laugh softly. "I can see a little Walker in bib overalls bopping around the lobby. It would be so damn adorable. But you'd need to keep little Walker away from little Peck. I can only imagine the shenanigans those two would get in."

Walker laughs the freest sound I've ever heard come from him. "It's little Lance that you'd have to worry about. Trust me."

I take his hand and lace our fingers together. "I told Graham I'd let him know this week."

"Do you want to go?"

"Do you want me to go?"

He takes a deep breath. "I don't want to keep you from doing what you want to do. I don't want to play a part in that decision."

"You don't think I'm taking into consideration leaving you when I think about going to Georgia?" With a final squeeze, I withdraw my hand. "I don't want to make things weird or put pressure on you or jump in too fast, but . . . the thought of leaving makes me really, really sad."

"Then don't go." Something changes and he roughs a hand through his hair. "I don't want you to go. Okay? I have to say it because if I don't and you leave, I'll never forgive myself for not telling you how I feel. But . . ."

"But what?" My forehead creases, my heart thumping in warning that this isn't a normal "but." "But what, Walker?"

"Nothing. I don't want you to leave."

Our plates are put in front of us, the scents of basil and garlic floating through the air. We pull our attention to our meals, avoiding the elephant in the room.

I'm ready to take a bite when Walker speaks.

"I want you to know that I want to be with you," he says, his eyes shining. "Only you. No other women. I want you to come to church and Nana's and let me take you to dinner and for you to bring me lunch at work just so I can kiss you in the middle of the day."

"Does this mean I'm fired?" I joke through tears that start to fall down my face at his sweet words.

"This means you're promoted," he laughs, shrugging. "I don't know what the fuck it means, to be honest. It's just me telling you how I feel so you can make whatever decision you want to make off it. There are things we'll have to figure out, but none of that matters if I let you go without you knowing. Right?"

"Right." I get up from my seat and walk around the table and slide into the chair next to him. He folds me into his arms, pulling me to his chest, and holds me in the middle of the restaurant. The clinging of silverware and hushed conversations of the other patrons suddenly don't exist. It's just me and Walker. "This is my favorite place in the world."

He holds me for a long moment, letting his sturdiness be the rock he seems to know I need. When I pull away a few moments later, he clears his throat. Something about it makes my skin prickle and I furrow my brow in anticipation of his words.

"I'm going to be leaving town for a few days coming up," he says, wrestling with each word. "I'll be gone a couple of days, a few at most. But I'll be back."

"Where are you going?" I go back to my seat, my food forgotten.

"I just have a few things to take care of that are overdue. I'll explain when I get back. I just wanted you to know."

"Okay." A sense of uneasiness settles over me, but is washed away with the simple way he touches my cheek. "Can I do something now that you've asked me to stay and promoted me?"

"What's that?" he smiles.

"I want to buy new towels for the shop."

He shakes his head, picks up his fork, and goes into a long lecture about frivolous spending that's both irritating and so freaking adorable I can't quite handle it.

chapter
Twenty Seven

Sienna

THE WEEK HAS GONE BY fast, the shop bustling with work and laughs and muffins. I've found myself there every day. Some of those days I wasn't supposed to be. I was supposed to be looking for a new place to rent since my lease is coming up or having lunch with Delaney. Instead, I've ended up at some point at the desk in Crank with a smile on my face.

The customers know me now. The old men that come in on Saturday mornings wearing their seed catalogue logo hats and cans of tobacco in their pockets bring me goodies. They entertain me with stories of Walker as a child, the "good old days" as they call them when Walker's dad, who seems to be more like him than his brothers, ran the shop. There are stories of coal mining explosions, tales of Vietnam, arguments over who makes the best lemon pie in town and who remembers the basketball game where the Linton Wildcats came in runners-up in the state tourney even as the smallest school in the state with a team.

I've been invited to an ice cream social at the Methodist church, a book club at the library with Ruby, to help Mr. Mitchell's wife bake ten pies for a raffle, and even filled in one day at Carlson's during the lunch rush when I stopped to get Walker and Peck a sandwich. Each day that goes by is another day that I fall in step with the sleepy town that's starting to win me over.

Walker taps on the window from his backyard and winks before disappearing again.

I think I've already started to fall in love with him.

I wipe off the counters in his kitchen, listening to him and Lance laugh outside the open window. My heart sings as I clean up the meatloaf lunch I had to call my mom and get the recipe for.

The kitchen is small and is in desperate need of a loving touch, but I'm afraid Walker will have a coronary if he comes in and I've completely redone the whole thing in one day.

When I was here earlier this week, I folded all the washcloths in the drawer and reorganized the silverware, putting them all back in the little compartments of the divider. Emboldened that he didn't say anything from that, I quietly redid the cabinet he had shoved full of plastic cups and container lids.

The front door squeals as it opens, Lance's laugh ringing through the house. Drying my hands off on a towel, I mosey through the kitchen and into the living room with the guys.

"Did you get the weed-eating done?" I ask, kissing Walker on top of the head.

"I did," Walker answers. "Lance sat on the mower playing with his dating app."

"You use a dating app?" I laugh. "Seriously?"

"Hell yeah. It's great. Women are so much more open about what they like without being face to face."

"But how do you know if you like them?" I ask, sitting on Walker's knee.

"They post a picture—sometimes of their faces, sometimes of their . . . you know," he grins devilishly. "You can see what you like and go from there."

"Oh my God."

"Wanna see some?" he asks, reaching for his phone.

"No," I flinch. "I don't want to see that. I can't get over the fact you look at . . . that," I say, making a face, "and then meet them and . . .""

"Fuck?"

Walker works his way around me until his hand is pressed against my stomach. I put my own hand on top of his, feeling his fingers flex against my shirt.

"Why don't you just meet a nice girl somewhere?" I ask Lance. "I have friends I could introduce you to. Nice ones. Pretty ones. Ones that like to have sex as much as you."

"I'm open to that."

"Don't do it," Walker chuckles. "They might never look at you the same again, Slugger."

"They also might consider you the best friend in the universe," Lance shrugs. "I don't want a relationship. Too . . . that." He nods towards our hands. "I don't want that."

"But you want to pick the girl you spend time with by the look of her vagina?" I ask.

"I don't always pick them like that," he scoffs. "Just the ones that look tight."

"Enough," I laugh, getting to my feet. "I can't deal with this."

"I'm leaving." Lance rises too, stretching. "I swiped for a little get together with a redhead this afternoon."

"Enjoy." I give him a little wave and head back to the kitchen. I no more than hear the door shut when Walker is twirling me around. "Hey you," I whisper, the sight of him all sweaty taking my breath away. "Want some dessert?"

"Why'd you think I came in here?"

"I was hoping for me," I admit, trying to ignore the butterflies taking flight in my belly.

"Damn right for you."

He backs me up to the counter, kissing me the entire time. His lips taste of salt and heat, a precursor of all the things I want him to do with them. Before I'm ready, he breaks the embrace.

"I wasn't done," I pout, trying to pull him to me again.

"Before I sit you on this counter and eat your pussy," he grins just before his face sobers, "I want to tell you something."

"Okay. What is it?"

"Two things, actually."

"Hurry up so I can say yes. You promised things."

He grins, but doesn't quite laugh. "I told Machlan we'd come by Crave tonight. I haven't seen him in a while and he wanted to catch up on a few things before I leave town . . . which is the second thing."

My throat squeezes shut, something about the look in his eye makes me nervous. "Right, I remember. For how long?"

"Hopefully I'll be back Monday. That's the plan."

"So just the weekend?"

"That's the plan," he reiterates. He brushes a strand of hair out of my face, then runs both hands across my head and pins my hair away from my face. He looks at me like he's never seen me before, like he's trying to memorize everything about me in just a few seconds. "When I get back, I want to sit down and talk. For real."

"We can't do it now?"

"Do you want to do it now?" He licks his lips, reminding me of his promise.

"No," I giggle, hopping up onto the counter.

"That's what I thought."

He slides between my legs. "This is the first time you've ever opted not to talk."

"Now you know how to shut me up."

He laughs, dipping his lips to touch mine. Even though it's not what he promised, I'll take it.

chapter
Twenty Eight

Sienna

"WHICH ONE OF YOU TOLD Blaire about the dating app?" Lance eyes his brothers and then Peck. "Was it you?"

Peck holds his hands up in front of him. "Wasn't me. I haven't talked to her in a couple weeks, not since I needed to know the legal ramifications of borrowing Kip's Sheriff cruiser."

"Why did you do that?" I laugh, snuggling against Walker's shoulder. He strokes my arm, leaning his cheek against my head while we listen to his family.

"It's a long story that really won't come out right," Peck winces. "You had to be there."

"What did Blaire say?" I ask.

He shrugs, bringing a bottle to his lips. "She called Kip. I don't think he's coming after me or anything."

"Back to the topic at hand," Lance says, "which one of you told her about the app? I got sixty-two texts from her today, detailing the hazards of using an app and meeting people online."

"Like she hasn't fucked some dude she met online," Machlan snorts. "I don't believe that bullshit for a second."

Nora places a hand on Peck's shoulder as she looks around the table. "Anyone need anything? Sure is quiet up there without you, Mach. The women don't want to talk to me, I guess."

Machlan smirks, his eyes as dark as Walker's are sparkling. "Give 'em enough whiskey and you can get them to do whatever you want."

"Ew," she says, wrinkling her nose. "I think I'm going to puke."

Peck scoots away from the table, taking his bottle with him. "Come on, Nora. I'll go talk to ya."

The bar is quiet for a Friday night; the "regulars," as Machlan called them, are the only ones in the place. The music isn't too loud, the chaos not as crazy as it has been in times past. I keep looking around for Tommy, but Machlan assured me he hasn't shown his face again since Walker rearranged it.

As if he knows what I'm thinking, he kisses the side of my head. "You okay?"

"I'm good," I say. Glancing around at the Gibson boys, Machlan giving Lance hell about a woman they both apparently know, Peck at the bar entertaining Nora, I realize just how good I am.

"What are you thinking?" Walker asks, his mouth pressed against my temple.

"I'd like to bring my sister here someday. She wouldn't have a clue what to do with your brothers, but she'd get a kick out of Peck," I say. "I should bring her in the winter and make her see what I've been dealing with up here."

"I love the winter," Walker says.

"You what? How could you? It's horrible."

"This year we're taking you to Bluebird," Machlan says, leaning forward. "It's old stripper hills that we've been sledding since we could walk. Funnest shit you'll ever do. Even Mr. Lame here goes."

"I'm not lame, you asshole," Lance snorts. "I'm often busy with work-related responsibilities."

Machlan looks at him out of the corner of his eye. "I know what you were doing and it had nothing to do with history."

"It's history now," Lance grins before taking a long drink of his beer. "But, yeah, we'll take you out there, Sienna. You'll love it. We fill thermoses up with hot chocolate and spend the day out there acting like idiots."

"Grown men sledding?" I laugh. "Do you go, Walker?"

"I usually take a car hood or two to use as sleds," he shrugs. "Don't knock it until you've tried it."

"Look at these pics from last year . . ." Machlan digs out his phone and starts swiping through the list. "Come on. Get over here, Slugger."

"Not you too," I whine, untangling myself from Walker. Moving around the table, I look at Machlan's phone. Pictures of all of them in the snow, bundled up in overalls and beanies, trying to go down this ginormous hill fill the screen. There are snaps of snowball fights, a little blood in the snow from a busted lip, and someone trying to stand on one of the car hoods.

It looks like one of the best days ever.

"That's amazing," I tell them, pausing on a picture of them with their arms around each other. "We need to print that."

When I look up at Walker, his eyes are trained over my shoulder. My smile fades as his jaw drops slowly towards the table.

"What?" I ask. Looking at Lance, he's looking the same direction. "What's going on, guys?"

I turn around to face the door, my heart sinking. Scanning the bar, from Nora and Peck to the wall of beer signage and mirrors on the other, there's nothing there. Just a group of people that have been there all night.

Just as I'm about to ask the guys what they're seeing, a ripple of goosebumps, a warning from something in my psyche, rolls through my body. It's so hard, so violent, that I actually shiver.

Then I see her. A woman with inky black hair that's cut into a bob with high cheekbones heading our way. Her steps are slow and pointed, her pink lips twisted into a "gotcha" formation. An eruption flares from my soul, a fire-breathing dragon shooting towards the woman walking towards us.

My shoulders go back, my face deadening in a self-preservation mode I've managed to develop over years of being in public situations with people I dislike. You stand still. Smile pretty, don't sweat it. Sweating it gives them an advantage.

Never lose the advantage.

"What did you do now, Lance?" I joke, but I'm not sure any of them hear me. I move away from Machlan and head towards Walker when I stop mid-step.

"Hey, honey," she says, a swagger in her shoulders as she looks at Walker. "I'm home."

Machlan's hand steadies me, resting on my forearm as I grab the back of the chair in front of me. Walker doesn't look at me. Neither does Lance. Nothing happens except Machlan angling himself between her and me, the same way he did the night Tommy grabbed my elbow.

"What are you doing in here?" Machlan roughs.

"It's nice to see you too," she grins. "What's happening, Lance?"

He looks at me, and despite her greeting towards Walker, despite the sickness curling my stomach as she walked this way, it's in this moment buried in Lance's eyes that I know this is much worse than I even imagined.

"Is this her?" she asks, tilting her head towards me. She looks at Walker with a familiarity that pierces my heart. He returns her stare with a level of intimacy that goes ahead and hammers my heart into pieces.

"What's going on?" I ask.

Walker steels, bracing as if he's about to be hit with a tidal wave at the last second. Jaw set, forearms flexed, shoulders broad and wide, I check off all the subtle ticks I know he has when he feels unsure. With each thing, my lip begins to quiver a little more.

"Sienna . . ." His voice wobbles, so unlike him. There's fear in his eyes as he pleads with me to wait a minute. To not press. To give him the second he's always asked me for.

"Sienna," the woman sighs. Sticking out a hand, she gives me the foulest, most saccharine-sweet smile I've ever been given. "It's a pleasure to meet you. I'm Tabby Gibson. Walker's wife."

"What?" I whirl around, shaking my head like I can shake off her words. Her insinuations. Her . . . truths? "Walker?"

It's in the bow of his chin, the drop of the corner of his mouth, the falling of his shoulders that gives me all I need. I open my mouth but nothing comes out.

My heart hits so hard, as if the staccato will somehow clear the confusion riddling my brain and allow me to understand what's happening.

My hand shakes as I look up at Machlan. "What's going on?"

The longer I wait for the answer, the more I bleed right in front of them all. Their eyes are on me, watching me absorb a truth they all knew.

A loneliness I've never known, a loneliness I can't imagine ever matching, takes over and tears begin to streak down my face. Tabby stands next to Walker, her arm resting on his shoulder so a diamond can be seen sitting on her left hand. He knocks it away, panic settling across his features, but I don't care.

Humiliated, her laugh behind me, I race towards the doors. Wiping away tears, ignoring Peck's call, refusing to even try to hear what Machlan is yelling behind me, I shove open the door and walk into the night.

I go north only because Walker's truck is south. My shoes click against the concrete as I half-jog, desperately needing to put distance between myself and whatever the hell that was. I don't know where to go. Who to call. What just happened.

A small patch of grass sits in front of Dr. Burns' office and before I can stop myself, I fall onto my knees in the damp blades and cry.

An arm goes around my shoulders. It's too thin, too narrow, smells too much like cedar. "Go away, Peck."

"Goddammit, Sienna," he sighs, pulling me into his arms.

"Is it true?" I ask, sniffling snot as the tears refuse to quit.

"Yeah, but it's not what you think."

"If the answer is 'yeah,' it has to be what I think."

Walker's energy finds me before he does, my body tugging towards his. I don't look up. I don't have to. I feel him kneeling towards me and his hand stroking my back. I pull away and into Peck, earning a growl from Walker.

"Peck, give us a second," he says.

"No," I insist. "Don't, Peck. Please don't leave me."

"Sienna, let me talk to you." Walker's voice sticks the knife in further. "Please, baby."

Sitting up straight, I look at him. The tears have stalled, an effect of the adrenaline, and in its place is all I can describe as rage.

My whole body trembles, actually shaking like I'm freezing. But I'm not. The longer I look at him, the hotter I get.

"You're married?" I ask, my teeth grinding against each other.

"Sienna . . ."

"It's a yes or no question. Are. You. Married?"

"Technically, yes."

"Fuck you." I get to my feet and head back towards the road.

He grabs my arm and spins me around to face him. "Listen to me."

"Yes, I will listen to you. I'll listen to you tell me why you just humiliated me in front of your whole family," I say, my voice shaking. "Does everyone know this? The whole town?"

"Sienna," Peck starts, "calm down."

"Go, Peck," Walker rumbles.

"I told you this was gonna fucking happen," Peck roars, ripping into Walker.

"What was I supposed to do?" Walker barks, his hands clenching at his sides. "I didn't fucking know where she was! How do you divorce a woman who doesn't want to be found?"

"You go find her," Peck seethes. "Like we told you. Like all of us fucking told you!"

"Get out of here," Walker warns.

"Peck," I say, resting my hand against his chest and gently moving him back. "I need a ride home. Will you take me?"

"Of course."

"Can you get your truck and pick me up? I want to talk to Walker alone for a minute."

He watches Walker over my head, pure disappointment scrawled across his face. "You sure?" Peck asks me.

"Yes."

With a final shake of his head aimed at his cousin, Peck stomps back down the road.

"Don't be mad at him," I tell Walker. "He did nothing wrong."

He runs a hand down his face, his eyes wide and full. "Sienna, listen to me. I haven't seen Tabby in four years."

"Tabby," I say, testing her name out on my tongue. "That's your wife, right?"

"Don't make this harder than it is."

"Me?" I ask in disbelief. "You're the one who led me on while you have a *wife*. A wife!" My laughter spills into the night, the sound haunting even to me. "Why would you do this to me? Why would you do this to anyone?"

The tears come again. I breathe in his cologne, look at his handsome face, and realize . . . he belongs to someone else.

"How could you humiliate me like this?" I croak. "What must everyone think? Oh, God . . ." I say, feeling like I might throw up.

"It's not like that," he says, extending a hand towards me. I step out of his reach. "Let me explain."

Spying headlights coming down the road, I shrug in the saddest, most defeated way. "You turned me into the kind of woman I hate. The ignorant, selfish . . ." My words break off, a sob capturing the rest of the thought. I shake off his hug and step towards the sidewalk as Peck nears.

"Sienna, please, don't walk away."

"You have no right to ask that of me," I sniffle. "You have no right to say anything to me."

"I don't love her. I don't want her," he insists. "Please, Sienna. I want to talk about this. Don't walk away."

I'm around the truck before Peck gets it stopped. Climbing inside, I refuse to look at Walker. "Go," I tell Peck.

He rips down the street. Before we turn the corner, I let myself look one last time in the mirror to see Walker standing in the middle of the street looking as broken as I am.

chapter
Twenty Nine

Sienna

"DO YOU NEED ANYTHING, SWEETIE?"

Delaney's mom stands in the doorway of her guest room, a light blue robe tied at her waist. She was so kind when I pulled up, mascara smearing down my face. But seeing her standing here, that maternal aura around her—I just want my mom.

"It's late," I tell her. "Go to bed. I'll be fine."

"Are you sure?"

"Yeah."

"I'll be down the hall if you need me." She steps into the hallway and pulls the door softly behind her.

The late night moon shines in the window of the bedroom I've never stayed in before. As soon as Peck dropped me off at home, I hopped into my car and drove here, not knowing Delaney went to Chicago for the weekend. I knew Walker would come by and I didn't want to see him. As I lie here, alone, so very, very alone, I replay every moment I've had with him over in my mind.

It's unbelievable to think he was married the whole time I was with him. The web of emotions is too tightly strung together to even make sense of them. The anger gives way to embarrassment which opens up to a sadness that I've never felt before.

The tears fall as I think back to twenty-four hours ago and the way Walker held me while he slept. Was all that fake? Did he not believe any of the things he said or mean any of the ways he made me feel?

Why would he do this to me?

A little alarm clock sits by the bed, the red numbering glowing in my face. I lift my phone and press the power button, only to see more texts and phone calls than I can count.

Scrolling through my contacts list, I find the only person who I know will be up at one in the morning and not livid I call. It rings twice.

"Sienna?" Graham's voice is full of concern and that only makes the tears fall again. "Sienna? What's wrong?"

"Oh, Graham . . ." I laugh through the tears, a little sister calling her big brother for help in the middle of the night. How pathetic can one person be in one day?

"What the hell is happening up there?"

"I just wanted to hear your voice."

He laughs. "We both know that's highly unlikely."

"Definitely unlikely." Lincoln's voice comes on the phone as I hear the speakerphone pick up. "What's up, Sienna?"

"Why are the two of you together at one in the morning? Don't tell me Mallory and Danielle kicked you out."

"We had a meeting in Atlanta and were supposed to stay the night but decided to come home," Graham explains. "Lincoln was just dropping me off."

"You let him drive?"

"Not my best choice, but yes," Graham sighs.

"I got us home in about half the time it would've taken you," Lincoln points out. "Stop complaining."

"Anyway," Graham cuts in, "what's up with you? Are you crying?"

"A boy . . ." My voice breaks and I can almost hear my brothers flinch.

"We can be there in a few hours," Lincoln says flatly. "Want me to bring Dominic?"

"No," I laugh through the tears. "You don't need to bring Cam's fighter boyfriend."

"So I can take him on my own?"

"Lincoln, stop," I sigh. "I need logical help here, G."

"I have you," Graham says calmly. "Shoot."

Taking a deep breath, I go for it. "I've been seeing a guy for a while. We've had fun—"

"We don't need this part," Lincoln interjects.

"We've seen each other pretty regularly," I continue. "Every day, really. He's been totally into me, taking me to hang out with his family, I've met his grandmother, and all that. And then I find out tonight that he's married."

"What the hell?" Graham barks. "He's married?"

"Yup."

"I'm gonna beat his face in," Lincoln seethes.

"Shut up, Lincoln," Graham says, his wheels turning. "Did you know this? No, of course you didn't," he grumbles. "Why didn't he tell you?"

"I don't know."

"Did his family know?"

"I guess. I don't really know. Some of them did." I look at the popcorn ceiling and can't even find it in me to want to scrape it off like I usually do. "Why would he do this to me?"

"That's a question you'll have to ask him," Graham says. "If you want to, that is."

Lincoln goes on a rant about how they should come to Illinois and teach him a lesson, Graham firing back that they have to think things through. That they have families now and can't go all crazy like they used to.

I listen to them banter, my mind going to Machlan and Lance. I find myself smiling and then realize they knew too. And not one of them told me.

"Sienna?" Graham asks.

"Yeah?"

"If you weren't pissed, I'd be pissed at you," he says. "But I think you need to give the guy a chance to explain."

"He was married!" Lincoln roars. "Fuck him."

"I'm with Linc."

"Both of you clowns better listen to me," Graham says. "Sienna has never once asked me for advice over a man. She's never called me crying, except for the time she ran over the kitten on Santa Monica Boulevard."

"Oh, don't bring that up," I say, trying not to cry again.

"The point is," Graham continues, "I can tell you care about this guy a lot. So even though he's guaranteed a few head cracks the first time we see him, if we ever do, and more than that if we tell Ford, you need to hear him out. For him, and more importantly, for you."

"You think so?" I ask.

"I know so. Do you remember what a mess Mallory was when I first met her?" Graham chuckles through the line. "She smelled like bacon every morning. Her desk was a disaster. She went on a date once just to make me jealous."

"I knew I loved her," I tease.

"But if I had written her off without giving her a chance, look what I'd have missed out on. Maybe you let the guy go. Maybe you give him another chance. Maybe you come home and get your ass to work for me," he cracks, getting that little slip in. "But get the facts together before you go making decisions. Be smart, Sienna."

"I'll try. Thanks for answering."

"Always. Goodnight."

"Night, G. Night, Linc."

"Love ya, sis."

I hang up, set my phone on the bedside table, and roll myself up in the covers and try to go to sleep.

Walker

I DON'T EVEN BOTHER TO turn on the light.

Sitting in the living room, the darkness surrounding me, I close my eyes and feel my world still crumbling. Sienna wasn't anywhere. I drove by her house, Crank, even Nana's, and nothing. Her phone is off, but I left so many texts and voice messages I wonder if it'll even turn on or just melt down when she tries.

I've exhausted myself. Every muscle in my body aches, every joint flaring from the adrenaline that shoved through my body for so long tonight. But now it's gone. Just like Sienna.

Tugging at my hair, I lift my head towards the ceiling and try to think of something other than the way she looked at me on the grass. Like her heart was broken. Like I'm some kind of monster. Like I did this to her on purpose.

This is heartbreak. As I sit in the unlit room, the organ in my chest responsible for pumping blood to my extremities is actually splintered. I can feel each piece puncturing me from the inside out. I've never felt this fucked up over anything outside of the death of my parents. And, just like that situation, I'm not sure I'll ever recover.

"Fuck," I hiss, tugging once more just to feel the pain before dropping my hands into my lap.

My face feels swollen, my hands achy from being clenched all night. I just want to close my eyes and sleep.

In the quiet, as the rest of the town is tucked happily in their beds, everything kind of settles. Like dust after the wind stops, everything finds its resting spot as I sit alone. Heaps of emotions, piles of mistakes, loads of truths that should've been shared aren't enough to fill the void that Sienna has created.

I should've told her. I knew it then and I know it now, but how could I? How could I tell her I wanted her more than I've ever wanted anything in the universe, but another woman legally has my last name?

Does that make me selfish? Probably. But I did try to stay away from her and keep my distance. I tried so damn hard to not get involved so I didn't hurt either of us, but I couldn't.

And I couldn't tell her the truth because that would ruin everything.

She wouldn't want to be with a married man, even though I haven't seen Tabby in years. Even though I didn't care enough about her when she left to chase her down to sign the papers.

Headlights turn up the driveway. Leaping to my feet, I race to the window to see a little compact car pulled up next to my truck and Tabby walking up the steps. She knocks once, then twice. Not sure of myself, not positive I can rein in my emotions, I wait to see what happens before opening the door.

"Walker, it's me. Open up."

Her voice is so odd. It takes me to days at the lake, planning a family, our wedding on that same lakeshore. What's even more odd is that I feel absolutely dead about it all.

I pull the door open and see her for the second time in years. She looks a little older, still incredibly pretty, her green eyes taking me back to so many years ago.

"Hey," she says, feeling me out.

"What the hell are you doing?"

"Can I come in?"

"No."

"Walker . . ."

I step onto the porch, shutting the house behind me. "What are you doing here, Tab?"

"I . . . I don't know, really."

My gaze settles across the front yard illuminated by the moon, to the spot Sienna and I had discussed putting a hammock. My chest feels like it's caving in and I jump, blasted out of my thoughts, when Tabby speaks.

"It's been a long time." She leans on the railing. "Your place is nice. I had to ask around to see where you lived. Imagine my surprise when I pulled up to our house and realized we didn't live there anymore."

I've waited for this conversation since the morning she walked out. This is the moment in time I've envisioned, when I tell her what an idiot she is, that I hand her the divorce papers Blaire had drawn up way back then and demand she sign them.

This is when I tell her I never loved her, that I knew she was sleeping around, and that I didn't even care enough to go after her. This is the moment I tell her what a bitch she was to leave me when I was dealing with the loss of my parents, that I throw in her face that the shop is still doing well despite her insistence it wasn't a way to make a living.

But now that we're standing here, none of that matters. I don't give enough of a fuck to inflict any pain on the woman, to tell her how I feel, to give a shit where she's been or that she knows my life is better without her in it. All of the things I've waited patiently for don't. Fucking. Matter.

Whipping out my phone, I check the home screen for what does matter. The glow shows no missed calls or texts.

"Why didn't you come for me?" she asks, her voice drifting through the night.

"Why didn't you come back?"

She slumps forward, weighed by the history she and I don't share. "Maybe we were too young to have gotten married."

I glare at her. "You asked why I didn't come for you. You sure as hell knew the way back."

"I'm sorry."

Checking my phone again, there's still no new messages. Bouncing my hand off the railing, I turn and lean against it.

"Who is she?" she whispers.

"None of your concern."

"Being that she's sleeping with my husband, I think—"

"I'm not your husband any more than you're my wife," I warn. "If you think you can trot your sorry ass back in here and act like you have some kind of say in anything I have going on, you have another think coming. And," I say, my voice rising over her start of an objection, "if you say a word about Sienna . . ."

She blanches, not expecting this reaction, and blows out a breath.

"This conversation would've been very different if I could've explained things to her before you came in," I sigh. "But that was probably your plan, huh?"

"She didn't know you're married?"

I just glare at her from the corner of my eye.

"Wow." She twists her earring, looking at anything but me. "I didn't know she didn't know."

"Guess you got a freebie."

"I . . . Damn it, Walker."

"No, damn you, Tabby," I say, spinning around. "Why the fuck did you do this? You don't give a shit about me. You never did. What is it? Do you need something? Were you bored? Just trying to piss me off for old time's sake? Because all of that I can handle. You can ride my ass about still being the poor mechanic at Crank—"

"Walker—"

"You can tell me how I can do so much better than this shitty little farmhouse—"

"Walker—"

"You can tell the entire fucking town I lost my shit when my parents died and almost lost us the house because I drowned myself in alcohol and couldn't get out of bed. You can do all of that and I don't even give a fuck, Tab. But what you just did tonight to Sienna is something even I didn't think you'd do," I growl, stopping to take a much needed breath.

"You think I should give a shit about her?"

I look at the woman I once thought I loved. "Peck warned me. He kept saying I should tell Sienna or go find you and end this sham fucking marriage before she found out, but I didn't. Despite all of their warnings, I didn't think you'd stoop this low. I figured I could wait a while. No sense in finding you if I didn't have to."

Folding my hands together, I press them into my forehead. My temper is creeping through the numbness and I'm not sure how to handle it.

I want to scream, tell her exactly what I think of her, dress her down in ways she's never imagined. But all I can see is Sienna's face and hear her laugh and that takes the fight right out of me. How do you fight with a broken heart?

"You love her, don't you?" Tabby's voice is soft, so soft, in fact, I almost don't hear it despite the peace of the night.

"What does it matter?"

She walks the length of the porch, her arms wrapped around her stomach like it's not eighty degrees outside. I check my phone once more. When I look up, Tabby is looking at me.

"Is she ignoring you?" she asks.

"Wouldn't you?" I huff.

"What are you going to do?"

I hate the way she asks, like there's a simple answer to fix this. Like I can make a quick try to get Sienna back and if that doesn't work, move on.

Fuck her.

"I'm going to get you to sign the divorce papers and then go find her," I say through gritted teeth.

Her features wash, becoming neutral, any sense of kindness or sadness wiping away. "You're going to try to find her?"

"No. I'm not going to try. I'm going to find her," I shrug, clutching my phone like it will prompt her to call me.

"But you didn't try to find me."

"Nope."

She looks out across the night. "Do you think we could've fixed things if one of us had come for the other?"

"If I would've found you, it would've been to get you to sign the papers," I tell her. "I just didn't care enough to even try. Our marriage was over long before you left. We both know that."

"Why didn't you fight for it?" she asks, a single tear rolling down her cheek. "Why didn't you fight for us?"

It's a fair question, even though I could turn it around on her. As I look at her across the porch, the gentle summer breeze playing with the ends of her hair, my heart squeezes with the answer to her question.

"I didn't fight for us then because of pride. I didn't fight for us through the years because of anger. I'm not fighting for us now because my heart is so tied up in Sienna that nothing else exists."

"Maybe we could fix things? Maybe we could fall in love again?" she asks, the words squeezed around the emotion filling the spaces between the words. "I miss you so much."

I hold her gaze for a split second before raising a finger. I go inside, flip on the light, and head to the old secretary's desk that used to be my mother's. There's a file at the bottom of the cavity, the little flags indicating spots for signature. I take it and a black ballpoint pen and head back to the porch.

Tabby is standing in the same spot, black trails streaming down her cheeks.

"I need you to sign here and here," I say, placing the file on a little table and showing her the spots with flags with "TG" tagged on them by Blaire.

She doesn't move. "You're so handsome, Walker. You remind me so much of your dad."

"Tabby . . ."

"I wondered if I'd come out here and you'd start throwing cans of pop out the door at my car the way you and Lance did that night of the bonfire at Tommy Jones'. Remember that?" she grins through the tears. "My God, you guys were horrible."

"He deserved everything he got," I say, remembering that night.

"Yeah, he did." She pulls her hair into a small ponytail at the back of her neck before wiping her face with the back of her hands. "You've really turned into a good man." Her lip quivers, the tip of her nose turning red. "Sienna is a lucky woman."

Without another word, just a sniffle as she tries not to dot the divorce papers with her tears, she takes the pen and signs her name to both spots.

"Tell Sienna I'm sorry," she says, climbing down the stairs. "And Walker?"

"Yeah?"

"I'm sorry to you too."

She gets into her car and backs down the driveway, honking the horn once before speeding away. I pull out my phone again, this time opening the texting app.

There are lines and lines of green text bubbles from the course of the night, all filled with me apologizing, begging her to call, begging her to text, me trying to explain. I don't know what else to even say. Still, I can't help but punching out another one.

> Me: *If you need someone to talk to and don't want to talk to me, call Peck. Please. Just let someone know you're okay.*

chapter
Thirty

Sienna

RAIN PELTS THE WINDOW, A summer storm rolling in just as I got home. Sitting on the sofa, gazing out the window, I wonder if it's a reflection of the weather outside or if I'm just imagining what my heart looks like.

Battered. Gloomy. Branches snapping off as they're flung back and forth.

My coffee went cold a long time ago, but I still grip the mug in my hands. It's like a life raft at this point. Something to root me in the present so I don't get lost in the past.

Climbing into bed earlier, his scent was all over the sheets and pillows. It would've been smart to get right back out. I think logical thinking was lost somewhere around two am. Curling up in the sheets, my face buried in the pillow he used, I whipped back and forth from crying to being so angry my fist hit the mattress again and again. I laid there long enough to get out of it with his cologne on my shirt.

My feet are cold against the hardwood, but I can't bring myself to find socks. If I can just stay in this half-muted state, I'll be better off.

There are so many decisions to be made and I ignore them all. What to do about the upcoming lease? Do I take Graham's offer after all? Do I bother talking to Walker or do I just skip town and forget this place ever existed at all?

Coffee sloshes in the mug as a score of emotions wave over me. The smell of Carlson's bakery, the sweet smile of the librarian, making pies with the little old ladies, and the feel of Crank in the morning all roll by, taunting me that I wasn't part of this place as I once thought.

My phone buzzes next to me and I look down, expecting it to be Walker for the eighteenth time since I woke up and turned it on. There were too many calls and texts last night to even process and I haven't read any of the messages or listened to the voice messages either. I reach for it and see it's Cam.

"Hey," I croak, putting the coffee down.

"Are you all right? Mallory called me this morning and said Graham told her you called last night."

"Yeah." I think back on the phone call with my brothers and squeeze my eyes shut.

"He's married, Sienna?"

"Yeah."

"I . . . I don't really know what to say," she breathes.

"Me either."

I grab an Arrows throw blanket and press it against my cheek. The softness of the fabric just reminds me of the way Walker's shirts feel against my skin. I toss it back on the floor.

"I wish I were there with you," Camilla says. "I hate being so far away when things like this happen. Do you want me to come? I will."

"I know you will," I tell her, expecting tears but they don't come. "But I think I'm going to come home."

She starts to say something, but stops before she gets it out.

"I don't know what to do, Cam," I say, my voice shaky. "Everything I thought was wrong. Everyone here must've been laughing at me. Heck, I'm laughing at myself. Do you know I was thinking maybe I could fit in here? Me," I laugh in a self-deprecating kind of way. "I was drinking the Kool-Aid with a straw."

"Sienna, stop it. There's nothing wrong with hoping for something."

"Yeah, well, I think this proves you wrong."

"No, it doesn't," she scoffs. "Have you talked to him?"

"Why does everyone want me to talk to him?" I say, getting to my feet. I pace the room, trying to stop my toes from freezing. "For the first time in my life, Lincoln is the only one out of you that makes sense."

"Oh, God. You're to the point of listening to Linc?"

"I'm not kidding," I fire back, annoyed at the laugh in her tone. "He's the only one who thinks Walker needs junk-punched."

"Well, junk punch him then. No one is stopping you." She sighs, getting her thoughts together on the other end of the line. "People aren't perfect. Sometimes they mess up. Sometimes they make a plan for things and then things happen that skew that and they don't know what to do. You know, maybe he was going to tell you. Maybe there's a reason he didn't."

I storm down the hallway and rifle through my closet until I come up with a pair of pink slippers. Shoving my feet in them, I sit on the edge of the bed. Looking over my shoulder, I see the messy sheets and moved alarm clock and remember Walker playfully asking me to dinner just a few days ago.

Choking down the bile that's creeping up my throat, I switch the phone in between my hands. "I do think he was going to tell me."

"You do?"

"He was going to go out of town," I say slowly. "I wonder if it had something to do with her."

"You'll never know if you don't ask."

"But does it matter?" I ask. "Can I even look his family in the eye again and know that they let him play me and didn't say a word?"

Her irritation sweeps through the line. "Think about this, okay? And it might not be apples-to-apples, so don't start arguing that it's not the same. I don't know the facts. I'm just making a point."

"Fine."

"Let's say Ford had gotten married when he was young, before he went into the Marines. Let's say the Marines sent him overseas and she left him and he came home preoccupied or something and never got around to finding her. Then let's say he met Ellie and brought her around and we all know he's still married to mystery woman, all right? Do we tell Ellie?"

"No," I say immediately. "It's not our place."

"Exactly. And we love Ellie. We don't want to push her away. She's great for Ford, right?"

Flopping back onto the bed, the stress of this whole thing too much to take, the lack of sleep and throbbing temples too much to work through, I close my eyes. "I need to go, Camilla."

"Are you going to go find him?" she asks, a hint of hope in her voice.

"Nope," I say, barely able to get the words by the dryness in my throat. "Going to sleep. Turning my phone off, so don't panic when I don't answer," I yawn. "I'll call you later."

"Call me if you need anything at all."

"I will. Bye."

"Bye, Sienna."

Walker

THE RAIN HAMMERS THE METAL roof of Crank. It's been a consistent downpour since I pulled up around five this morning. I drove around town and over to Merom and couldn't find her. Couldn't sleep. Couldn't stand the house for another damn minute, so I came here. Peck showed up around six. On his day off. Fucker.

He's kept busy all morning in the shop, tying up a few loose ends and getting shit organized. He's not supposed to be here today and none of the stuff he's doing is urgent. I want to send him home, but I'm afraid if I open my mouth, I'm gonna lash out, and I'm smart enough to recognize that and that Peck doesn't deserve it. I just can't find out how to kick my own ass.

Maybe it's the rain. Maybe it's the feeling of helplessness that's shoved me into a hole. Whatever it is, Crank feels remarkably quiet.

I try to work on a few things, but I can't focus on anything unless the phone rings. That's the only thing that spurs me in to action. As I type in a part number, the ringer goes off and my hopes rise and then fall when I see it's Blaire.

"Hey," I say, bracing myself.

"Good morning. Imagine my surprise when my secretary brings me in signed divorce papers from you at seven this morning."

"Why are you in the office on a Saturday morning?"

"When you have plans to take over the world, Walker, there are things to be done. Now, let's get back to my original point. I'm assuming you saw Tabby."

"She strolled into Crave last night," I report, flipping an ink pen between two fingers. "Nice of her, huh?"

"I'm not hearing much in your voice that leads me to believe that went over well."

"You're talking to your brother," I remind her, tossing the pen on the desk. "No need to pretend you ever felt neutral about Tabby."

"You're right. There's never been a neutral bone in my body about that useless excuse for a woman. I loathe her. Seeing her signature on those papers this morning ultimately made my month."

"So glad I could help ya out."

"Do I get details? Because I've waited on this since you said, 'I do.'"

Watching Peck push a broom across the floor of the shop, I roll my eyes. It feels like a fucking funeral in here today and I just want to snap everyone out of it and go back to the way it was. Peck's stupid dancing. Sienna's reorganizing shit. Tractors that piss me off and muffins on the counter.

"Well, in typical Tabby fashion," I say, feeling my teeth grit, "she managed to do it at the absolute worst time."

"She came back for a divorce. Let's not get picky on timing."

"She came back because someone told her I've been with another woman more than a night or two. I'm figuring someone was at the restaurant I took her to."

"You did? You've been really seeing this girl? Why did no one tell me?"

"Lance probably couldn't work it in between all the dating texts you sent him."

She laughs, her chair squeaking in the background. "I always figured it would be Machlan who would need my legal defense first. I'm beginning to think it's Lance."

"It might be me if I don't figure out how to stop wanting to smash something this morning."

I pick up a stack of papers Sienna stuck on the corner and bounce them on the desk. My skin crawls with the need to move, to do, to fix this shit that I can't sit still.

"I'm less interested in Tabby, more interested in the new woman."

"Well, since Tabby ruined that last night, I'm pretty sure she's the old woman now."

"You didn't tell her you were married?"

"Blaire . . ."

"You fucking idiot."

The door chimes and I don't even look up. "I gotta go. Someone came in."

"Call me later. We have to discuss this."

"Love ya."

"Love you, Walker. Call me."

I end the call and look up to see old man Dave standing in the lobby. His hair is dripping wet, his clothes soaked. I spring off the chair and rush around to him.

"Are you all right?" I ask.

He seems physically uninjured, yet sopping. But it becomes increasingly obvious that an injury is there. I just can't see it.

Grabbing the chair, I work it around to the front. "I need to just get a chair for out here, huh?"

He tries to smile as he sits. "My wife passed this morning."

"Oh, Dave." I rest a hand on his shoulder, not sure what to say. "I'm so sorry."

"She went peacefully. The nurses called really late last night and I headed up there to sit with her. I held her hand," he says, his gaze settled on something in the distance, "told her stories. Reminded her of all the things we'd done in our lives and how much I loved her."

I squeeze his frail shoulder, a loss for words.

"The rain started around five o'clock," he says, his voice so hollow it's painful for me to even hear. "I was in the middle of a story about a Thanksgiving turkey she cooked one year when she turned her head and looked at me. It was her again . . ." His voice breaks and he coughs into his hand, taking a minute to regain his composure. "Her eyes were blue and bright and she said, 'Well, hello, David.'"

He bends over and cries, catching his tears in his hands. I feel so helpless. Rubbing his back, I try to figure out what to say. This is a devastation I don't know, one I can't imagine. I know the pain of losing my parents, but I can't imagine spending my entire life with someone and not having her there. The emptiness of not having Sienna already kills me.

"She's not struggling anymore," he says, sitting up and looking at me through cloudy eyes. "I don't know what I'll do for breakfast now and don't know why I'll get out of bed. But I suppose this is a part of life and I'll manage. At least I had her back for a few minutes before she passed."

"If there's anything I can do, please tell me."

He pats my arm. "Thank you, Walker. I wanted to see if Sienna was around today."

Biting back a lump in my throat, I shake my head. "She's not."

Despite his grief, even though he just lost his wife, Dave looks beyond the surface. "You two have a falling out?"

"That's nothing you need to be worried about."

"She reminds me of my wife. As kind as she is pretty. Wanting to fix everything," he says, a small smile slipping across his lips. "Take it from me, do whatever it takes to keep her around."

"I think I messed up pretty good on this one."

"Well, we all do that from time to time. Nothing is bad enough it can't be fixed." He stands, swaying a little on his feet. "If you see Sienna, please tell her I said thank you for the breakfasts from Carlson's this past week."

"What?"

"She had something brought over to the nursing home every morning this week," he admits, shaking his head. "It . . . It was appreciated."

A clap of thunder hits outside and I run to the back and grab an old coat of my father's. "Here," I say to Dave, throwing it over his shoulders. "Let's try to keep you warm."

He starts in on a story about my dad and this jacket as I open the door and help him to his car. He gets settled in, the rain pelting my back. "If you're lucky enough to get a shot at love, Walker, it's worth whatever you have to do to keep it."

I watch him pull away. Standing in the middle of the parking lot, getting drenched, I know he's right. I just don't know if it matters.

chapter
Thirty One

Sienna

"**I** REALLY DON'T FEEL LIKE lunch, Delaney. But thank you," I say, trying not to let her hear how much her insistence drives me crazy. She goes on and on about how I need someone to hang out with today, how Cam asked her to check on me, how she'll take me for coffee cake at Carlson's.

She means well. I know that. But I also know what it'll be and that's a huge anti-Walker fest. While I've wanted someone to join my grumblings, as the day has worn on and I really consider listening to it, it doesn't seem appealing.

"Delaney," I say, cutting in. "I need to go. I have a call coming in."

"Call me back."

"Okay. Bye."

I end the call and toss the phone on the sofa.

The sun is out, but a little creek has formed in the back yard. It flows from the neighbors on the north to the ones on the south. The kids at the top of the hill have made these little boats and are floating them down to their friends below. Like a busybody old lady, I stand at the window and watch them play in the water. They're so happy. So carefree. Not old enough to have their hearts broken.

A knock at the front door startles me. Expecting to see Delaney with a bag of takeout, I pull it open without asking who it is. But it's not Delaney. It's Peck.

The mischief that typically riddles his eyes is gone and is replaced with a concern that rushes back all the events from last night. I lean my head against the door and expel a sigh. "What are you doing here?"

"Came to check on my buddy."

"Don't make me cry," I say, choking back a sob.

He gives me his goofy smile. "You doing all right?"

"About as well as you might've guessed when you realized I found out what you all already knew."

I let that hang in the air, a little jab to let him know how I feel. He takes the hit, actually flinching, before removing his hat and running a hand through his wild, blond hair.

"I fucking told him to tell you," he says, shaking his head. "We all did. Every single one of us, Slugger."

"But none of you did," I say, standing upright. "I can see why Machlan didn't. I don't really know him. Maybe not even Lance. But you?"

His face falls as I stand before him, calling him out on what certainly feels like a betrayal.

"You were the one lugging me to Nana's," I point out. "You were the one shoving us together and making sure we had enough opportunities to connect. Hell, Peck, you were the one who came up with the idea for me to work there."

"You wanna know why?" he shoots back.

"I'd love to."

"Because I could tell from that very first night that Walker needed someone like you. Did I know he was gonna fall on his ass for you? No. But I was thinking, at a minimum, you and he could spend some time together and it would pull him out of the fucking fog he's been in for years."

"So maybe I'd sleep with him and he'd get over Tabby?" I ask, my brows shooting to the ceiling. "Gee, thanks."

"That's not at all what I mean," he swears, plopping his hat back on. "He's been over Tabby for years. He's just been kind of stuck."

My head slips from the door.

Peck dips his chin. "He's a great guy. I just hoped maybe I'd see the Walker I knew before he married Tabby. And you know what? I did."

"At my expense."

"Was it?"

"Absolutely."

"What does the fact he married a woman who ran off, one he didn't even care enough about to chase down for a divorce—how does that hurt you? Did we know he was married? Yeah. I was there that day. I watched him almost drink himself to death an hour before the ceremony. The whole town saw him with her and the whole fucking place saw the aftermath. You think people are judging you because of this? Think again."

"Then why didn't you tell me?"

"It wasn't my place." He teeters on the edge of the step. "I don't know why Walker didn't. I know he hated falling for you knowing he still technically had a wife. It's why he pushed back so hard against it. He was going to tell you after he got back this weekend with her signature on the divorce papers."

All of this makes my head spin. The stress in my shoulders aches, the acid in my stomach almost eating it raw. I just want to be happy again, to smile, to want to go do something instead of sitting on the sofa and being miserable.

I want to see Walker. I want to kiss him and hold him and make him laugh. But the man lied to me, omitted something beyond significant, and I don't know if I can ever trust him again.

"Go for a drive with me," Peck says, offering me his hand. "Some fresh air will do you some good."

"I don't look fit to go anywhere."

"My truck won't care," he says, shaking his proffered palm. "Come on. Trust me."

"The last time you said that I ended up at Nana's."

"Not today. No Nana's. No Crank. No Walker's house. Promise. Just me and you and my ol' truck."

I consider going inside and sitting by myself. I think about pacing the floors, taking a bath, overthinking everything.

With a deep, uncertain breath, I take Peck's hand. "Don't let me down."

"I won't. Promise."

———

THE RAIN MISTS AGAINST THE windshield of Peck's truck. It's not heavy or hard but consistent enough that I can't see Dr. Burns' building anymore.

My breath starts to steam the cab as I wait for Peck to come back. He disappeared inside Crave fifteen minutes ago, leaving me in the truck when I refused to go back to the scene of the crime—and I'm not even sure which crime, exactly, I was referring to.

Despite the warm temperatures, the rain works its way into my bones. A chill settles over me and I hold myself, rocking back and forth, wishing he'd hurry up. Like I used to do when I was a little girl, I make a deal with myself: if he's not out by the time I count to one hundred and twenty, I'm going in to get him.

The counting starts in my head as I think I see Walker's truck. But it's not. It's actually a midnight blue truck that's a slightly different model than Daisy. As the numbers keep going up, I tick back through the night I hit her with the bat, the first day at Crave, the church service. I remember every stare, every kiss, every accidental and purposeful touch. I yearn for more. Need them, even, and wonder if I'll ever feel normal without them.

Hitting the magic number, I groan and open the truck door. The warm water mists around me, almost like a thick, wet fog. The street is empty as I jog across and lug on the door to Crave. It opens easily.

There are a few lights on around the bar, mostly advertisements that glow in a variety of colors. My eyes dart to the back table, the one Walker frequents, and where the bomb that blasted me apart last night. It's empty, the chairs neatly arranged around it, the pool balls in their pockets, everything in order.

"Peck?" I call, my voice echoing off the walls. "Where are you?"

When he doesn't answer, I consider taking a spritzer out of the cooler and sitting down. It's not my thing, but I'm not exactly me today. Instead,

I walk over to the cork boards that line the wall beneath the television.

Notes of every size and color are pinned, some serious and some not. A napkin stuck to the cork with a nail reads, "Someone tell Denise to get her ass home." There are three pictures of two football players wearing Legends hats hanging at the top. There's an advertisement for a wood chipper and a poem with more words I can't read than words I can.

"Hey."

I jump at the voice. I don't turn around though because it's not Peck. I don't move because my feet refuse to walk away from him.

"Where's Peck?" I ask Walker, feeling his energy move around behind me. I close my eyes and breathe in his cologne, tears filling my lids.

"He's in the truck. Just went out the back door."

"So this was a plan to get me here?"

"Actually, it wasn't," he says. "There was a plan but it involved me coming to your house after Peck made sure you were all right. This is just happenstance."

Second-guessing everything I think and everything I do, I turn to face him. His eyes have dark rings around them, his clothes the same he wore last night. I refuse to let the tears spill over.

"It's a pattern, huh?" he chuckles. "You. Me. Crave."

"Now we have your wife to add to that," I throw back.

He nods, struggling to stay composed. "Fair enough."

"There's nothing fair about it," I tell him. "You set me up."

"No, I didn't. I was going to tell you."

"When? When did you decide was a good time for me to know the man I was falling in love with was married to someone else?" I realize my slip, but it's too late. His eyes go wide and he starts to step towards me, but I shake my head. "Don't."

"I didn't tell you because, at first, I didn't think it mattered. The marriage was a joke and only was intact legally because I didn't care enough to chase her down for a divorce. You were probably leaving anyway and I figured why get into it?"

"Because it would've been nice to know."

"And I apologize." His eyes cloud as he runs a hand through his hair. "God, I'm so fucking sorry."

"You lied to me. I told you everything about me. I contemplated turning down a job with my brother for you," I say, my face damp despite my best efforts to keep it from happening. "I made decisions that I hoped would give us a chance to figure things out between us and you made decisions that you knew would be worse the longer you waited."

"I tried to tell you," he says, watching the tears fall. "Every time I tried, I got scared. Afraid you'd leave. Afraid you'd be pissed or would have your feelings hurt. I thought it would be a hell of a lot easier if I had a signed set of papers in my hand that said it was over. A thing of the past."

Despite my glare, he stalks across the room and stops in front of me. He searches my face, his own full of the same misery that's torn apart my soul.

"What are the odds we'd end up back here?" He reaches out and touches my face. My brain screams to pull away, but my heart wins. I lean against his hand, the warmth of his palm caressing my cheek. "Let this be our starting point. Let us try again."

"Have we ever really tried? Or was that all a lie?"

"Nothing I said to you was a lie. Nothing I insinuated or whispered in your ear while you slept."

Furrowing a brow, I don't dare ask.

"Slugger, please . . ."

Standing on my tiptoes, my heart bleeding into my chest, I press a kiss to the side of his face. As if he knows what I'm saying, he closes his eyes and drops his hand from my face.

"I need to go," I whisper turning to the door.

"Sienna, wait . . ."

"I've given you a second," I smile sadly. "I don't know what else you could want at this point."

He calls out after me, but I swing the door open and run across the road. The rain drizzles on my head as I climb into the cab of Peck's truck.

"Go."

Without a word, Peck steps on the accelerator and starts down the street. Only when we're ready to turn off do I look back to see Walker standing in the middle of the road again, his head bowed to the asphalt, the rain creating a foggy haze around him.

chapter
Thirty Two

Sienna

WE DON'T EXCHANGE A WORD as Peck drives me home. I want to ask if he went there on purpose, but I'm pretty certain I know the answer and I can't blame him. If I were in his position, I'd have tried it too.

The truck slides into the driveway of my little rental and he jams it in park. "Don't be mad at me," he says.

"I'm not."

"Nah, you are. I have broad shoulders. I can take it."

"I'm not mad at you," I sigh. "I don't even know what I am, to be honest."

"You'll figure it out." He cocks his head to the side, narrowing his eyes. "Are you sticking around?"

I lift my shoulders and let them fall, not sure what to do when all I really want to do is climb under the covers and sleep for ten years.

He nods. "Well, you'll do what's best for you. You're a smart girl."

"I don't feel like it."

"Yeah, well, I don't always feel awesome and I know I am."

A chuckle escapes my lips, even though I don't expect it. I grab the door handle and then stop. "Peck?"

"Yeah?"

"Thank you."

He sends me his lopsided grin. "For what?"

Sitting quietly, my hand still wrapped around the door handle, I try to focus on this one thing. I think back to all the nice things he's done for me since I've known him. All the times he hasn't just sided with Walker because they're family, but almost treated me like family too.

My gaze softens, my shoulders sag. "I hope Molly McCarter realizes how special you are sooner rather than later."

"Me too," he sighs with a smile.

"You're gold, you know that?"

"I do. But thank you for noticing," he winks. "Go on and get out of my truck before this gets all sappy and I have to report back to Walker a bunch of shit that he'll tease me for. Okay?"

"Sure." With a heavy heart, I shove open the door. Before I shut it, I peer inside the cab one final time. "Thanks for the ride."

"If you need anything, you know who to call. Just remember—if you're in Georgia, I'll need lead time."

With a laugh and a tear sliding down my cheek, I swing the door closed and head up to the door. In typical Peck style, he doesn't leave until I'm in the house.

As I hear the engine take off down the street, my back slides down the wall and I drop onto the floor. I don't know where my sobs sound harder—in the empty house or in my desolate soul.

THE FOG ON THE MIRROR fades as the cool air from the house rushes into the bathroom. It tickles my skin, still sensitive from standing under the shower for what felt like a lifetime but wasn't quite long enough.

Camilla and I always say that a hot shower can cure just about anything. It can't cure a broken heart.

Heading into my bedroom, stepping over the sheets I ripped from my bed before putting on new, non-Walker-scented ones, I climb up on the mattress and curl up into a ball.

I didn't die. My heart got trampled, my trust broken, my ego bruised, but I didn't die. I thought I might. I also thought I might just pick up the phone today once Peck dropped me off and call Walker and talk to him. I didn't do that either.

My eyes drift closed and I concentrate on my breathing, listening to the air smoothly enter and leave my body. As I lie in bed, in a semi-awake, semi-sleep sort of twilight state, there's a sense of peace that covers me.

I've taken everything the last few days have thrown at me. I got bumped around and hurt but I didn't break. I fell in love, but I didn't lose me. I didn't give in, I didn't roll over, I didn't sacrifice anything about myself to stay in a relationship.

I wasn't my mother.

Thinking of her sweet face and warm hugs makes my chest hurt. Pulling my legs tighter to my chest, I imagine being at the Farm, surrounded by my family, and although it doesn't seem like it'll fix things, it's a better solution than lying here alone.

Decision made, I find my phone buried in the blankets on the floor and scroll until I find Graham's name. I hit the green button.

"Hey," he says immediately. "How are you?"

"I'm coming home," I tell him, ignoring his question. "Is the job still open?"

"Of course . . ." A paper crinkles in the background. "You okay?"

"No, but I'm going to survive."

"That's good news. Mom will be happy."

I look around the room and spot a packet of gum Walker left lying next to the television. The stupid little package makes my heart burn in my chest and I know if this can make me feel so sad, what will driving by Crank do? Or Peck? Or if I run into Walker at the gas station?

"Think I can stay at the Farm for a while?" I ask. "I'm going to try to grab a flight in the morning."

"I'll have someone go over and make sure it's ready for you. You coming back for good then?"

"I think so, G."

He waits a long minute before responding. "You know I want you here. I feel better when we're all in one place."

"Yeah."

"But I want you to take a breather. Don't make any decisions until you're more steady on your feet, okay?"

"The way I feel . . ." My voice cracks before drifting off. I pace a circle, trying to rein in the lump at the bottom of my throat. "The way I feel, it might take a while to be steady on my feet. I can't wait that long to move on."

"You know I'm behind you one hundred percent. But can I give you some advice?"

"That's what I call you for, isn't it?" I laugh, sniffling.

"Don't bring him here. Lincoln got Ford all wound up and you know how that ends."

"Oh great."

Graham laughs. "Okay. I'll have my secretary secure you a plane ticket for morning. The Farm will be waiting."

"Thanks, G. Love you."

"Love you too. See you tomorrow."

"Bye."

chapter
Thirty Three

Walker

THE LAST TIME A WOMAN left me, I almost drank myself to death. It wasn't because she left. Her actual leaving was symbolic; she was out the door months before that. It was because I wanted to forget everything that had happened. I didn't want to remember our farce of a wedding, deal with the house she wanted to buy that I hated from the start, see her things lying around that only reminded me of a woman who betrayed me over and over again. Being drunk delivered the sweet peace I couldn't find elsewhere.

This time? I want to remember it all.

The tractor seat beneath me bites into my ass. The engine is now cold, the sun just starting to fall behind the trees. I should get up and go inside, get a shower, probably a sandwich, but I can't make myself move. If I get up, there's a better-than-average chance I'll find myself in my truck headed to Sienna's, and that'll just make things worse.

She needs time. That's what Blaire told me, it's what Lance suggested, it's what my gut says. Give her time. But I don't want to give her time. I want to hold her in my arms and kiss her until she remembers what we are together.

Everything.

We're everything together.

My palm slams off the steering wheel, the crunch of the bone against the hard plastic twisting under my skin. It registers, but I don't really feel the pain. It pales in comparison to the ache everywhere else.

They say you don't know what you have until it's gone. That's not true. I knew what I had long before she left. What I didn't know for absolute certain until Tabby came back and I looked in to her eyes and felt absolutely nothing was that I absolutely, without the shadow of a doubt, love Sienna Landry.

A pair of headlights sweeps through the field before Peck's pickup truck comes into view. He shuts it off a few yards away, climbing out and heading my way.

He tosses me a little wave, testing the waters, and I can't deny I'm happy to see him.

"How are ya?" he asks when he gets close enough for me to hear.

I shrug.

"Decided to mow the back forty, huh? Been a long time since this has been cut."

"Seemed like a good, productive way to not get a restraining order," I laugh.

He chuckles, leaning against a tire. "Well, what do we do now?"

"About what?"

"Losing our girl."

"Our girl?" I ask, eyes wide. "What the hell are you talking about?"

"I mean, she's your girl," he scoffs. "But I like her too. She's fun. She makes you a decent guy. She just . . . fit in, all right?"

Scratching my head, I sink into the seat. "I can't just go get her. I want to. I want to throw her over my shoulder and handcuff her to the bed and make her listen to me until she loves me back."

Something flickers in Peck's eye, but he doesn't say anything. Instead, he nods his head.

"You know, her brother offered her a job in Savannah and she never said she would or wouldn't take it," I note.

"Maybe she won't."

I look at him. "Maybe she needs to."

"What are you saying, Walk?"

"I didn't realize how unhappy I was until she came around. I'd forgotten what it feels like to want to get out of bed, to not loathe the idea of going to work."

"You mean you don't skip out the door every day to see me? Fucker," he teases.

"Sorry," I laugh. "I'd fallen into this slump and nothing sort of mattered anymore. I didn't think there was anything out there for me. Now I know that's not true."

"So you're going to let her walk away?"

Gazing into the sunset, the final rays of light shining through the trees, the emptiness of not having Sienna settles into my soul. It claws at me, pierces me, makes me uncomfortable in the worst way. "I have to," I whisper.

"I don't understand."

"I could go get her like I want to and tell her all the things I know are true. That I love her. That she loves me. That we belong together. But she needs to realize that on her own."

"What if she doesn't?"

"A girl like that . . ." I can't fight the laugh that comes falling past my lips. "You can't tame a girl like Sienna. She still has things she wants to do, things she wants to figure out. And I'd be a cocksucker if I tried to convince her she doesn't."

"Okay," he says, holding a hand in front of him, "I get what you're saying. But it's risky as hell."

"Everything's a risk, isn't it? I've already fallen in love with her. That's where you really take the chance and I'm all in. It's too late for that." I climb off the tractor and look at my cousin. "How late is Terry's Lumber open?"

"Till nine? I think?"

"Wanna give me a lift over there?"

"Yeah, but I control the radio . . ."

chapter
Thirty Four

Sienna

"COME ON," I GROAN, THE wheels of my suitcase getting stuck. I jerk it forward and it springs loose, catapulting me into the back of my car.

Blowing out a breath, I stand with what little energy I have left and get it situated in the trunk and close the lid.

The little house Delaney and I called home for the last year looms overhead as I walk back up to the door. Its little black shutters were my favorite part from the moment I rolled up here months ago. Although it's small and odd-shaped and the grass never grows evenly, my heart twists as I check the door for a final time.

As I head back down the sidewalk, Peck's truck slides in behind my car. "Hey," he says, getting out. He pulls his brows together. "Going somewhere?"

"To Savannah," I say, trying desperately to keep my voice free of emotion. "I have a flight in a couple of hours."

"Why didn't you tell me?"

"Am I supposed to tell you everything?" I laugh, letting him pull me into a hug.

"Not everything, but this is kind of a big deal."

"I just . . ." Shrugging, I blow out a breath. "I don't know what else to do."

"You staying there for good?"

I shrug again. "I need to go though. I can't miss my flight."

He opens his mouth, but nothing comes out. Instead, he pulls me into a hug again.

"You're the best, you know that?" I say against his t-shirt.

This time, there are no witty comebacks and no cute one-liners. He just squeezes me tighter.

Fighting tears, I pull away and refuse to look at him.

"Here," he says, his voice full of emotion. "Take this."

"What is it?"

He hands me a white envelope with my name scrawled on the front. My thumb goes immediately to Walker's writing as if touching his pen strokes allows me to touch him.

"I don't know what it is, really. But it's from Walker," he says. "Are you going to tell him you're leaving?"

"Is Tabby still around?"

"Hell, no," he sneers. "Even if she was, it wouldn't matter. You get what I'm sayin'?"

Blowing out a shaky breath, I circle around to the driver's side door. "Take care of yourself, okay? Don't let Walker give you too much hell."

"If you need anything, call me," he says, as I get into my seat.

Tears welling in my eyes as Peck reaches me, he closes the door softly. Leaning down so we're eye-to-eye, he smiles sadly. "I hate seeing you go."

"I hate to go," I choke out. "But I have to."

He nods, patting his hand against the roof of the car. "Then you better get going. Be safe."

I watch him in the rearview mirror get into this truck, throw it in reverse, and zoom off down the road.

The tears start and they don't stop even after I hit the highway towards Chicago. By the time I hit the Linton exit, my shirt is soaked and I can barely see.

On auto-pilot, I take the little offshoot into the little sleepy town.

Instead of going right towards Crank like I do every morning, I turn left.

The streets are lined with American flags that billow in the warm summer breeze. Cherry smiles, broom in hand, as she sweeps the front of Carlson's Bakery. I wave back, wishing I could stop and get one last piece of coffee cake.

Passing Nana's church, I stop at the little stop sign at the end of the street. Ruby, the librarian, is checking the mail at the road. She, too, waves and points to a little sign about the upcoming speaker she's been telling me about. I give her a thumbs up, making her smile as the tears just keep flowing.

Passing Goodman's gas station, I see a bunch of the old men who hang out in Crank sometimes and I honk. They recognize my car and lift their coffee cups high above their bib overalls, the little hello they have worked out for their friends.

Me. Their friend.

Funny how this little town that I once thought of as a pit stop in the adventure of my life has my heart all twisted into a knot. I take a quick left and head back towards the highway, a road I don't usually take. There's a sign painted a bright shade of blue with a white arrow that reads, "Bluebird."

Pressing on the gas, I force myself forward on the on-ramp and head to the airport.

chapter
Thirty Five

Sienna

"LAST CALL FOR FLIGHT 3086 to Atlanta, Georgia."
With a long, frazzled breath, I watch the steady stream of people board the jet. I should've been one of the first between my first-class ticket and the fact that I've sat here for an hour. Yet, here I am, still stuck in my seat staring at a coffee pop-up in the middle of the airport.

Like a zombie, I reach for my bag and drag it to my lap. I poke around, searching for my boarding pass when I stumble upon the envelope Peck gave me earlier. It's leaned up against my wallet, cuddled in amongst my things, like it has all the time in the world to sit there until I decide to open it.

The line still has a handful of people in it, so I go ahead and retrieve the envelope. It's heavier than I remember and uneven as I hold it like a bomb waiting to go off.

I don't want to open it. Something tells me to not be antsy and leave it be. I get up and start to gather my things before sitting down and tearing the top open before I can talk myself out of it again.

A key falls to the floor, dinging as it hits the metal leg of the chair. I pick it up and unfold a piece of carefully creased paper, the words hard to read from the tears in my eyes at the first word.

Slugger,

I've made a lot of mistakes in my life, but there's only one I'd go back and fix if I could. That's hurting you. I'm so damn sorry. Once I realized I was in love with you, I panicked and tried to find Tabby to get everything taken care of. I should've just told you, but I didn't. And now we're both paying for that.

I am in love with you, Sienna. I don't expect that to absolve me from any guilt for my mistakes, but I want you to know that. I've never been in love before now. I know that because I've never felt this way about anyone else and I know I could never stop feeling this way or feel it for another person.

The key is to the front door of my house. I waited four years to get a divorce. I'll wait an entire lifetime for you to come back. Go explore the world. Work for your brother. Whatever it is you want to do. Just know that when you realize you can't live without me, you know where I'll be.

Love,
Walker

The paper shakes, my hands trembling, as I make it to the last words. I want to be mad at him, I want to be so jealous that I hate him for having a wife. But both of those things leave me sitting here. Without him.

Looking around the airport, at the man sitting across from me reading a paper with his wife's head on his shoulder, at the young couple sitting against the wall, laughing at something on her phone, my lips begin to tremble.

The flight attendant at the gate looks at me and I nod, gesturing for her to give me a minute. Wrapping bag straps in my hands, I still don't get up because reality hits me like a ton of bricks.

If I get on that plane, I'm everything I say I'm not.

Leaving is the weak option. Fleeing is the childish answer. Not fighting for what I want is a betrayal to myself.

If I go, I'm sacrificing everything.

Laughing out loud, I realize everything my mother has ever said and done is true. She didn't give up a life to stay with my father. Her life was with my father. Just like staying here won't be giving up my life. It might actually be where it was all along.

Slinging my purse over my shoulder, I turn to head back to security when the seat next to me is taken.

I sense him before I see him. His cologne finds me before he does. That little flame in my belly that makes me excited and simultaneously calm flickers and I whip my eyes to meet his deep, dark gaze.

"Walker," I breathe, my bags falling out of my trembling hand to the floor. "What are you doing here?"

"Well," he says, sliding his hands down his jeans, "I came to catch a flight to Atlanta that I see I'm about to miss." He cringes, nodding up towards the flight attendant who's watching me with annoyance.

"You got a flight? Why?"

My heartbeat pounds. I can feel it in my temple, my entire body heating as I hold my breath and wait, *hope*, for his answer.

"I thought I could let you go," he says, his voice full of uncertainty. "I thought I could just wait around and you'd come back." He leans forward, taking my chin in his calloused hand and angling my face so he can see all the way into my soul. "But I can't."

"Why?" I say, my voice cracking with emotion. I lean my cheek into his arm, trying to stay rooted in the seat and not jump into his arms.

"Because I love you."

It's the simplest thing he could say, but the most powerful too. His handsome face gets cloudy as I bat back tears.

"I may have let Tabby go for years, knowing she'd come back to nothing but a divorce, if she ever did. But I could do that because it didn't matter. Thinking about you leaving for even a day kills me, Slugger."

"Oh, Walker . . ." I throw my arms around him, burying my face in his neck. He pulls me in tight, his body so hard, yet so welcoming, against me. It's where I belong.

"Madam, I'm sorry, but are you going to get on this flight or not?" The flight attendant's voice sounds behind me, crisp and clear.

"She's not," Walker answers for me. "She's going home with me."

"Very well."

I pull back and look at him. "Are you divorced yet?"

"Blaire says she'll get it through the system, but it'll take up to three months. Seems it takes longer to break up a marriage legally than it does to create one." He takes a deep breath. "I should've told you. I was wrong."

"I know." A slow smirk kisses my lips. "I'm going to expect a lot of favors to make up for this."

"I'm going to expect to do a lot of favors, although nothing will make up for hurting you." He kisses my cheek. "Will you go home with me?"

I look over my shoulder to see the doors to the jetway are closed. Twisting back in my seat, I take a deep breath. "What would you think if I told you I might be looking forward to those Illinois winters after all?"

"I'd say that's a good thing," he says, standing and pulling me to my feet. "Because I might be looking to spend a few decades with you cuddling."

"Next to a fire?" I grin.

"Wherever you want, Slugger."

chapter
Thirty Six

Walker

I FOLLOWED HER LIKE WHITE on rice all the way from Chicago, afraid she'd get cold feet and veer off and go back to the airport. She parked her car at her house, only because it's the first opportunity I could get to get her in my truck.

I haven't let go of her hand since she got in my truck. She's tried to pull away a few times, but I just clamp down harder.

"Get used to it," I say, bringing our interlaced fingers to my mouth and planting a kiss on our knuckles. Pulling into my driveway, I pilot the truck all the way to the end near the barn. She gives me a confused look when I turn off the key. "I want you to feel free to ask me anything. I'll answer whatever questions you have."

"Do you love her?" she asks.

"No."

"Do you love me?"

"Yes."

She nods, biting her bottom lip. "I do have questions I want to ask you later. Just so I understand what happened. I think it's important."

"Whatever you want."

Her phone rings and I let her hand go so she can find it in her purse. She pulls it out and smiles wide. "Hey, Graham." She laughs, nods, and then winces. "Yeah, I think I've decided to stay here. Can you get my checked baggage in Atlanta?" She nods again. "Yeah. Have Barrett send Troy. Just tell him not to go through it," she laughs. "No. Absolutely not." Her eyes close before she hands the phone to me.

"What?" I ask.

"My brother wants to talk to you."

"Really?"

"Really."

"This should be fun," I grumble, taking the phone. "Hello?"

"Hello. This is Graham Landry. Who is this?"

"Walker Gibson. How are ya?" I make a face at Sienna. She buries hers in her hands.

"I'm going to cut to the chase because we both don't care about the weather or how the other person is, correct?"

I like him already. "Correct."

"What we both care about is my sister. We haven't had the pleasure of meeting yet, but I would like you to know one thing: if you do anything stupid, I have people who are capable of just about anything you can imagine. Okay?"

"Let me put it to you this way," I say, looking at the beautiful girl beside me. "I've been to jail one time in my life and that was for doing something similar to what you've insinuated to a guy who thought he could get away with a few things with my sister. If anyone ever touched Sienna, I'd never get out. So I hear you loud and clear."

"Oh." He pauses, letting that sink in. "Maybe we're going to be all right."

"Maybe so. Nice talking to you." I hand the phone back to Sienna and then get out of the truck.

There's a gentleness to the air as I fill my lungs with it, blowing it out into the freshly-mowed field. The pile of lumber Peck and I got last night sets at the edge of the woods. I wonder how long it will take me to finish the project and hope I can get it done before fall comes and it gets cool and muddy back here.

Sienna joins me, wrapping her arms around my waist. "I told Graham I'm not coming back. Not for good, anyway."

"Not for good?"

"I have to go back and visit them," she laughs. "And they'd like to meet you." The toe of her shoe kicks at a clod of dirt, breaking it apart. "Graham is going to free up some of my money so I can try to grow my business. I know a few people who have fashion lines coming out next year and I've been offered to submit some designs for them. There's more to it than just sketching pretty dresses and I need money for that. Graham seems to think I can do it, which is nice."

"That's great," I say, kissing her forehead. "And of course you can do it."

"It's exciting. There's just one problem."

Looking down at her, I take in her pinched nose. "What?"

"I don't have anywhere to live. My lease is up next week and I'm kind of homeless."

"Well," I say, untangling her arms and taking her hand, "I might have an extra part of a bed."

I guide her across the field, butterflies scattering as we pass.

"Part of a bed?" she asks.

"Yeah, you'll have to sleep with me," I tease. "Hope you can handle that."

"What's all this?" She points to the wood freshly bundled and marked with red flags so other driver's didn't run into it last night when Peck hauled it home for me.

"Wood."

"No shit," she laughs. "What's it for?"

"Come on." I tug her towards the trees. We step inside the little forest and follow a little path a few yards in. Then we stop.

I turn to watch her expression change as she realizes just what it is. "Walker?"

"I just started on it this morning," I tell her, my chest tightening. This was a risky idea, one I wasn't sure she'd love, but I find myself rambling away while she decides what she thinks. "There will be a trap door like the one at Nana's, but only two windows so you can hang stuff up and have some privacy on the other two sid—"

She silences me with a kiss. It's her in control this time as she moves her mouth against mine, backing me up to the tree that will house her new treehouse.

"And I got you purple curtains," I mutter against her lips.

She giggles, pulling away. "Walker Gibson, I love you."

"It's a good thing. Because I'm so fucking in love with you."

Epilogue

a month later

"ANYONE WANT PIE?" NANA TOSSES her napkin onto the table next to her glass of tea. "I made chocolate, pecan, and coconut."

"Coconut," says Peck.

"Chocolate," Machlan chimes in, shoving the last piece of meatloaf into his mouth.

Lance doesn't bother to look up from his phone. "Chocolate."

"Are your legs broken?" I ask from my perch on Walker's knee. "At least get your butts up and bring the pies in here for her to cut." I'm cinched closer to my man, his arms locked at my belly as the Gibson boys look at me like I just asked them to scale Mount Everest. "Did I stutter?"

"You go get them," Lance chirps. "I'm busy."

"Busy doing what?" Walker leans forward, taking me with him, as he tries to snatch Lance's phone from his hand. "Whatcha doing there, bud?"

The grin on Lance's face says it all. "Nothing I'm going to describe as we sit at our grandmother's familial table."

"Good boy," Nana laughs, resting back in her chair. "But Sienna is right. You boys bring the pie in and I'll cut it."

"We had a good thing going until you showed up," Machlan teases, sending a wink my way.

They get to their feet and traipse into the kitchen. I nestle back into Walker's chest again, closing my eyes as the sunlight warms my face and his heartbeat warms my soul. The only imperfect thing about today is the little splinter in my pointer finger from helping with the treehouse last night.

I never thought, in a million years, that I would feel as comfortable with another family as I do my own. But I do. This crazy, foul-mouthed, not quite politically correct gaggle of boys and their Nana have changed my entire world.

Walker's home is becoming mine as we paint the walls, strip the cabinets, and replace flooring. The only argument we really have is that I want to just pay for it all to be done now and he wants to wait and get it done as he can afford it. It drives me insane, but I respect it. He's frugal, not so different than my brother Graham, really, except Walker is this way because he has to be. Graham watches the bottom line because he doesn't want to ever have to worry about watching it. The two of them bonded over talk of savings accounts interest rates the other day.

The sound of a plate breaking in the kitchen is enough to get Nana to her feet. "Should've just done it myself."

Giggling, I watch her disappear through the doors. "She's one of a kind."

"That she is," Walker says, his voice hot against my ear. He burrows his face into the crook of my neck and presses a sweet kiss in the bend. "And so are you."

My heart flutters, the smile on my lips that's been there for the last few weeks growing even wider. I place my hands on top of his at my stomach and just melt into him. "How long do we have to stay here?"

"You wanting round three?" he grins against my skin.

"Yes," I breathe, flushing.

His hand slips from under mine. It slides down my stomach, over the top of my jeans, until his palm is lying just above my clit. The pressure incites every nerve ending in my body to fire and I wiggle, needing more contact.

"I can feel how hot you are through your jeans," he growls against my cheek. "Damn it, girl."

Rotating my hips, digging my ass into his lap, his cock pushes back. "That," I almost moan, "is hot."

"Will you two stop it?" Lance snorts as he walks back in with two pieces of pie. "You shouldn't be fornicating at Nana's table."

"My dick is in my pants. Sadly," Walker points out, his fingers tapping against the denim between my legs.

"I'm eating this," Lance says, scooping up a chunk of chocolate pie, "and then I'm off to get my dick out of my pants."

"Nobody wants to hear that," Walker laughs.

Clenching my legs together to keep his hand in place, I try to refocus. "Who are you meeting?" I ask Lance.

"Nerdy Nurse." His fork pauses mid-air. "Sounds like a good time to me."

"You don't even know her name?" Walker asks.

"I don't need her name to fuck her," Lance shrugs, shoveling more pie into his mouth. "I just want to get off, and by the look of the messages she just sent me, she is up for the challenge."

"Don't talk with your mouth full." Cringing, I grab a napkin and hand it to him. "You aren't eating with her, are you? Because that's a huge turn off."

"He won't be eating *with* her," Machlan chuckles, coming back into the room. "Eating her, maybe." He switches his attention to me. "Did you get the design contract you were after?"

I wriggle until Walker sighs and releases me from his clutches. Just thinking about the job I just landed keeps me from sitting still. It's driving Walker crazy that I'm up all night playing with designs, colors, and fabrics, but I can't help it.

"I did," I almost coo. "I'm so excited. I'll have to make it my sole focus for the next six months or so and will probably even have to go to Los Angeles once or twice to meet with the owners and get a good feel for what they're after. But this is so, so exciting. I'm in heaven."

"Too bad she's not saying that about your bedroom," Machlan says, looking at Walker.

"Oh, that's beyond heaven," I say, moving behind Walker and laying my arms across his wide shoulders. "That's perfection."

Lance's phone chimes. It takes him all of two seconds to get his plate on the table and the device in front of his face. "It's been fun, but I gotta run," he says, not looking up. "Holy shit. She can do that?"

"Let me see," Machlan says, craning his neck. "If there's anything left of her, I'll have a shot of that."

"There won't be." Lance gives us a little salute and disappears into the kitchen, Machlan on his tail.

We watch them move past the windows on their way to their cars, Walker reaching up and taking my hand. He holds it reverently, kissing the top.

There's something meaningful about the moment, but I don't quite understand what.

"You okay?" I ask softly, laying my cheek on top of his head.

"Just thinking you're still here."

"Should I be anywhere else?"

"Is that a loaded question?" he chuckles, urging me around the chair so I'm sitting on his lap again. "Thank you."

Gazing into his sweet, brown eyes, I smile. "For what?"

"For being you. For being here." He holds me, cuddles me so close that I can barely breathe. "I have one request though."

"I'm not into anal."

His chest bounces as he laughs. "I heard you last night."

"Good. Because I was serious." Pulling away, I can't keep the grin off my face.

"Dave was in yesterday and he thanked me for not charging him for the catalytic converter Peck put in his truck."

"Oh," I say, trying to get off his lap. "Not where I thought this was going."

We both look up as Peck walks in. He stops as soon as he enters. "I'm coming in the middle of something, aren't I?"

"You need to go," I say, shooing him away.

"Stick around," Walker offers. "Pull up a seat."

Peck laughs and takes a step back. "I definitely want to go now."

Walker leans back, the most peaceful smile in the world planted on his kissable lips. "If you two don't stop giving my stuff away . . ."

"She's the boss," Peck says, holding his hands up. "I can't argue with her."

"You argue with her about every-fucking-thing else!"

"Not *totally* true," Peck challenges. "And you told me whatever she wants, to do it. She wanted to fix the truck."

Walker looks at me. There's a twinkle buried in his eye that makes me want to kiss him, but I don't. Instead, I cup his cheeks in my hand. "I owe you."

"You've owed me since the day you met me."

"And you haven't let me get even yet," I say, kissing him. Our lips touch sweetly, at first, and as his fingers dig into my hips, his tongue swipes across mine. "Oh," I moan, feeling the ache building in my thighs.

He breaks the kiss, his breath as strangled as mine. "I can't let you get even. You might leave me."

"Oh, baby," I laugh, pulling his hand until he stands up. "There's not a chance."

He lets me lead him through the house, pausing to tell Nana thanks for dinner. In no time at all, we're out the back door.

Nana's sheets are hanging off the clothesline, the last of her tomatoes lined up along the railing of the porch to ripen in the late afternoon sun.

A breeze trickles through the yard, a slight hint of the cold that's sure to come. I used to blanch at the idea of winter in Illinois. It doesn't seem so bad now.

Looking up, I see Walker watching me. "Where are we going?" he asks, his voice alight with humor.

"You can have sex with me on a random dirt road or at Crank because it's fairly close," I say, as he opens the passenger's side door of Daisy for me. "But pick. Quick."

"Ah," he says, leaning against the truck. "There is a Mustang pulled in one of the Crank bays now. Could be fun."

Leaning out of the truck, I grab the door handle and pull it closed. "Get in."

His laughter finds my ears, his love fills my heart.

As we pull out of Nana's and onto the gravel road, I watch the fields go by.

Just a few months ago, I didn't know where I belonged and I definitely didn't think it was in a place with cornfields and snowstorms. But I was wrong.

You belong in a place where you can plant your roots and feel safe enough to let them grow. You belong somewhere your tank is filled as much as you take from it. You belong in the little niche of the world where you can't imagine waking up anywhere different.

As Walker takes my hand and gives it a gentle squeeze, this is it for me. This is the place I'm spreading my wings and trusting the rowdy Gibson boys to have my back. It's somewhere I feel like it would be impossible to give as much as they give to me. Despite the cold on the horizon and the miles away from anyone or anything Landry, being anywhere else isn't an option.

I, without a doubt, belong here. With him.

"Hey," Walker says, shaking my thigh. "What are you thinking about over there?"

I could tell him and get all sappy and find myself gushing over how much I love him. Instead, I grin. "I really hate going to the laundromat."

"That's what you're thinking about?"

"It smells funny and I hate lugging in the soap and sitting there forever."

He pulls back a little and looks at me with a furrowed brow. "Why do I think this is a lead-in?"

"What would you say if I told you I bought all new towels for the shop?"

"Sienna . . ."

"Walker . . ." I mock, scooting into the middle of the truck and leaning my head on his shoulder. "It's a good thing you love me."

His arm settles around my shoulders and tugs me into his side. "It's a damn good thing I do."

The End

Coming Soon

Vincent, Peck's brother, will have a novella coming out in December called CROSS.

CRAFT will follow Lance Gibson and will release in January.

About the Author

USA TODAY BESTSELLING AUTHOR ADRIANA Locke lives and breathes books. After years of slightly obsessive relationships with the flawed bad boys created by other authors, Adriana created her own.

She resides in the Midwest with her husband, sons, two dogs, two cats, and a bird. She spends a large amount of time playing with her kids, drinking coffee, and cooking. You can find her outside if the weather's nice and there's always a piece of candy in her pocket.

Besides cinnamon gummy bears, boxing, and random quotes, her next favorite thing is chatting with readers. She'd love to hear from you!

www.adrianalocke.com
Facebook—*www.facebook.com/authoradrianalocke*
Twitter—*www.twitter.com/authoralocke*
Instagram—*www.instagram.com/authoradrianalocke*

Acknowledgements

THANK YOU TO THE CREATOR for blessing me with life, family, love, and opportunities. I'm so undeserving but equally grateful.

Mr. Locke: thank you for loving me for the past twenty-two years and teaching me things every day. You'd never believe it, but you are the better half of our team in so many ways.

Little Lockes: hugs to my four little boys, the reasons I get out of bed every day. I love your patience, enthusiasm, and sweet, sticky hugs. Just stop bringing home stray animals, okay? We have enough.

Mom: the older I get, the more I appreciate you. It's doubtful I tell you that enough, but I'm putting it in print so hopefully that counts for something, right?

Kari: you're one of the best people I know. Gorgeous, talented like crazy, and kind. Thank you for being my friend.

Mandi: I love you. That is all.

Tiffany: my right hand, my friend, the person that makes sure all the things get done. You are the bee's knees, my friend.

Jen: I'm glad you still love me. I was worried for a minute. Ha! We just rocked out book number fourteen. How wicked awesome is that?

Susan: you're one of the sweetest people I know and I'm honored every time you meet one of my projects with your bright enthusiasm. Thank you for being you.

Carleen: there really are no words. Your patience and kindness and ability to get things through (even if it takes twenty minutes of voice messages) is unparalleled. You are the yin to my yang. Thank you a million times over.

Kim: I still can't believe you agreed to read this thing for me. Thank you for your willingness to help a girl that was struggling out. Huge, massive hugs.

Kara: the best eyes out there! You keep things clean and organized and working with you is a dream. Thank you for rearranging a few things so you could work on this project.

Candace: your messages always make me smile, your enthusiasm for my stories keeps me going. Thank you for reading Crank and sending me your thoughts. I cherish you.

Ebbie: you keep the group moving! Thank you for maintaining our group step activities every month. It means so much to the ladies in Books by Adriana Locke and to me. You're making a difference in so many lives—thank you.

Lara: you've been such a help to me these last few weeks with your advice, support, kindness, and laughs. Thank you for being a light in the book world and an advocate of authors. I love you, friend.

Lisa: every time I send a book to you for editing, I assume you'll reject it. Yet, you still work with me, and for that, I will forever be grateful. (How would I make it without your little asides as we go?)

Becca: thank you so much for taking me on. I learned so much from you during this process and your eye is fantastic. (Make me feeeeeeel it.) I adore you, my sunshine friend.

Christine: your interior design is always gorgeous. Thank you for working me into your schedule for Crank.

Give Me Books: thank you for your professionalism, efficiency, and kindness. I love working with you.

Books by Adriana Locke: you are the best thing ever! We are more than a reader group; we are a group of friends. I treasure each and every one of you. Thank you for the love, support, memes, videos, and silly posts. You're my happy place.

Bloggers: you're the glue that keeps everything together. Your job is thankless and I know sometimes you feel overlooked, but please know I see you out there, slaving away, and I appreciate you. Thank you for all you do.

You: yes, you. Thank you for taking a chance on my book. I know you have so many choices and I'm beyond honored you picked up Crank. I hope you enjoyed it, I hope it gave you a break from the daily toils of real life. Take this sentence as a giant hug from me to you.

Xo, Adriana